"So you want to f... sure, do you, Diana?" This wasn't the voice she remembered. It throbbed and seethed and demanded with all the passion she'd set loose. It stirred her deeply, causing her breath to come in wispy gasps. "His obsession with that treasure has destroyed my family and, I suspect, caused his own death. Would you like to see what it did to *me?*"

He jerked his jacket open and flung it in one furious motion across the room. Then he savagely ripped his shirt off and sent it flying in the jacket's wake. As he did, Diana saw the criss-crossing of scars on his chest and his arms. When he turned his back to her she saw the faded tracks left by the cat-o'-nine-tails.

"Now tell me," he spat out, facing her again. "If my jailers couldn't break me, what makes you think I'd bend to your will?"

Her eyes had been riveted by the scars. Rather than deform him, they gave his finely honed body a sense of reckless adventure and romantic mystique.

Dragging her gaze back to his face, she said, "Because you owe me."

Written in the Stars

Katherine O'Neal

BANTAM BOOKS

NEW YORK TORONTO LONDON SYDNEY AUCKLAND

WRITTEN IN THE STARS

A Bantam Book / September 1998

ISBN 0-553-57380-2

Published simultaneously in the United States and Canada

PRINTED IN THE UNITED STATES OF AMERICA

WCD   10 9 8 7 6 5 4 3 2 1

For Bill,
for Janie,
and
in loving memory
of
Dr. Q

PROLOGUE

London
June 1894

*D*iana was startled out of her concentration by
the sound of something crashing in the back
room. It was a storeroom, rarely used, with a
single window that would be an ideal invitation to a
burglar. She glanced at the clock. It was after midnight. As always, she'd lost all track of time as she'd
pored over the rubbings of ancient Egyptian hieroglyphs. The British Museum was completely deserted
at this hour. She vaguely remembered the guard, Mr.
Brownlow, saying, "I'm gone for the night, now. I'll
be locking you in, Miss Sanbourne."

As she sat frozen at her desk, she heard the distinct sound of someone maneuvering his way through

the storeroom with its unpacked boxes from expeditions all over the world. There could be no doubt of it now. Someone had scaled the rear fence, climbed through the window, and was coming her way.

In a panic, she glanced about the office for something she could use as a weapon. There was nothing but the stacks of reference books she used in her study of ancient languages, rolled papyrus scripts, and her empty teacup. The footsteps came closer. She shot up from the desk. Her mind flashed on all the stories she'd heard of Jack the Ripper, how he'd cornered lone women late at night to brutally butcher them. Or, if she was lucky, maybe it was a skilled thief—someone after priceless antiquities. The museum's security was paltry at best. Only two guards patrolled the vast mausoleum, neither one especially reliable, as they'd been known to take a nip or two throughout the lonely nights.

She stared at the door. The knob began to turn. *I'm twenty years old,* she thought. *I'm getting married the day after tomorrow. How can this be happening to me?*

Spurred to action, she kicked off her shoes and ran out the side door into the dark hall. She paused at the entrance of the Egyptian wing. The intruder was following her. She could hear the determined tread of his boots resounding against the marble floors. Darting into the wing, she was immediately surrounded by the eerie shadows of giant obelisks, colossal granite statues, a long file of sphinxes, brightly painted New Kingdom caskets, and immense stone sarcophaguses with their carved instructions for the afterlife.

She felt small and vulnerable amidst the ghostly splendor. But she realized she had the advantage of knowing the layout of the room. Surely the intruder wouldn't try to follow her into its dark recesses.

She paused to get her bearings. The footfalls continued in her direction, growing louder with each step. She was shaking now and her breath was coming fast. He seemed to be coming not for booty, but for her. As if he knew she'd be alone and unprotected at this hour.

Quietly, on her stockinged feet, she raced through the wing toward the passage that led to the Greek and Roman displays. The curator's office was just beyond the Elgin marbles. Surely she could find a weapon there. Or perhaps she could commandeer a heavy object along the way. But no. The archaeologist in her was loath to risk damaging some irreplaceable artifact, even if her life was in danger.

She passed the Rosetta Stone, out of the Egyptian section, and entered the larger, high-ceilinged chamber that housed the Graeco-Roman statuary collection. Weaving a shortcut through the marble fragments that had once adorned the Parthenon, she came to the office door. But when she turned the knob, she realized with horror that it was locked. The footsteps were growing louder by the second. There was no way out.

She turned, her back pressed against the door. The footsteps stopped. Across the vast hall, through the shadows of the flowing statues, she could see the silhouette of her pursuer. He stood like a phantom in the darkened archway. His breathing was heavy, ominously loud in the silent room.

Then she remembered. There was a fire ax on the wall just opposite her. She took two steps and yanked it free. It was heavy, the wood of the handle seeming to cut into her palms. She raised the ax above her head. "Take one step closer and I'll chop you in half," she told him, her voice echoing through the stillness, her tone shockingly calm.

"I believe you would," came a deep voice from the shadows.

"Jack!"

She let the ax drop to her side. As he struck a match, the flame formed a candescent wreath around him. Awash in relief, she knew she'd never seen an image quite so welcome. Or so arresting.

At twenty-five, her fiancé, Jack Rutherford, was tall and dramatically handsome in a rugged, commanding way. There was nothing soft or boyish about him. The sun-bronzed, virile features and his unflinching glare spoke of a seasoned confidence that was rare in a man his age. His hair was streaked a light bronze from his many years spent in sun-drenched lands. Tonight it fell about his head with shaggy disregard. Broad-shouldered and lean, his powerful body was draped in a dark suit that looked as if he'd slept in it, the jacket falling open, the shirt unbuttoned at the throat. He appeared disheveled, which gave him a rough-hewn, devilish demeanor she loved. His strong jaw sported the slightest trace of a stubble, as if he'd forgotten to shave. It was a casual disregard for decorum that never failed to stir her.

But her heart was still pounding madly from her scare. "You idiot!" she cried. "You nearly scared me to death."

"I had to see you. The museum was closed, so I let myself in."

Now that she was calming down, she wasn't too surprised. Jack was nothing if not ingenious. A locked window would pose little challenge to him. Still, it was an uncharacteristic appearance. Many of his actions lately had baffled her. Indeed, the past month had been a difficult time for Jack. His father, Niven Rutherford, had unexpectedly passed away in May. Jack had suddenly inherited the earldom and all its inherent responsibilities. Diana had suggested postponing the wedding, but it had been dear Niven's last wish that they go ahead with it as planned. She'd seen little of Jack in the past few weeks and even when she had, he'd seemed distant and preoccupied. She understood. He'd been close to his father, as she was to hers. But still, he'd seemed to be taking his loss harder than she'd expected.

He shook out the match and in one motion, crossed the distance to her. In the darkness, she felt his hands grasping her shoulders with a firm grip, slamming her against the solid wall of his chest so her breath left her lungs in a single gasp. His arms went around her, clutching her to him, enclosing her in imprisoning bands of steel. He found her mouth with his and smothered her in a devastating kiss.

She began to tremble again, but this time not with fear, clinging to him as he stole her breath, loosing her hands to run her fingers through his hair. "Jack," she cried when her mouth was free. "You impulsive fool. I never know what to expect with you." Her voice took on a teasing tone. "I should be angry with you. You've stayed away so long, a girl could begin to wonder if you still wanted her."

He loosened his embrace and raised his head. She could feel his eyes boring into hers. Then, with a savage jerk, he thrust her up against him and buried his lips in her hair. "Diana, God help me, I want you more than life itself."

His intensity was overwhelming. He was kissing her again, holding her so powerfully that she felt her feet leave the floor.

"Oh, Jack," she murmured, "I want you, too. And in two days—"

He straightened abruptly.

"What is it?" she asked, sensing more to his mood than he was divulging.

"Do you love me, Diana?"

"You know I do."

"But do you love me enough? Enough to—" He stopped again, faltering on the words.

"Jack, how can you ask? You're such a blessing in my life. Sometimes I feel so grateful for you that I don't think my body can hold the force of it."

He didn't move. "But do you love me," he asked quietly, "enough to withstand anything? If I did something—if I disappointed you—if I—"

"Jack, stop it! How could you ever disappoint me? I know you as I know myself. What is this? Wedding jitters? I know we can't tell what the future will bring. I know there will be hardships. But I know it won't matter. You could never do anything—"

"But if I did," he insisted.

She tenderly ran her fingers along the stubble of his jaw. "What's happened?" she asked at last.

"No questions, love, please. I need to know. Is there anything I could do—*anything at all*—to make you turn from me? To make you—hate me?"

"Nothing," she cried, her conviction causing her voice to throb. "There's nothing you could ever do that would make me hate you. How could you even think it?"

"Swear to me."

"I don't need to—"

He grabbed her arms and shook her. "Swear to me, Diana. *Swear it!*"

She was so surprised, it took her a moment to find her voice. She rubbed his cheek in a gesture of comfort and said, "I swear to you, Jack Rutherford, that nothing and no one will ever cause me to love you any less than I do now. Don't you believe me?"

He took her in his arms, more gently now, and whispered, "If you only knew how I want to. I need you, Diana."

He'd never said those words before. She wrapped her arms about him as he kissed her hair, his mouth moving to the flesh of her neck. She felt a sweep of longing coil inside. She turned her head to his, felt his mouth seize hers, felt dizzy from the onslaught of his kiss. In an instant, she was hoisted up into his arms and he was carrying her, his mouth locked on hers, through a maze of hallways and into an atrium they knew well. There, in a re-creation of a Roman villa, he laid her on a daybed beneath the window. She was suddenly bathed in moonlight. She stretched her arms to him and he went to her, covering her with his heavy frame, so she could feel the heat and iron of his erection on her thigh.

"Love me, Diana," he pleaded against her mouth.

She stilled in his arms. They'd agreed to wait until their wedding night, fighting their desire for each other to keep this sacred vow. Not that it had been easy. Jack's persuasive seduction had made her hunger for his body so many times, she'd had to tear herself from him to keep that promise. She looked at him now, bent on reminding him once again of their pledge, but she saw in the moonlight a proud man who'd never begged for anything in his life, pleading with his eyes for the love only she could give.

"Love me," he whispered again.

She'd never loved him more. He seemed like a lost child, this strong, decisive man who would boldly break into a locked museum because he wanted to see her. She'd never seen him like this, unprotected, needy, seeking assurance when he'd always been the one to reassure. And in that moment, when he needed her most, when he craved proof of all the love she had to give, she knew she couldn't deny him.

She smiled at him, and slowly, with fumbling fingers, unbuttoned the bodice of her gown. She'd unthinkingly worn his favorite dress, but now she was glad. She parted the midnight blue silk and brought her hands to cup her breasts, offering them in invitation.

He stared for a moment at the creamy, moon-kissed mounds of flesh with the nipples standing erect from the knowledge of his gaze. And then, like a starving man, he dropped his head and took one, then the other, into the moist cavern of his mouth, feasting on her with an insatiable appetite that made her loins cry out with need.

It wasn't the first time she'd felt these longings while lying in his arms. But never before had she been possessed of the knowledge that tonight, now, this very minute, she would open herself to him for the taking. The knowledge thrilled yet frightened her. She felt more of a woman than she ever had, savoring the enveloping succor of his mouth on her breast, the grazing of his stubbled jaw. She felt like molten liquid, melting, dissolving, flowing like warm lava toward his rapacious mouth. Yet she quivered with longing and with fear, not knowing what to expect once she'd passed the boundaries of the last frontier of her girlhood, the roadblock that had kept her agonizingly disconnected from the man she loved. She didn't know what to do, or how to please him.

But he sensed it, as he'd sensed her every thought since she was six years old. He lifted his head and caressed her mouth with his lips to put her at ease. And then he trailed loving kisses along her cheek until his mouth was at her ear and he was whispering, with an intimate huskiness to his voice, "As long as I live, Diana, I'll never love anyone but you."

It sounded like good-bye. And because it did, she lost her fear, lost her reticence in her desperation to give that which he sought—reassurance that their love would withstand the ravages of time.

She began to kiss him with all her inflamed passion, pressing her pliant body to his. Then she was drowning in the sensation of his mouth as it roamed her curves, grazing her shoulder, her throat, the small hollow between her breasts. Worshiping every inch of her as her dress slid from her like hot wax from a flame. Before she knew it, they were both naked and she caught a glimpse in the moon's enchanted glow of his firmly muscled chest covered by a thick, seductive smattering of hair. It traversed his chest, pointing like an arrow down his stomach to the—

Suddenly she froze. "Are you sure, Jack? Are we doing the right thing?"

"I'm sure," he growled.

The magic of his hands parted her thighs, expertly and in a fashion not to be denied, before his mouth found her and caused a strangled gasp. His exquisite, hot tongue made her forget everything—her abandoned work, her surroundings—everything but the wicked sensation of opening herself completely before him. She was on fire, thrusting into his mouth as her breath burned her lungs like a torch. She cautioned herself to be quiet, even clamped her teeth upon her lower lip, but then, to her amazement, she felt herself unfolding completely beneath his mouth, felt the blood rush to her head, felt an explosion of such majesty that she clutched his head and cried out with her panting breath.

As she was still swirling, still awash with astonishing pleasure, he heaved himself up. He moved between her thighs and she felt the head of his erection. She wanted him inside, wanted him as she'd wanted nothing else. Lifting her hips, she beckoned to him, whimpering her need.

As he entered her and pain ripped through her, it was as if the door of some internal cage had been cast open, and her soul had been set free. She glimpsed the woman she was meant to be, in all her glory, free and fearless, not a creature full of doubt and trepidation. She saw herself standing in the light, whole, complete, glowing with a radiant joy.

The moment was as fleeting as the pain. She felt shaken, as if she'd glimpsed something just out of reach. But then Jack's mouth closed over her own, muffling the cry she hadn't known she'd made, as he lay atop her, in her, not moving, only kissing her and soothingly stroking her hair. She realized the courtesy he was affording her—giving her a chance to adjust to the invasion of his body, holding back the impulse to pump and plunge his way to bliss. Controlling all the unleashed passion of a decade of waiting—waiting still, to be certain she was ready in these final moments before he allowed himself to sate his long-held lust.

Wanting it as much as he, she moved beneath him. He took her lead, stroking cautiously so as not to hurt her. She felt so full, she marveled that she could take all of him inside. She felt closer to him than she ever had, felt that she'd become a part of him and he of her. And she knew, as he began to thrust in her, that this was as it was always meant to be. They were soul mates, destined to be one through eternity and beyond.

The guests waited patiently amidst the hushed splendor of St. Paul's Cathedral as the pipe organ played selections from Mozart. It was an assembly of remarkable distinction. The marriage of the new Earl of Birch Haven to the daughter of Sir Stafford Sanbourne was itself a cause for special celebration. But what brought the core of fashionable nobility—earls, countesses, marquesses, dukes and duchesses—to mingle with the scholars, professors, and museum curators who made up the couple's world, was the unending fascination society had for the relatively new science of archaeology.

For most of the past decade, the British public had thrilled to the exploits and discoveries of the two noted archaeologists, Stafford Sanbourne and his more aristocratic best friend, the late Niven Rutherford. But no aspect of their celebrated careers had ever captured the collective fancy as much as their

long-standing quest for the fabled Cleopatra treasure—the legendary legacy of Egypt's last queen.
Eight months before, they'd found what they considered a decisive step toward that goal, a shipwreck of a
Roman galleon off the Egyptian coast containing artifacts they believed belonged to Cleopatra herself.
The discovery was called the Alexandria Collection.
It had created more excitement than any discovery
since Schliemann had found Troy. The ceremony
joining the offspring of these two heroes, archaeologists in their own right, was being hailed as the wedding of the year.

The rumors surrounding their romance were as
enchanting to the public as any of Mrs. Spencer-
Campbell's fanciful tales. But only the couple themselves knew how magical their childhood had been.
They'd largely grown up together, spending their
summers accompanying their fathers on archaeological expeditions. As young children, they'd played
among the ruins of Pompeii, Jack taunting Diana to
keep up with him as he scampered through the city.
As early teenagers, they'd shared a first kiss under the
moonlight of the Athenian Acropolis, thrilling at the
touch of soft lips and playful tongues. As older teenagers, they'd felt their first sexual stirrings—and had
fallen madly in love—on an excavation of Druid
ruins on the wild Irish coast, certain that no lovers
since the dawn of time had felt such passion and
longing.

As young adults and budding archaeologists,
they'd discovered that even their intellectual gifts

complemented each other. Bored with the library and laboratory, Jack came alive in the field, displaying an uncanny ability to sniff out seemingly impossible finds. Diana, on the other hand, was an unusually talented linguist who could speak several languages and read ancient Greek and Egyptian hieroglyphs as well as anyone in the world. Together, they felt the excitement of being pioneers in a profession that was young and filled with endless promise. It was only natural that they'd be married, joining the Sanbourne and Rutherford families and teaming their unique abilities to become what they knew they were destined to be: two halves of one remarkable whole.

Diana would never forget the day he'd asked her to marry him. He'd taken her on a Sunday picnic at Birch Haven, his family estate in Bedfordshire. With an irresistible romantic flourish, he'd carried her to a waiting rowboat and laid her gently in a luxurious bed of brocade pillows. Snaking their way through the reeds that lined the narrow curves of the River Kennet, they'd whiled away the lazy afternoon. As Diana lounged, barefoot and filled with a sense of peace and contentment, Jack had spoken quietly but with heartfelt candor of all he wanted his life to be. He'd described for her the crucial moment when he'd first understood his destiny.

"My father told me something when I was ten years old, which I've never forgotten. He said that what he did—what we do, Diana—is more important than the work of any kings or prime ministers. Because when people see for themselves the legacy of the past, they understand history in a way they otherwise never could. It ignites in them a passion and curiosity they'd never feel from reading the dry volumes of dead writers. By digging up the lost past, we make it live again. And the only way our species will ever improve itself or learn from its mistakes is to know exactly how we reached this point in time. Archaeology connects us in a very real way to our roots, makes us realize we're all one human family."

Even now, as Diana stood before the mirror in a side room of the church, adding the finishing touches to her bridal finery, the memory of those words brought tears to her eyes. On that exquisite afternoon, she'd looked directly into Jack's soul and glimpsed there an unshakable bond—a bond that few couples on this earth would ever be privileged enough to share. As precious as this ceremony would be, it was merely a formality.

In the reflection, she caught a glimpse of her mother, Prudence, looking triumphantly out the door at the sea of important faces. Prudence was a dedicated social climber, the daughter of a merchant who'd thought Stafford Sanbourne a good catch when she was young, only to become disenchanted with his long absences and to regret that she hadn't held out for an earl, at the very least. Diana glanced again at her own image, at the bold and striking features, the sleek black hair, the catlike ebony eyes. So different from the blond frailty of her parents, her mother sharp-featured and small, her father gentle-featured, his skin eternally tanned from years spent in the sun.

She'd always disliked her looks. They were too exotic, branding her as different from the rosy-cheeked children at school and their pale, aristocratic parents. But now all she saw was the happiness that seemed to glow like a light from within her.

Getting into position for his march down the aisle, Stafford, who cared nothing for the social ramifications of his daughter's marriage to an earl, gave Diana a wistful smile. "I knew this day was coming the first time I saw you and Jack together. I think you were two, and he seven. Some marriages really *are* written in the stars." He cast a haunted look at his wife. "I only wish Niven could have lived to see it."

Diana squeezed his arm, sharing a somber homage for the passing of their dearest friend.

At that moment, the wedding coordinator gave the signal to begin and the wedding party scrambled into position. As the organ music changed, and her bridesmaids made their way up the aisle, Diana glanced nervously at the assembly. The Rutherford family side of the aisle was filled with nobility, the cousins, aunts, and uncles having come from as far away as Northumberland for Niven's funeral and having stayed on for the wedding. In the front pew, Jack's younger sisters, Primmie, eighteen, and Edith, sixteen, proudly watched their brother take his place at the altar. Diana followed their gaze to behold the handsomest groom she'd ever seen, formally attired in black cutaway, fawn-grey trousers, and a black and silver striped cravat—vestments that strangely made him appear more rugged than ever, even as he gave the impression of elegant assurance. He turned to look at her and their gazes locked as the music cued her to begin the procession.

She couldn't take her eyes off him as she made the journey that would lead her to a new life. Standing before the altar, Stafford placed her hand in Jack's, kissed her cheek, and stepped back. Jack's hand was warm and steady, his gaze roaming her face. He seemed at ease, very much his old self as he crooked a knowing grin. As if their love two nights before had made the ceremony an anticlimax, and he couldn't wait to have her alone, in his arms, once again.

But his ease was shattered and his eyes flashed alarm when the sound of a disturbance echoed through the vast cathedral. All heads turned to the rear as an officious, red-haired man and three stone-faced constables charged up the aisle. The music faltered, then died on a sour note. Diana's father stepped forth to cut them off.

"What is the meaning of this?" he cried.

"I'm terribly sorry, Sir Stafford, but—"

"Who in blazes are you?"

"Excuse me again, sir. I'm Inspector Worthington of Scotland Yard."

Stafford was by now red with rage. "Do you realize what you're interrupting? We're in the middle of a wedding."

"I realize that, sir. But information has reached my office that makes this wedding highly inadvisable. I think you'll thank me when—"

"What information?" Stafford demanded.

Diana glanced up at Jack and felt her heart skip a beat. She'd seen that look in his eyes before, the day he'd rid his schoolyard of a bully and had been taken to task for ruining his good clothes. The look of a man who'd done what he had to do, and was now willing to take the consequences.

Inspector Worthington was also looking at Jack. He said, "Lord Rutherford, it is my unfortunate duty to arrest you in the name of Her Majesty the Queen."

"This is preposterous," Stafford argued as murmurs hummed through the church. "Of what possible crime?"

"The crime is theft."

The murmurs converged into a collective gasp. Prudence rose from her pew.

"My office has acquired evidence that Lord Rutherford has surreptitiously sold off a significant portion of what has become known as the Alexandria Collection. Priceless relics that were promised to the British Museum. In other words, sir, stolen from the British nation. An act not only of theft but of high treason."

The sudden silence in the church was suffocating.

"Where did you get such outlandish information?" Stafford cried.

"From none other than Sir Bunky Haversham, president of the Royal Geographical Society. An unimpeachable source, I'm sure you'll agree."

Stafford blinked. "But why would young Rutherford do such a thing? The Alexandria Collection is our greatest discovery yet. His father's and mine. The lad himself contributed enormously to—"

"It doesn't belong to any of you. It belongs to the British people. It was merely in your trust. As to why the lad did it, we'll leave that to the courts to determine."

At the Inspector's signal, the constables moved forward and began to clamp irons on Jack's wrists. Cries of outrage and disbelief reverberated from the guests.

"The Queen herself will hear of this travesty," called a male voice from the crowd.

The unperturbed Inspector replied, "Her Majesty will not condone a theft of this magnitude, even from a member of the peerage."

Diana had heard enough. Turning on Jack, she cried, "Tell him you didn't do it!"

He said nothing, just looked at her with sad resignation in his eyes. His silence inflamed her. Why didn't he defend himself? Bold and impetuous he may be. But a thief? Never!

"For God's sake, Jack. Tell this sanctimonious little man that you didn't do this despicable thing!"

Taking up his chains, the constables began to lead him away. In a panic, Diana rushed to Jack and grabbed his arm. "Jack, tell *me* you didn't do it."

He stood for a moment, looking into her eyes. "I can't do that, Diana," he said in an eerie, unemotional tone. "Because I *did* do it."

*D*iana drifted through the crowd at the Wapping dock, full of nervous anticipation, the mysterious telegram clutched in her gloved hand. She still wasn't certain why she'd come. It could be a hoax. Her father's death the month before in Egypt had been highly publicized. Any prankster could have sent the wire. Why, then, did Diana feel so compelled to come?

Through the fog, she glanced at the telegram once again. "I have important information about your father." It wasn't signed. It contained instructions to meet the ship, where she would be recognized and hailed. She had no idea who the author might be or what he could possibly tell her about her father. But

here she was, awaiting the arrival of the ship from
Cairo and the passenger who she hoped would clear
up the mystery.

Perhaps it was Diana's need to feel connected
with her father once again that had caused her to take
this summons seriously. She'd had a month to mourn
his death—a hellish month during which the newspapers had dragged up the old scandal, raking over
Stafford's sad downfall, portraying him as a pathetic
failure with his head tragically in the clouds. A man
who'd wasted his life seeking a treasure that didn't
exist.

The treasure. The Cleopatra love treasure that had
caused so much excitement . . . and over the last
five years, so much grief.

The quest for it had begun even before Diana was
born, on her father's first expedition to Egypt. He
and Niven Rutherford had stumbled upon tantalizing evidence that the great queen Cleopatra and
her Roman lover, Mark Antony, had hidden a priceless horde of gold and jewels shortly before their joint
suicide in 30 B.C. When word of the potential treasure had first leaked out, the world was thrilled by
the wildly romantic notion that a legacy might have
been left by two of the most notorious, glamorous,
and ultimately tragic lovers in history. Fleet Street
quickly dubbed it "The Love Treasure."

But when the antiquities of the Alexandria Collection couldn't be conclusively authenticated as belonging to the queen, the tide of public opinion had
turned sharply against Stafford Sanbourne. Three

months later, the all-powerful Royal Geographical Society suddenly dropped its support. The quest was criticized in the *London Times* and savagely lampooned in *Punch,* and the love treasure came to be regarded as a fantasy, in the same league with unicorns and leprechaun's gold.

But Stafford had never given up. He'd invested every shilling he had, all the money he could beg or borrow, to finance his expeditions to Egypt. He'd always felt that a breakthrough was just around the corner. Diana had worked long hours at the British Museum, translating hieroglyphs and helping to catalog antiquities from the museum's numerous expeditions. She was the most talented translator they had, acknowledged as the foremost expert in reading ancient Egyptian texts. She'd used what money she earned—half of what a man would make, which was little enough—to help fund her father's quest, devoting her life to helping him prove to the world that he wasn't the fool they thought him, after all. And to extricate him from the taint of Jack's crime.

Now poor Stafford had died an ignoble death, perishing of fever in some Egyptian hovel, far away from any loving care. Diana should have been with him. She should have insisted on accompanying him, even when he'd so adamantly refused. If she'd been there, maybe he'd be alive now.

She'd found out later that he'd spent precious money before leaving for Egypt to take out an insurance policy in her name. Had he sensed that this might be his last trip? It chilled her to think so.

She'd unexpectedly been left the tidy fortune of thirty thousand pounds, but she hated the money—considered it blood money—and couldn't think what to do with it. She'd lost the entire focus of her life. Every waking moment had been dedicated to helping in her father's quest. What stability and purpose she felt had died with Stafford. The money he'd left should have afforded her a welcome independence from her mother. But even that was little comfort. She'd happily trade every shilling of it to have her father back again. She missed him terribly. She couldn't stop mourning his death. She couldn't stop thinking about him. And now, this incredible message . . .

She looked about her at the eerie figures drifting through the dense fog. All around her there was an air of expectation, mostly from families awaiting the arrival of soldiers returning from the Suez garrison, or red-coated officers about to assume their posts in Anglo-Egypt. The latter stood about in groups, discussing the continued troubles in the Sudan, or complaining that they'd be so far from home when the new century—scarcely two months away—dawned.

Diana scanned the assemblage, watching children scamper through the fog, thinking sadly of her own childhood. She'd always been an outsider at school. The fact that she'd spent her summers with her father, traveling to foreign places and embarking on adventures her companions would never know, had made her an object of envy and suspicion. She wasn't like the other children. She even looked different, with her exotic features and her honey complexion. They perceived her as being foreign, mysterious, even aloof, when in reality her differences had made her shy, longing to be accepted, but not knowing how to go about bridging the gap. So she was left alone. It was one of the things she'd had in common with Jack, early on. He, too, had spent his summers with their fathers on archaeological digs. He understood the loneliness of trying to fit in with playmates who couldn't possibly understand his way of life. It had bonded them together, despite the difference in their ages. She hadn't had to explain herself to Jack. They spoke with a shorthand that was born of shared experience.

She drew herself up short. It had been some time since she'd thought of Jack. But now, when she felt so vulnerable and alone, Jack's specter came back to haunt her. She never thought of him without feeling humiliated all over again. As painful as it was, the scandal that had followed his confession—the subsequent trial, the stripping of his title, his prison sentence, the Sanbournes' rejection by the same polite society who'd trooped to her wedding, the endless hounding by the London press—had been nothing compared with her personal sense of betrayal.

Around her, the restless crowd perked up in anticipation. A foghorn blew, low and melancholy. Diana glanced up the Thames to see the ghostly silhouette of a ship gliding up the river. She straightened, steeling herself against this new ordeal.

It seemed forever before the ship docked and the
gangplank was lowered. Dock workers unloaded baggage as passengers began to descend. Children
squealed as they recognized fathers, and wives flew
into their husbands' arms. Diana felt a pang as she
remembered all the times she, too, had rushed into
her father's arms when he'd returned from a journey.
Now he'd never return again.

She waited, straining to see the descending passengers, wondering who her mysterious correspon-
dent might be. She watched as the last of the
passengers left with their families. As the baggage
was all cleared. As the soldiers embarked. Soon, the
dock was all but empty. Diana sighed, crushing the
telegram in her hand. It had been a hoax after all.

She turned to leave. As she did, she sensed a presence in the fog. Someone was standing a few yards or
so ahead of her, watching her. The hair at the nape of
her neck prickled in warning. Had she been foolish to
come, after all? Was there danger here?

She stood where she was, clenching her fists,
barely breathing as she waited. For many moments,
she saw nothing but impenetrable fog. Finally,
through the mist, a figure began to emerge. She saw a
faint outline, then, slowly, the image of a woman
appeared. A tall woman with skin the color of honey,
dressed in a form-fitting sheath of emerald silk beneath her cloak.

Diana stood staring as the woman approached like
some mystical apparition. As she drew closer, Diana
began to distinguish the features of her face. Bold,

striking features, dark almond eyes. She looked to be in her forties, yet she was still beautiful, without a touch of grey in her ebony hair. Her slender hands were adorned with jewels. She walked with a grace, a dignity that was bewitching. But as she advanced, Diana's heart gave a panicked lurch. She felt for a moment as if she were seeing herself as she might appear in twenty years' time.

On impulse, she turned to run. Some instinct warned her to flee while she still could.

But as she did, she heard the woman's voice behind her. "Diana, please. Don't go."

The sound of her name stopped Diana short. She turned and watched as the woman continued toward her.

"Who are you?"

The question seemed to unnerve the woman. "I—" She stopped, as if struggling for the proper words. "I knew your father."

Diana shivered. "How?"

The woman glanced about. "Couldn't we sit and talk for a while? I've come so far to see you." She gestured toward a bench.

Her legs feeling as if they might collapse beneath her, Diana dropped onto the seat. The woman joined her.

"My name is Sheila," she began. "I knew your father in Egypt, many years ago. And again just before he died. It is difficult to know how to begin, after all this time."

"I think it best that you tell your story quickly."

A flicker of pain darkened Sheila's eyes. But she said softly, "Very well. I was married when I was twelve to an important man. A—diplomat. He was much older than I, and the marriage was arranged by my uncle upon the death of my parents. I never loved my husband, who proved to be a cruel and domineering man, but I endeavored always to be a good wife to him nonetheless. I was alone much of the time, for he traveled extensively. Those were the times I lived for. You see, we were childless, and my husband blamed me. He beat me when he was home, berating me for my lack. It was vital to him to have an heir to carry on the family name. Because I had failed to give him one, he was ashamed of me, and so he kept me home when he went on his frequent trips abroad."

"It must have been awful for you," Diana sympathized.

"Life to me was a misery. Until I met your father."

Diana shifted uncomfortably.

"I met him one day at the Great Pyramids of Giza. I was accustomed to walking there when my husband was away. We spoke as strangers do, yet there was something about him that intrigued me. It was his first trip to Egypt, yet he was so knowledgeable about my homeland. Not a typical tourist at all. He asked if I would show him the Cairo I knew and loved. I saw no harm. In the course of these outings, he told me of his belief in the Cleopatra treasure."

She turned to Diana with wistful eyes. "I wish you could have seen Stafford then. He was so young, so enthusiastic, so full of hope. Yet he carried an air of sadness about him. He'd been married to your—to Prudence for two years, and they had discovered that she was barren. This was a great disappointment to Stafford, who so longed for a child. This gave us something in common. Also, his wife took no interest in his search for the treasure, and I believe he felt happy to find someone who took pleasure in hearing him speak of it."

Diana looked away, out into the rolling fog. She imagined her father, young, robust, being squired about Cairo by this lovely creature, pouring out the secrets of his heart.

"You became lovers," she said dully.

"Not merely lovers, my child. Stafford and I fell deeply in love. We fought our feelings. After all, we were both married, and took our vows seriously. It seemed a tragedy to us that we had met under these circumstances, when neither of us was free to belong to the other as we wished. But eventually, yes, we became lovers. And after a time . . ." She paused. When she spoke, her melodious voice broke. "I conceived his child."

In a rush, Diana felt the air leave her body. *They had discovered that Prudence was barren . . .* "I don't think I want to hear this."

Sheila was quiet for a moment. Then, softly, she asked, "Have you never wondered why Stafford kept you from Egypt?"

It suddenly made sense. Even though Diana had learned to read ancient hieroglyphs better than perhaps anyone, Egypt was the only field of her father's archaeological endeavors to which he hadn't taken her. She'd sometimes thought he was afraid to take her there, but she couldn't begin to guess why. Throughout her life, every time she'd prepared to accompany him, he'd found some excuse to prevent it. In her youth, he used the excuse that he couldn't take her out of school. Later, he'd invariably invented some vital mission she must perform in England that he couldn't entrust to anyone else. The most magical and mystical place on earth, and she'd never come closer to it than the average layman in England.

Was it possible that *this* was the reason why?

"You can't imagine my joy upon hearing the news," Sheila continued. "It was not my fault, after all, that I had given no children to my husband. It seemed that destiny had taken a hand. To give me the child of the man I so loved—"

Diana felt her knees trembling uncontrollably beneath her dress.

"Stafford and I were so happy that we put aside all thoughts of what was to come. We knew, I think, that we must selfishly hold what happiness we could, even knowing that there was no way for it to last. Oh, Stafford spoke often of divorcing Prudence, and of entreating my husband to divorce me. I even allowed myself for a time to believe it might be possible. If my husband knew of the child, surely he would want me no longer. But he was away, and it was convenient not to think of what would occur when he discovered the truth.

"Those were the most enriching months of my life, feeling my child grow inside me. Stafford was ecstatic. I could see the joy in his eyes every time he looked at me. One night, we took a carriage to the pyramids where we'd first met and walked hand in hand, speaking of our child. But something went amiss. I began to have pains and I knew the child was coming fast. There was no time to get back to the carriage. I had our child there, by the Great Pyramid, in the sand beneath the stars. Stafford and I both cried as he took his daughter in his arms and held her up to the night sky."

Diana's mouth was dry. "You're my mother."

Tears welled in Sheila's eyes. "We named you Diana, after the goddess of the moon."

She reached over and tentatively put her hand on Diana's. But Diana was too stunned to return the affection. She quietly took her hand away.

"What happened?"

"We had one glorious week together, enjoying you. Everything you did was a miracle. You were, indeed, our miracle child. But then, my husband returned unexpectedly. When he learned of your existence, he flew into a terrible rage. He refused to divorce me. He threatened my life. He told me the only way that I would live was if I gave you to your father and sent him back to England, never to see either of you again. I begged and pleaded, to no avail. I told him to kill me, for life would mean nothing without my baby girl. But he had an answer even for that. He swore if I did not do as he demanded that he would have both you and Stafford killed."

By now, tears were splashing on the backs of Sheila's hands. Diana stared at her, aghast. "You can't be serious."

"I have told you my husband was a powerful man. I knew he had arranged the murder of those who opposed him in the past. I knew this was no idle threat. He swore if I ever tried to contact either of you that he would kill you. He would not suffer the humiliation of having his wife leave him for another man and the child of that union. Instead, he would spend the rest of his life making me pay for my betrayal. This, you see, became his greatest pleasure in life. To see me humiliated as I had humiliated him."

"What did you tell my father?"

"I could not tell him the truth. I knew he would confront my husband, and would pay with his life. I loved him so dearly that I could not bear for him to come to such a fate. So I told him I no longer loved him. That I was too ashamed of what I'd done to ever keep our child. I told him to take you and never try to see me again. It was the most difficult thing I have ever done, but in the end, I made him believe me."

Diana ached inside. "How he must have suffered all those years, not knowing why."

"You must believe that I have cried myself to sleep every night of all these years, thinking of the pain I brought to my beloved. But I could not risk his life—or yours." She was quiet for a moment. She glanced at Diana with an ember of hesitation in her eyes, as if struggling to come to a decision. Then, slowly, she reached into the neckline of her emerald dress and brought forth a gold chain. On it were fastened two small gold talismans. One Diana recognized as a cartouche, a small oval frame with a name embossed upon it in hieroglyphs, much like the pharaohs had worn in ancient times. The other was an oddly shaped amulet, like a misshapen fish. "I have worn this always. Do you know what it says?"

She lifted the cartouche and Diana scanned the symbols that ran from top to bottom.

"Diana," she read.

Sheila nodded. "Despite my absence, I always kept you close to my heart."

It was too much to digest. Diana's mind was reeling, struggling to battle with the truth and make some sense of it all. She couldn't bear to look into Sheila's eyes, so much like her own. "Yet you never tried to see us. Not once."

A silence followed her words as Sheila sought to compose herself. "You can never know how desperately I wanted just to see you, to—"

"Why didn't you?"

"Because in the end, I knew the scandal would ruin you both. If I came forward with the truth, I would destroy you as surely as my husband would have. So, as painful as it was, I stayed away, even after my husband passed on. But when I learned that Stafford was in Egypt, and dying, something died inside me. I had to go to him."

Diana looked at her. "You saw him?"

"He was very ill. I tried to nurse him back to health, but all I did was to no avail. He died in my arms."

Diana had to fight back her tears. But she couldn't help feeling it should have been her, and not Sheila, at Stafford's deathbed.

"Just before he died, Stafford gave me a message. He pleaded with me to come and find you and deliver his last words."

"His . . . last words?"

"He asked me to tell you the treasure exists."

"The treasure . . ."

"It is real."

Diana sighed. Even to the end, he was consumed with his eternal quest. Even from the grave, he was singing the same stale song.

"Is that all?"

"No. He said for you to find Cleopatra's cats. Statues. Three of them. They will show you the way."

Diana cast about in her mind, her face puckering into a frown. "What cats? I don't know of any statues belonging to Cleopatra."

"I do not know. His final words were, 'Tell her . . . Alexandria.' "

"But what does that mean?"

"I have told you all he said. But Diana, I will tell you, he died with these words on his lips. He believed them with all his soul. All through his illness, all he wanted was to share his new findings with you, so the two of you could at last begin the real journey.

He died with but one wish. That you should take up his quest, and find the lost treasure in his name."

Diana said nothing.

"I came with your father's message, but I never intended to tell you who I really was. I only wished to see you. To see the woman you'd become. But when I saw you today, when I saw the sorrow on your face . . . perhaps it was selfish of me to reveal myself. I wonder if I haven't done more harm."

"I don't know," Diana said. "I don't know what to think. Do you know how many times I wished—"

She stopped. She couldn't go on.

"Diana, I know not what you must think of me now. But you must know one thing. In all those awful years, I never stopped loving you. My arms never ceased their longing to hold you. No, I will not go on. I can see that you are not yet ready."

Diana felt seized by a strange mixture of longing and dread. "No. I need time to think. It's still a shock. I wish I could give you what you want. I wish I could throw my arms about you and welcome my long lost—mother. But I can't. Not now. I have to sort out my feelings. All those years and you never once came to see us . . ."

"I understand. Very well, my dearest child. I shall return to Cairo with this ship, and give you the time you need. If you find that you wish to know your mother, come to me at this address. I shall welcome you whenever that time may be. And if you care for it, I shall tell you of your heritage, that you might begin to understand more about who you really are."

Diana took the card and held it limply, not looking at it. Sheila sat for a moment, hesitant, as if there was so much more she wanted to do or say. But finally she rose and began to walk toward the ticket office.

On a sudden impulse, Diana called after her. "I was told that I was born in September of 1874. Is that true?"

Sheila turned with a tender look. "No doubt they told you that to make it appear that you were Prudence's child. But no. You were born the eleventh of December, 1873."

With that, she left as she'd come, disappearing into the fog.

When Diana closed the door to her house in Russell Square, she was greeted by Prudence's shrill tones. "Diana, is that you? Where have you been? You've completely missed dinner. If you think I have any intention of coddling you just because—"

Coming into the hall, she spotted Diana's stricken face and stopped.

"I know the truth," Diana told her softly.

"The truth about what, pray tell? I have neither the time nor the patience for riddles."

"I've seen—Sheila."

The color drained from Prudence's face. She said nothing.

Even in the face of this new revelation, Diana felt small before Prudence, as she had as a child. Guilty, trembling, as if she'd done something wrong. Her words, when she spoke, seemed to trip over one another. "I always wondered why you never seemed to—love me the way other mothers loved their children. It must have been dreadful for you, not being able to have children of your own, having to pretend I was your daughter."

"It was more than dreadful," Prudence said in a softer tone. "It was humiliating."

Prudence's acquiescence shook Diana. She'd expected a denial. Now there could be no doubt that what Sheila had said was true. "Why did you go along with it? Did you love father so much?"

"*Love* him?" she sneered. "How could I love him after what he'd done to me? I did what I had to in order to prevent a scandal."

Diana should have known. But she'd just been liberated from a lifetime of deception and mortification. She stood before Prudence now, not as a wicked child awaiting punishment, but as a woman, her equal. The past had been shattered. And before them was the basis for a new beginning, an opportunity to establish a new bond, unfettered by the falsehood that had stood between them. Perhaps they'd come to some understanding. Perhaps even some shared affection.

"Still," she offered, "you took me in when you didn't have to. For that I'm grateful. I'm sorry it was so difficult for you. I'm only beginning to understand what I must have put you through."

But all Prudence said was, "Now that you know, I think it best that you leave this house as soon as possible."

Her words seemed to echo through the silent hall. Diana stood rooted, truly shocked by this cold slamming of the door. It was a moment before she could bring herself to speak.

"Mother, surely we can—"

But Prudence cut her off. "There's no need for you to ever call me that again."

The satisfaction with which the woman spoke these words chilled Diana's blood. All through the lonely years, she'd genuinely wanted her mother's love and affection. But she realized now, staring into the glacial divide, that Prudence had never—not once—wanted Diana as a daughter.

"Very well," Diana said.

"I do have one request, however."

"What is that?"

"If you would be so kind as to not make this common knowledge. I've had enough scandal thrown upon my head because of your father."

It was the first time Prudence had ever shown the slightest vulnerability. But even as she did, she spoke proudly, her head erect, her eyes cold and hard. There would be no softening.

Diana made the promise and went upstairs to spend her last night in Prudence's house.

The hours that followed seemed endless, her loneliness and sense of loss acute. When she finally fell into a fitful sleep, her last conscious thought was that she'd been rejected by not one mother in her life, but two.

2

The next morning, Diana took up residence in a small hotel between Lincoln's Inn Fields and Drury Lane. As she moved her belongings, she felt haunted by her father. It pained her to realize how he must have suffered in silence all those years. Had he seen Sheila's face every time he'd looked at Diana? It surely must have torn his heart out. But he'd never held it against her. He'd loved her, no doubt, with all the devotion he'd longed to lavish on Sheila. She felt strangely closer to him than she ever had before. She knew what it was to be abandoned by someone she'd loved and trusted with all her heart. If she'd known, maybe she could have helped him. The way he'd helped her after Jack . . .

But no. She could do nothing to alter the past. The only way she could make up for the suffering her father had endured was to take up his quest. His final wish. To find the Cleopatra treasure and use it to exonerate his name.

But how to make that wish come true?

She welcomed having a focus once again, something to take her mind off the succession of events that had left her feeling battered. So, settling herself into her cozy room, she set her mind to the puzzle of her father's last words. *Find Cleopatra's cats . . . Alexandria . . .*

She had no idea what this meant. Was she to go to Alexandria? And if so, how would she know where to begin her search? She had no knowledge of any cats belonging to Cleopatra. None of the queen's effects had ever been found, her palace and tomb in Alexandria no doubt buried beneath the extensive rebuilding of the modern city. Even the Alexandria Collection—

Suddenly, her mind gave a jolt. Could that be it? Was her father steering her not toward Alexandria the city, but toward the ill-fated Alexandria Collection?

She thought back to the time when Stafford, Niven, and Jack had found the collection. Stafford had discovered evidence that, after Cleopatra's death, her possessions had been ordered back to Rome. The ship containing them had never reached its destination. In an early Christian-era document unearthed in a nearby monastery, Stafford had found accounts of witnesses who'd seen the ship sink just off the Alexandria harbor. Jack, with his infallible instincts, had calculated the route of the ship, the currents in that area, and the way the storms played off that particular spit of land, and was able to determine where the ship would be. The find had aroused great excitement, even when none of the articles could be conclusively linked to the infamous queen.

Diana, engrossed in wedding plans at the time, had never seen the portion of the collection that Jack had sold off. Was it possible the artifacts had, after all, belonged to Cleopatra? And could her cats be part of the stolen booty?

It was an astonishing thought. But on the heels of her excitement, Diana realized what it really meant. The only person capable of telling her where to find the stolen relics was none other than Jack Rutherford.

The last person on earth she ever wanted to see again.

She thought of everything she could to get around it, but finally it was inescapable. Jack was the only person who could tell her what she needed to know. She'd have to go to him and somehow get the information.

She didn't fool herself into thinking that it would be easy. The Crown's barristers had done everything possible to get Jack to reveal the name of the corrupt collector during the course of the trial—all to no avail. She could only hope that Jack's sense of obligation to her would loosen his tongue.

But the next day when she arrived at the Savoy Hotel, where Jack had taken up residence, she felt like a nervous adolescent. She scolded herself, recalling that this was a matter of business and nothing more. She would simply procure the information she needed and leave the way she'd come, unscathed by her confrontation. Jack meant nothing to her now except as a means to an end.

She was informed at the reception desk that Mr. Rutherford was in the dining salon. She'd heard that he held court there, sometimes for hours in the afternoon. She knew, too, that Jack had become a celebrity in the ensuing years: a kind of archaeological mercenary who had no official affiliation but was invariably the last resort called upon by governments, museums, or private collectors when they'd reached a dead end in some expedition or treasure hunt. Always for a whopping fee. His amazing discoveries of the last three years included the lost Inca palace of Machu Picchu, the Zulu diamond mine of Botswana, and the Viking tombs of Erikson Fjord. Each had rated a front-page story in the *London Times*.

This would have been enough to keep his name in the papers, but his fame was given a special luster by the scandal of his past. Jack was celebrated not in spite of this skeleton in his closet, but *because* of it. The London press chronicled every move he made, dragging out the story of how this fallen aristocrat had spent two years in Wormwood Scrubs prison for "stealing from the British nation." Hinting that he was secretly a smuggler, a gunrunner, a pirate.

While all this made Jack Rutherford a pariah to polite society, it afforded him a unique attraction to the bohemian crowd. Artistic people flocked to him. He was seen in theaters, concert halls, in fashionably eccentric salons, surrounded by poets and painters who were thrilled by his edge of danger and scandal. He squired around some of the most alluring and seductive actresses the boards had ever served up. He was rumored to have had an affair with Lillian Russell before abruptly breaking it off. He never dallied with any woman for long, but those he chose were the ripest flowers of the West End.

Diana tried to reconcile the vile things she'd heard with her memory of the young man who, on a lazy river dappled with sun, had spoken with such passion of using his talents to make history come alive. She couldn't.

On the threshold of the salon, she looked across the room and saw him for the first time since their aborted wedding. She wasn't prepared for the sight of him. He was sitting at a round table with three other men, superbly attired in a dove-colored coat and striped cravat, lounging nonchalantly in his chair with his arm draped over the back, holding a cigarette that sent spirals of smoke to the ceiling. She'd forgotten the way his hair—tamed to perfection now in a debonair sweep off his forehead—glinted like an ancient Roman coin. How his face had a life and character all its own. A thoroughly manly face, as rugged as a mountain crag, sculpted lean by exposure to exotic winds, crinkled now about the eyes by lines made from scanning distant horizons, squinting into the sun.

A new aura emanated from him. As if a live electric wire lay sparking in the street, riveting everyone's attention, yet keeping each frozen in his tracks, fascinated yet afraid to come too close. He wore it the way a dangerous man might assume an air of courtesy. He wore it like a shield.

He was speaking easily with the men at his table, his grin flashing briefly so Diana saw for the fleetest of moments the man he'd been. She felt the shock of it directly in her loins. She'd expected to hate him, and so she did. But she'd forgotten one simple truth: never had she been in the same room with Jack Rutherford without wanting to throw herself into his arms and drown in the possession of his kiss.

Her heart was thumping like a shutter banging in a storm. She was seized by an impulse to turn and run. But she couldn't. For the sake of her father, and for her newfound self, she had to stay. She had to bolster herself to face what she must.

"May I be of some 'elp, then, miss?"

She turned to find a bellman peering at her. He was short, barely five feet, dressed in a smart green uniform that he wore like a bantam cock, chest thrust out with an air of self-importance.

"I'm 'Enery, miss. At yer service, I am."

Diana reached into her bag and withdrew a calling card. "Well then, Henry, I'd like you to take this card to that man at the corner table."

His eyes followed the small gesture of her hand,

then he turned back to her with a wary gaze. "Mr. Rutherford, is it, miss?"

"Yes. I have some business with him."

His face assumed a look of long-suffering refusal. "I can't be botherin' Mr. Rutherford. Honest, now, you women'll be the death of me. When are ye goin' to learn, ye can't jest march in 'ere and barge in on a man like Mr. Rutherford?"

His implication that Jack had women barging in on him day and night rankled her. She gave him an imperious look and said, "I'm an old family acquaintance. I assure you he'll see me."

"Isn't that wot they all say, then? Don't get me wrong, miss, I'm not sayin' 'tis always a pleasure. But 'Enery 'ere 'as to tyke care o' Mr. Rutherford. 'E depends on me, see? Look yonder. Y'see that bloke sittin' there with him? That's Mr. Gilbert 'isself. The bloke what makes those musicales with Mr. Sullivan. Wot d'ye think 'e's after? Jest wants to make one about Mr. Rutherford, that's all. 'Bout 'is adventures in the jungles of Java, or some sech thing. With songs and wot."

Diana's patience was at an end. "I don't need a résumé," she snapped. "I just want you to take this to him." She was still holding the card in her hand.

"Listen to 'Enery, missy. Wot 'Enery don't know about don't 'appen in this 'otel. 'E'll break yer 'eart, will Mr. Rutherford. Yer a fair-lookin' woman, but 'e's already got a liedy fer the noite. 'E's spoken fer with Miss Lucy Brannigan." Diana was staring at him with a blank look. "Ye know, that new actress wot's playin' in the theater next door. 'E never laid eyes on 'er, but she's a woman, ain't she? She sent word she'd loike to see 'im after the show." He leaned toward her with a proud, conspiratorial tone. "She's a stunner, that Miss Lucy. Ye don't want to compete wi' the loikes of 'er. I'm to bring 'er to his room at eleven o'clock. So ye can see 'e's booked up fer the noite. Ye might try tomorrow, though."

Her female vanity smarting, she felt the urge to show this self-important little twit a thing or two. Through gritted teeth, she insisted, "Just take the card to him. That's all I want you to do."

He held out a silver tray with a shrug. "Very well, miss. But tyke it from 'Enery. 'Enery knows."

She dropped her card onto the tray. "Believe me, when he sees my name he'll come running."

She watched him walk across the dining room, relishing the anticipation of the sheepish look on his face when Jack proved him wrong. Henry stopped beside Jack and, bowing at the waist, held forth the tray. Jack was engaged in animated conversation. He spoke, took a puff on his cigarette, and blew out the smoke as he chuckled at something someone had said. He didn't even look at Henry. As he spoke again, he took up the card, and glanced at it while finishing his story. Everyone laughed as if he'd just told a riotously funny joke. Still laughing, Jack put the card on the table, took the pen Henry handed him, and scrawled something on it before tossing it back onto the tray, never once giving any indication that he'd noticed Henry's presence. As Henry moved away, Jack spoke again and a burst of male laughter filled the room.

Diana smiled confidently as Henry returned. She snatched the card from the tray and glanced at it, preparing to scold Henry for his rudeness. But when she saw the card, her smile and her superior air exploded in her face.

Without so much as a pause in his conversation, Jack had scrawled across her card, "Not interested."

"Sorry, miss. But I tried to tell ye. 'E's already got a liedy fer the noite."

As he left, Diana stood frozen, feeling as if she'd just been kicked in the stomach. She realized now, some small part of her had always believed that—despite everything—if she really needed him, Jack would come to her aid. This casual dismissal seemed the ultimate proof of his betrayal. She felt her illusions shatter, felt herself at the dead end of her quest before it had even begun.

But as she stood there, glaring at his contemptuous words, something began to take hold of her. A new spirit, an absolute unwillingness to accept defeat. Her shock crystalized into a brittle anger and fierce determination. Dismiss her, would he? She'd just see about that!

The moment she left, Jack dropped his bantering grin. The sight of Diana's card had been a shock, but he'd disguised his reaction with a steely will. Now the pain of seeing her standing there so boldly, so imperiously, hit him full force, bringing with it raw memories of her betrayal. He recalled again how she'd looked meltingly into his eyes and sworn her loyalty and her love. And how, just days later, she'd turned on him so readily, not even bothering to show up for his trial. It angered him to realize how fresh the hurt still was. Damn her for bringing it all back again, when he thought he'd finally put it all aside.

He felt his hand shake with the force of his rage. The conversation flowed around him, unheard. He saw in the shallow, smiling faces of his companions the sham his life had become. Empty. Hollow. Going through the motions of living with a deadened heart.

He'd had enough. Not even bothering to cloak his scowl, he crushed his cigarette and threw a wad of bills onto the table.

"You'll have to excuse me, gentlemen," he said, before abruptly rising and marching through the room.

They watched in abashed silence as he left, wondering what had caused this sudden change of mood. But then they shrugged in silent agreement. Rutherford was volatile, driven by dark impulses they couldn't comprehend. It was one of the traits that fascinated them most.

3

As was his custom, Jack strolled leisurely along the Strand, heading toward Covent Garden to clear his head before bed. It was early for him, hardly past midnight. But his engagement with the actress hadn't gone as planned. She was a beauty, no denying it. But try as he had, he couldn't seem to concentrate on her. He couldn't shake off the vision of Diana standing proudly in the aftermath of his snub.

That vision had haunted him until at last he'd cut the evening short and headed off on his own for a nightcap at the Lamb and Flag. The fresh air didn't help. He was still churning with a dozen emotions he'd just as soon dismiss. The memory of those endless nights in prison, reliving Diana's words. *There's nothing you could ever do that would make me hate you. How could you even think it?* Words that had proved cheap when he'd needed her the most. All the nights when he'd tried to hate her, knowing in his most secret heart that he'd give anything—*anything*—for just one forgiving smile. To hear that she understood.

He shook his head, determined to erase the painful memory even if he had to drown it in rye. But as he turned the corner onto Bedford Street, his desire to forget was given assistance in a most unexpected way. He felt a heavy club to the back of his head. The next moment he slumped, unconscious, to the ground.

With a soft groan, he came back to consciousness, slowly, by agonizing degrees. He felt groggy—so much that his head ached and he had to fight to open his eyes. When he finally did, he realized that he was surrounded by pitch black, a smothering darkness in which he could feel the heat of his breath. Too dark for night, too enclosed for—

Suddenly, he realized that there was something covering his head. A hood of some sort. He jerked, bent on yanking it off, and found that his arms were bound. He tried again. He began to struggle, a little at first, then increasing his jerks until he felt something beneath him nearly topple over. Only then did he realize, with the numb horror of someone awakened to a nightmare more real than his dreams, that he was tied, sitting upright, to a chair. He fought the incessant, drowsy layers, wondering who? Who could this foul kidnapper be?

Distantly, he heard a movement, a swish of fabric, before the hood was snatched from his head with a single tug. A rush of air assaulted him as light pierced his bleary eyes. He caught a quick impression of a large drawing room, empty but for a few scattered pieces of old furniture—something familiar that caused his gut to churn. He heard the crackling, felt the heat, of a fire blazing in a grate at his side. But these impressions were fleeting. For when he raised pain-racked eyes, he saw a woman standing before him, the black hood dangling from her fingers.

"You!" he cried, in a voice that sounded rasping in his ears.

His eyes bored into her, contemptuously taking in her appearance. Diana had taken great pains with her attire, wearing a form-fitting evening gown of soft white chiffon overlaid with dainty seafoam blue-green flowers and vines. The sleeveless creation dipped into a low cleavage, the fabric smooth across one breast, draping in a lacy diagonal to the opposite side of her tightly corseted waist, the other breast swathed in a fluttering of pleated chiffon that riveted his eye to her lushly swelling flesh. The thin, horizontal pleats continued a tantalizing path down the side of her hips to fall into a softly gathered train that appeared as delicate as spun sugar as it flowed about her slippers and drifted behind her. Her creamy shoulders were enticingly bare beneath the foamy chiffon flowers, which were repeated in a diagonal line from the left side of her waist to her right knee, and down the softly rounded curve of her backside. The dress hugged her hourglass figure so perfectly that she gave the impression of having just stepped from the sea, with the seafoam frothing and spilling in a caressing stream down the majestic contours of her frame. She was stunning. He could almost smell the sweetness of her artfully displayed flesh. He hated the sight of her.

"You were out for longer than I expected," she told him, backing away. "The men I hired to kidnap you forced a dose of laudanum down your throat. I was beginning to think they'd done their job too well."

His eyes burned as he stared at her, anger and hatred warring for supremacy in his heart. He was still groggy from the drug, but he jerked at his ropes again, seething inside, wanting to lunge at her and wrap his hands around her delicate throat and shake some sense into her. When his exertion failed, he slumped back in the chair and looked about him, trying through his haze to comprehend where he was.

His eyes took in the nearly empty room. Then his gaze flicked to the window, a magnificent stained-glass rendering of the Rutherford family crest, artistically fashioned in shades of gold and blue. The fading light of dusk cast blue shadows across the wood floor. Beyond the window, an avenue of birch trees stretched to the horizon, their leaves golden in the late afternoon light, their trunks as white as snow.

Horrified, he demanded, "Where am I?"

"You know where you are," she told him, her voice maddeningly calm.

"You brought me to *Birch Haven*?" He couldn't believe it. How, in all conscience, could she do this to him? She'd professed to love him once, yet she'd brought him to this, of all things. Knowing what it would do to him.

"Why not?" she shrugged. "It's the perfect place. It's deserted. Even the caretaker's gone this time of year."

His chest seized up, empty, hollow, hurting. Seeing his home again was like looking at the woman he'd once loved and lost. It hurt more than he'd thought possible. More than he cared to admit. As he glanced around him, coming face-to-face with his vision of hell, his fury burned away the last lingering effects of the drug. Through clenched teeth he ground out, "Have you no concept of the pain it causes me to even *think* of Birch Haven?"

"I thought it might help bring you to your senses. Give you an occasion to make up for past grievances. What better destination? Birch Haven is the symbol of everything we had together and all we lost because of what you did. The past and the future you destroyed."

"*I* destroyed?" He fought against the ropes so violently that the chair moved several inches across the floor, giving a fearsome scrape. "*Your father* destroyed this. Why do you think I did what I did? It was to save Birch Haven."

As he glared at her, he saw the slowly dawning

realization in her eyes. If she'd guessed his rash action five years before was to pay family debts, it was clear from her expression that she hadn't suspected his motive was quite this specific. How could she not know? he wondered. Had she known him at all?

She stood looking down at him, her hands balling into fists at her side. "You mean to tell me the reason you stole from us, from the museum, the reason you betrayed everything and everyone that had ever meant anything to you—was merely to pay the mortgage on this place?"

"Of course it was."

"You did it to hang on to a piece of property?"

"Birch Haven is not just a piece of property. This place is—" he stopped abruptly and amended his words, "*was* the embodiment of my family's heritage. But why waste my breath? You have no concept of what it's like to feel your roots belonging to a special place."

"You're right. I don't."

"Well, I do," he snarled. "And someday I'm going to get this place back. Nothing else in this world matters to me."

"I can see that now. No matter what you have to do, no matter who you have to betray. Even yourself."

He looked around the room again, his gaze coming to rest on the stained glass. Torment filled his eyes before he turned to her with all the hatred and rage blistering his soul. "You have the gall to speak to me of betrayal? Your father came to mine, right here in this very room, and told him he was 'almost there.' The treasure my father had already nearly bankrupted himself to finance was within his grasp. 'One more time,' Stafford said. 'All we need is this last bit of capital.' He didn't give a damn that my father had already given everything he had out of love and friendship. Believed in him beyond what anyone had a right to expect. Was your father grateful? Was it enough? It was *never* enough. He wanted more and more, until he sucked that poor man dry. And my father, in his foolish trust of his best friend, made the ultimate sacrifice. He mortgaged his family legacy. He gave your father what should have belonged to my sisters and me."

"You misguided fool! Your sisters have been so humiliated by what you did, they won't even speak to you. They've been forced to live as poor relations to your distant cousins in the dreariest corner of Northumberland—"

"That, too, will change once I get my hands on the deed to this place again."

"You can't be serious! Edith and Primmie care nothing for Birch Haven. Even if you get it back, they won't set foot here again. Don't you understand? You *ruined* their lives. No decent men will marry them because of you. They may never have families of their own. If you thought they'd thank you, you're out of your mind! If it was your sisters you were thinking of, you could have found any other way. You didn't have to steal, to deceive everyone who believed in you—"

"I believed I had the financing arranged. But I lost it, suddenly, just two days before the note was due. I found myself in a corner. I needed an enormous sum of money, and I needed it fast. What would *you* have done?"

"Anything but what you did."

"You're so bloody sanctimonious. The virtuous Diana would never commit a crime to get what *she* wants. Never mind that kidnapping is a felony."

"It's not the same," she snapped.

"It's never the same when it happens to you. Yes, I committed that crime. And what did I get for my pains? Two years in hell. But I'd do it again."

"You have absolutely no remorse, do you?" she asked, incredulous.

He looked out the window, down the long row of birches, gazing down a path of memory. Memories too tormenting even now to remember without a rush of raw pain. Some deep well of passion and pain that had been dammed up for years erupted now from the very depths of his soul.

"What do you know about it? The prospect of losing Birch Haven was tearing my father's heart out. Birch Haven and the earldom that went with it were awarded my family eight generations ago for meritorious service to the Crown. No money, not even a shack to live in, just a piece of the most glorious land in all of England. We didn't inherit a windfall. We were a self-made family. Each subsequent generation added to the estate with the sweat of their brows and the love in their hearts, building it bit by bit so that someday the estate would be a place of pride and honor to pass down to all the generations of Rutherfords. It was more than a home or a piece of land. Birch Haven *was* the Rutherfords. I was going to bring you here after the wedding, thinking, fool that I was, that you'd realize what that meant. And your father, who claimed to love mine as a brother, callously stripped him of everything he owned and held dear to serve his demented obsession."

She moved closer, crouching down before him and resting her arms on her knees so that she was looking up at him.

"But you see, Jack, that's the whole point. My father *was* close. That's why I'm here. The Alexandria Collection *did* belong to Cleopatra. A clue to the whereabouts of her treasure was in it. I know where that clue is. Father sent a message to me before he died. It's not in the museum, so it must be among the portion you sold off. That's why you *must* tell me who the buyer was."

He could feel his expression harden as she spoke. He stared at her in silence for a time, attempting to digest what he'd heard. The treasure. It always came back to that bloody treasure.

Finally, he said, "You're no better than your father. Stafford stood in this very spot telling the same thing to my father. You've just inherited his lunacy. It's like the working out of some tragic Greek myth."

"It's not a myth, Jack."

He lunged toward her, his arms straining against the ropes. She jumped up, alarmed.

"You Sanbournes will trample on anyone to get what you want. You'll destroy them, take every last shilling, even kidnap them."

"All you have to do is tell me what I want to know and I shall set you free."

"I'll tell you when hell freezes over," he growled. "Do what you like, you witch. Beat me, starve me, *kill* me, for all I care. But I'll tell you nothing."

She breathed deeply. Her hand trembled as if repressing the urge to slap his face. But she brought herself under control and said calmly, "Very well. Let's see how you feel after a few days without food. Because you're right, Jack. I will stop at nothing. You may think what you like of me, I don't care. You may revile me to the heavens and back, it won't alter my course. Because sooner or later, you *will* tell me what I want to know."

Grabbing the hood, she jerked it down over his head. Seconds later, he heard the door slam and knew he was alone. Alone with his pain and frustration. Alone with his rage.

Diana walked along the avenue of ancient birches, enclosed in the shelter of their overhanging leaves. A brisk breeze ruffled her hair and cooled her hot cheeks. The last of the evening sun was setting in the west, infusing the sky with iridescent hues of rose and pink.

When she'd thought to bring Jack here, she

hadn't counted on the memories that would assault her. She recalled a particular sunny afternoon when they were younger, when they'd first realized how well matched they were. The greatest legend of this estate involved the theft two hundred years before of the jewels of the third countess of Birch Haven. A crazed servant had stolen them in the night and buried them somewhere on the extensive grounds. The earl had come to suspect the poor woman and a week later, while she was on her way to dig them up, he unleashed the dogs on her. Unfortunately, they killed her before she could reveal where she'd buried the jewels. For generations, Rutherford descendants had scoured the grounds unsuccessfully for Crazy Mary's stash.

In the summer of Diana's thirteenth year, a renovation of the servant's wing had uncovered Crazy Mary's diary, written in some outlandish personal code that none of the experts Niven called in were able to decipher. When everyone had given up on it, Diana and Jack took it upon themselves to give it a try. Diana cracked Crazy Mary's code within thirty minutes, and it led them to the general area—the Butterfly Meadow—where Mary had hidden her loot. There, Jack took over, and deduced exactly where she'd chosen to dig: at the base of the stump of an ancient oak tree.

As they dug, sweaty with excitement and anticipation, bathed in the liquid afternoon sun, they realized in an epiphany of joy just how perfectly their talents complemented each other's. It was like two souls coming together. They'd found those jewels, but had found more. They'd found themselves.

Until Jack had ripped that future apart. For what? For this piece of earth.

She looked about her, at the vast acreage stretching toward the sea, the spectacular rock gardens with their waterfalls, the mermaid fountain in the midst of manicured lawns, and wondered who owned it now. She'd heard something about a consortium of businessmen having bought it at auction. With the immense fees and commissions Jack had racked up over the last three years, she wondered why he'd been unable to buy it back.

She realized that she'd never really understood how much this place had meant to him. Even when he'd spoken of his plan to bring her here and raise their children on his ancestral home, she hadn't comprehended the depth of his attachment. In the long view of history, did anyone really own anything? It seemed to her like a delusion, an enormous trap, an empty excuse to ignore what was really important.

He'd spoken angrily of his family's lost legacy. But she had a legacy of her own. She was her father's daughter. She understood that to unearth that great depository of Egyptian pride and give it to the world was more important than any personal ambition. She remembered that long-ago day when Jack had bared his soul. *What we do, Diana, is more important than the work of any kings or prime ministers.* She believed that with all her heart. Jack had believed it once. But he didn't now. She'd thought him better than that. But when it came down to it, all he'd really cared about was saving his own petty piece of England.

She took a breath, trying to calm her thoughts. What was she going to do? Somehow, she must make Jack understand. Or if that was too much to ask, she must at least get the information she needed out of him. Her father had given his life for this dream. She couldn't let it die.

But she knew enough about Jack to know that in the face of his profound hatred and bitterness, he'd starve to death before he gave in. Underneath the facade of the reckless Victorian adventurer beat the heart of a deeply disillusioned and self-destructive man.

She felt despondency seep into her soul. She could see no easy way out of this impasse. They were locked in a battle of wills. Neither was likely to back down. Least of all, she vowed, herself.

Feeling discouraged and at a loss for ideas, she returned to the house. Walking through the grand hall, she went into the drawing room, only to stop short just inside the doorway

The chair was empty.

She felt a flash of terror. She heard a sound behind her and wheeled around. Jack stepped from behind the door.

He had a rope in his hands. With a motion of startling swiftness, he looped it around her so her arms were pinned to her sides.

"Now it's my turn to play the captor," he snarled.

Diana gasped, "How did you get loose?"

He jerked the rope so she came up hard against him. "You don't spend two years in prison without learning a trick or two."

She looked about in a panic, feeling the rope imprisoning her, wondering desperately how to get loose. But he wound it around his fist, tightening the hold. Slowly, she became aware of his proximity, of the fresh, manly scent she'd forgotten that was uniquely his. He was still, holding her bound, so still that she raised her eyes and looked up into his face. Something sparked between them, something raw and primitive. She was conscious suddenly of the breadth of his shoulders, the power that seemed to flow through his arms. She felt helpless, her knees threatening to buckle beneath her, jolted by the magnetism of his body pressing into hers.

It frightened her more than the furious glower of his face. She saw in one quick glint of his eyes that he felt it, too, the primal surge of inexplicable longing.

In one desperate motion, she hauled back and kicked him in the shin. He groaned and reflexively loosened his grip. She lunged back, felt the rope drop free, and darted for the door. But the steel grip of his hand was on her arm, hauling her back, before he slammed the door.

"Oh, no, Diana. You called this game. You're going to play it to its end."

"Get away from me," she breathed.

"Foul play, Diana. How does it feel when the shoe's on the other foot?"

She felt the fireplace mantel against her shoulders as she cringed backward.

"You want to know the buyer's name, do you? Enough to starve it out of me."

"That and more," she hissed. He looked huge in the gathering darkness, the glow of the fire sparking off the irate features of his face.

"You must want it badly."

She stared up into the blue blaze of his eyes and felt the shocking truth of all she really wanted thunder through her. *I want you to want me like you've wanted no other woman. I want you to know the foulest mistake you ever made was to betray me. I want you so mad with desire for me that you can't sleep, can't eat, can't take a breath without shrieking my name. And then I want to laugh in your face and tell you what a fool you were to play false with the likes of me!*

"Enough to do whatever it takes," she told him, willing her voice to stop its trembling.

"Thinking you could kidnap me and force me to talk. When all the turnkeys in London couldn't beat it out of me?"

She turned and tried to bolt, but he grabbed her again and pushed her back against the mantel so her shoulders bit sharply into the marble.

"So you want to find your father's bloody treasure, do you, Diana?" This wasn't the voice she remembered. It throbbed and seethed and demanded with all the passion she'd set loose. It stirred her deeply, causing her breath to come in wispy gasps. "His obsession with that treasure has destroyed my family and, I suspect, caused his own death. Would you like to see what it did to *me?*"

He jerked his jacket open and flung it in one furious motion across the room. Then he savagely ripped his shirt off, buttons scattering against the wooden floor, and sent it flying in the jacket's wake. As he did, Diana saw the criss-crossing of scars beneath the thick hair and bronze expanse of his chest. His arms, sleekly muscled, were similarly scarred. When he turned his back to her she saw the faded tracks left by the cat-o'-nine-tails.

"Now tell me," he spat out, facing her again. "If my jailers couldn't break me, what makes you think I'd bend to your will?"

Her eyes had been riveted by the scars. Rather than deform him, they lent him the rugged, dashing quality of a martyr stoically holding his tongue beneath the most unimaginable torture. It actually made him more attractive, gave his finely honed body a sense of reckless adventure and romantic mystique.

Dragging her gaze back to his face, she said, "Because you owe me."

"I owe *you?* I'm the one who spent two lousy years in that hellhole, wanting to die. I'm the one who had to wake up in the middle of the night to the sound of a turning key, knowing they were coming again, and wondering if I could take it one more time. *I'm* the one who didn't get so much as a *visit* from the woman who just two nights before I was arrested had sworn to love me no matter what. If anything, baby, you owe *me!*"

He was scaring her. She thought she'd seen him in all imaginable circumstances, but she'd never seen him like this. She used her anger as a shield, attempting to bluff, to conceal the fear that he must surely sense.

"You're mad! Whatever you've been through, it must have warped your mind."

"It did more than that. It taught me never to trust a woman's promise again."

She felt the outrage burst in her like a broken dam. "You insufferable boor! You wrested that promise from me under the falsest of pretenses. How could you have done that? To betray me so miserably after I gave you something I'd given no other man. I made *love* with you. I trusted you, Jack, with everything I had. And after all that, you didn't even have the decency to trust me with the truth. *Damn* you for what you did to us. If you rot in hell you can't make up for a *minute* of it."

That was why she hated him. That was why she'd do anything to see him on his knees before her.

But he wasn't on his knees. He was looking at her through a narrow, bitter gaze that spoke of his own betrayal at her hands. Yet it was the shrewd gaze of a quick mind ticking off the possibilities.

Jack remained as he was, stubbornly silent. There were things he hadn't told her, things that would help explain his actions. But now wasn't the time. He'd be damned if he'd give her the satisfaction.

Diana straightened her shoulders, as if pulling together what was left of her dignity. His glance dropped to the outthrust swell of her breasts.

"Tell me," he said, hooking one thumb beneath her jaw and lifting it to study her face. "Have you been with another man since our last encounter?"

"That's none of your concern," she snapped, jerking her chin away from his hand.

"No, but it would make the payment all the sweeter."

She narrowed her eyes. "What do you mean?"

"You want something from me. You've made it clear you'll stop at nothing. Should I leave now, no doubt you'll hound me until I tell you what you want to know. I hate to think what lengths you'll go to next. So the prudent thing would be to give in to your demands and be done with you once and for all. But that brings up the question of payment. You wouldn't expect to get something for nothing. And my services don't come cheaply, as you may know."

"Mercenaries never do."

"So, logically speaking, what have you to offer me?"

"Money," she said, a little too quickly.

"Money is of no use to me now. You don't have enough to make it interesting."

"What then?"

"What, indeed? What could you possibly have that would be worth my time?"

He was looking her up and down.

"*Two minutes* of your time."

"Two years and two minutes," he corrected.

"That's not my fault."

"I'm a bitter man, Diana. I'm not ashamed to admit it. I despise you and your family every bit as much as you scorn me, if not more. I see it in your eyes that you want me punished for my sins. Well, guess what, sweet? I want you chastened just as much. So I ask myself, what could you possibly give me that would make your flesh crawl to hand over? What," he asked idly, tracing the back of his finger in a path from her collarbone to the soft mound of her breast, "indeed?"

She slapped his hand away. "If you think I'll stand still and let you blackmail me this way, you're madder than I thought."

"Cheeky words, coming from a kidnapper. We might as well be honest. We loved each other once, or thought we did, but we're adversaries now. We don't trust each other, and we each feel we have good reason. So any personal appeal you might make to me is guaranteed to fall on deaf ears. I'm on to you now, and am not bloody likely to fall prey to your trap a second time. I don't give a damn if you find your father's precious treasure. But since you do, here are my terms. I'll give you the information you want and you give me what you've—*given no other man.*"

4

ℳoments passed before she digested his words. "You *are* mad!" she said.

"Mad? If I am, I earned the right to be."

"You must know I'd never agree to such an—"

"Abomination?" His brows shot up sarcastically. "I know you'd never do so unless you had a compelling enough reason. And since the only way you're going to get the information you want is through me, my question is: How much do you want it? Enough to sell yourself to a man you despise? Either that, or say good-bye to all your plans. All the years of struggle your father went through will be for naught. His death will have meant nothing, and his twisted vision will die with nothing but the word 'no' for eulogy. Would you see that happen, Diana?"

"I'll never agree."

"Won't you?"

It was impossible not to stare at the vast scope of his chest as he stood his ground before her. In a rage she cried, "Damn you! Damn you to hell for the devil you are!"

He grabbed her shoulders to anchor her as his mouth descended to nibble at her neck. Her flesh tingled and she felt an electric shock inside.

"Are you a rapist now as well as a thief?"

"Oh, no, Diana. I'll not rape you. And I'll not take you like some two-shilling whore. I want seduction. I want you to feel every hated caress, every touch of my fingertips, every taste of my tongue. To feel it until you can't help but cry out in agony. Until you can no longer bear the touch of me against your skin."

She moved away but he followed and pinned her shoulders in the prison of his hands. "I want you to know what it is to suffer, Diana. The way I suffered from my traitorous desire for you in my cell every minute of seven hundred and thirty agonizing nights. To want something so badly, you think you'll go out of your mind. So desperately that even the grinding, unrelenting lash of the whip can't force it from you. So despairingly that you pray at night for the agony of the flogging because it isn't as rancid as the pain in your heart. I want you to know what it's

like to want so badly to be free of that torture that
you'd gladly sell your sorry soul."

He snatched her to him, holding her to his chest.
He bent his head and kissed her, blindly, angrily,
branding her lips with the torch of his own. "You
smell like a woman in heat," he said against her lips.
"You smell like a woman who wants a man so badly,
she'd beg him to take her."

He kissed her again, lifting her slightly so her feet
left the ground and she was dangling in his arms.
"You're not just going to spread your legs for me,
love. You're going to beg me to take you before I'm
through with you."

"Over my dead body," she breathed, gasping for
air.

"If that's what it takes. Maybe then, I can forget
the way you look in that gown. How it makes you
look more naked than without it. How it makes me
feel to see you standing there, knowing you went to
such trouble for me."

"How does it make you feel?" she challenged.

"Like this." Taking her hand in his, he shoved it
onto the erection that was straining against the front
of his trousers. She tried to move away, but he held it
there, forcing her to rub him up and down, to feel
the chiseled proof of his desire on the palm of her
hand.

"You're so much lovelier than I'd remembered.
What is it, Diana? It's a look in your eyes. It's the
way you hold your head. It's an elusive quality—an
attitude. You look at me the way a queen might look

at a lowly subject. Like I'm dirt beneath your feet. You didn't used to look at me that way. It makes me rue the day I ever heard your name. But it does something more."

"What?" she asked, completely breathless now.

"It makes me want to tame you. It makes me want to see you panting beneath me, all sweaty and rumpled and forgetting everything as you wrap your legs around me and beg me to slam into you. That's what I want from you, darling. *That's* the price you'll have to pay."

"You'll have to make me," she told him in a voice that didn't sound like her own.

He crooked a lopsided grin. "That's what I've been living for, baby. I didn't know it until just now. But that's what's kept me going all these years. I'll make you, Diana. Have no fear of that."

"You *do* make my flesh crawl." She tried to dislodge her arms from his hands.

"Not for long. The pity is that it will be so easy. I'd like to see you suffer the indignity of my touch. But don't you feel it, Diana? Do you recognize the truth when it stares you in the face?"

"Truth!" she scoffed. "A fine word, coming from you."

"Lust, then," he conceded. "It's like a force in the air. It's that feeling that comes when the skies won't rain, yet the clouds are crackling with thunder. That feeling that if something doesn't happen soon, you'll go out of your bloody mind. You know why, Diana?"

She shook her head so violently, some of her up-swept hair fell in curling tendrils to her shoulders.

"Because hating each other as we do, our bodies don't lie. My body remembers the touch of yours as it recalls no other woman's. I'd give anything to deny it. Because I do hate you, Diana. I hate everything you stand for, and all you're trying to do. I hate the sight of your perfect face. I hate that smug little smile of yours that seems to hold the answers to questions I haven't even thought to ask. I hate those piercing cat eyes that strip a man of his very pride. But I love your body."

His hands began to roam about her, stroking her heaving breasts, spanning the tiny measure of her waist, reaching behind her to cup her backside and yank her close so that her breasts were crushed against the stronghold of his chest.

"God help me, but you've got a body made for love. If I were a pirate, I'd want nothing more than to capture you for my prize. Where did you get this body? I don't remember you like this. I don't remember this need——" He looked down at her, clutching at her dark hair, brushing it back off her face in desperation as the pins fell unheeded to the floor. "This need to have my mouth on you . . ." He unfastened the top buttons of her gown with startling skill, and, almost in the same motion, dropped his head to taste of the flesh above her cleavage. Impatient with the remaining restraints, he grasped the fabric in his hand and yanked it free, claiming her nipple in his wet, greedy mouth, so that she cried out helplessly beneath the exquisite shock. "It's like a gnawing in the gut, this thirst for you. If I'm mad, you've made me so. I detest you, yet I must take you, must possess you . . ."

She felt the exhilaration of his words. That's what she wanted. Nothing more than what he sought to elicit from her. She wanted him groveling at her feet. She wanted him driven so crazy with lust for her that he'd do anything . . . say anything . . . to assuage his need.

"Tell me the name," she whispered.

He laughed, his breath warm against her breast. "Mad I may be, but I'm not dull-witted. Yet."

He trailed his mouth upward, kissing, nibbling, licking her with his tongue, until at last he reached her parted, panting mouth. Then he clutched her head between both hands and consumed her lips in a domineering kiss. As he did, he drew his fingers through her hair until it tumbled free, brushing her naked back. His hands moved and his fingers began to massage the sensitive lobes of her ears until shock waves of lust sparked her loins with hot, raw desire. Beneath his lips and the play of his touch, she felt herself melting into him so that she couldn't tell where his body ended and hers began.

He'd never kissed her this way before. He'd kissed her tenderly, passionately, even desperately. But never with this sense of command, as if claiming his right to take her in any way he pleased. To use her body with no thought of gentleness or love or anything even approximating fondness or regard. But what appalled her was the way her body responded, as if it had been born for this, as if there was nothing more thrilling than to be claimed like some buccaneer's booty and carried off to bed. Her arms clung to his head of their own volition. Her legs were shaking so she could barely stand. And her heart was thumping wildly as her breath discharged in helpless gasps.

She gritted her teeth, determined to show him that she would suffer him with dignity and restraint. But when his lips left hers, she felt such anguish, it was like losing a part of herself. She had a mad impulse to drag him back so she could taste the compelling nectar of his mouth, but his head dipped lower and once again pronounced his dominion over her. Cupping her breasts in his hands, he kneaded the soft, pliant mounds, as he licked and sucked and nibbled and flicked his tongue and gulped at them like a famished man in need of sustenance for his soul. It was as if he said, with his mouth, with his hands, *You're mine. You belong to me. If only for this one night.*

But oddly, in his resolve to humiliate her, he was making her feel more radiant than she ever had. Because he was more than dominating her. He was worshiping her.

He moved lower, and as he did, she felt his hands everywhere, skillfully removing the rest of her gown so it seemed to fall from her in the wake of his stroking palms. Before she knew it, she was standing before him wearing nothing but her corset, her silk stockings, and heels, with her dress pooled about her ankles. He dropped to his knees as his mouth traveled the slender length of her thighs and she thought victoriously, *Yes, on your knees.*

But he didn't tarry for long. Folding her across his back at the junction of her hips and thighs, he carried her over his shoulder across the room. Along the way he grabbed a large chair and dragged it behind, positioning it where he wanted it. Then he bent and flung her back into the cushiony comfort of the seat.

It was a wide chair with padded, carved wooden arms, upholstered in a deep blue watered silk. When she looked up, she saw that he'd positioned her in front of a large gilt mirror. He rounded the chair to stand behind her, leaning down to caress her shoulders and cup the breasts that spilled lushly over the bondage of the tightly laced stays.

"Look at yourself, Diana."

When she jerked away, he grabbed her head and turned it back to face the mirror. "I want you to look. Do you look like a woman who's being forced? Or like a woman who wants me as much as I want you?"

She looked. What she saw was a woman in sensual disarray, her black hair tumbling in mad profusion, her moist lips swollen and pursed in a silent entreaty to be kissed. As she watched, he played with her breasts, softly, slowly, agonizingly teasing her as she watched her eyes grow dewy and indistinct. Then he reached lower and took the crooks of her knees in his hands, lifting them and draping them over the arms of the chair at either side so she was completely open and exposed to his view.

She was so shocked, she would normally have looked away. But she found that she was mesmerized by the sight. By the way she looked at the mercy of his expertly roving hands. How her eyes took on the sultry, faraway look of a woman transported to a land of unimagined delights. How she did, indeed, look as if she were on the verge of begging him for mercy, to unleash the full sorcery of his arsenal and make her scream for all he could give, and more.

Flushing with shame, she brought her legs together, cutting off his view of her juicy core. But he wasn't fazed. He eased around the chair and knelt before her, putting his hands on her knees. Then, grinning up at her with the insolent, lopsided grin of Lucifer himself, he slid his hands down the silky smooth skin of her calves until he'd caught her slippers in his hands. He wrenched first one, then the other shoe from her feet and flung them aside. Then, yanking off her stocking, he raised her foot to his mouth and began to suck on her toes.

She thought she'd go out of her mind. Her need for him began to throb its desperation. Jolts of unspeakable pleasure and reckless desire shot up her legs to settle themselves between her clamped thighs. She lost track of her thoughts and resolutions as his mouth traveled like a sweet marauder up the curve of her calf to the back of her knee to the warm, velvety summons of her inner thigh. As he feasted on her, she felt herself open like a wanton as she cried aloud into the stillness of the fire-crackling room, arching her spine and throwing back her head in unbearable delight. She felt his mouth form into a grin against her throbbing flesh as he lifted her other leg and spread it wide, draping it once again over the side of the chair, this time without resistance or reproof. As she felt herself arch into his mouth in her hunger and need, she saw a flash of truth that was as stark and real as her desire. And she knew the secret motive behind bringing him to this remote hideaway in ropes. She'd had him kidnapped because every word he'd said was true. She wanted him.

She couldn't stand the sight of him. She wanted him punished before her gloating eyes. Her mind rejected everything he was and said. But her body wanted him in that moment as badly as it had wanted anything. More than food or water or air to breathe, more than happiness and hope, more than any treasure that might come her way—she wanted Jack. She wanted to feel the pleasure she'd shut from her mind, with his mouth tormenting her, moving closer and closer, but not close enough, to the throbbing axis of her heat. She'd looked at his naked chest, at the scars he bore as a testament to his heroic insurrection against those who'd sought to break him, and she'd wanted him to take her just as he was, without love, without tenderness, without sentiment of any kind to get in the way of feeling the mastery of his touch. That's what she'd wanted when she'd bathed and perfumed and powdered her body. She'd wanted him to rip the clothes from her and take from her what she couldn't bring herself to honestly give.

The realization forced her eyes open. She saw herself in the mirror, sprawled open before him, looking hot and lusty as he buried his tongue between her legs. Watching him as she exposed herself to him made her heart beat so wildly, it seemed to pound in her ears. She'd never looked more like a woman in all her life.

In that instant, he glanced up at her with the dreamy blue eyes she remembered from childhood, and gave her a look that seemed to say, *I knew what you wanted all along.*

Then he brought his tongue at last to her center and she whimpered helplessly as her pleasure soared like the steady surge of a tidal wave, higher, higher, mounting in intensity, scaling heights she'd never known, until it seemed impossible to take even a moment more, finally breaking with a thundering rush as she began to explode inside to the crescendo of her sobs ringing in her ears.

Instantly, he replaced his mouth with his hand, urging her higher as his mouth claimed hers. "Tell me you want me," he commanded as his breath mingled with her strangled gasps.

"No," she snarled.

He kissed her hard, cutting off her breath. Still, his fingers played her like an instrument he'd been practicing all his life. "Say it," he demanded.

She did want him. She wanted his mouth on hers, crushing her rejection into willing submission. She wanted to feel the length and breadth of him inside her, taking the place of the fingers that were driving her wild.

"Yes," she spat out.

"Yes, what?"

She said nothing, just rebelliously jerked her head.

He pulled back on her hair and made her look him in the eyes. "What do you want, Diana?"

"I want you. Damn you, yes, I want you."

He didn't move. He just held her head pinned back by her hair, staring into her eyes, waiting with infinite patience until she gave him the price he'd demanded. "Yes," she said more softly.

But when he brought his lips just a fraction from hers, when he wouldn't move closer and take her mouth, her tone changed and she sighed, "Jack, please . . ." meaning it now, surrendering at last.

"Yes, baby," he whispered against her mouth. And softer still, "Now . . ."

He crushed her lips with his. She thrilled to the touch of his hands beneath her, hauling her to the front of the chair. She leaned back, watching as he stripped his trousers with expeditious speed to let them drop in a heap to the floor. Watching as he took the rock-hard hoard of his lust in his hand and fed it into her like a sword.

And then she knew, at last, the appalling emptiness of all she'd missed and all he'd stolen from her with that one thoughtless act. She knew what it was to be fully alive, pulsing to the mystifying rhythm of spirit with the zeal and ardor of one truly whole. And in her joy, in her crazed torrent of pleasure, she felt anew the weight and horror of his betrayal. And as he pounded into her, giving her everything she'd wanted, she beat at his back with her fists and cried out in her mind, *How could you have destroyed this? How?*

5

*J*ack lay slouched on the floor before her, his head resting on her knee. Diana remained collapsed in the chair, her arms hanging limply over the sides, her breath coming in labored gasps. She could hear Jack's breath, equally arduous, mingling with her own to form a counterpoint to the occasional soft pops of the fire.

They were both slick with perspiration, both in a state where full consciousness had not yet returned. Their headlong passion had left them not only physically drained, but mentally shattered as well. Their lovemaking, magnified as it had been by animalistic fury, had left behind a bittersweet feeling that this had been more than lust, more than anger, more than revenge. It felt uncomfortably like . . .

Diana felt Jack's head turn, felt the leisurely graze of his cheek against the curvature of her knee. It was oddly intimate in the hushed setting, like a devoted lover nuzzling his adored in the afterglow of shared affection. She opened her eyes at the same instant he opened his, and saw in the startled blue glare the reflection of her own sentiments, the abrupt discomfort, the recognition of something they wouldn't dare admit. And as their eyes held, the dreamy languor was replaced by a spark of suspicion, and a recollection of distrust.

Diana sat up hastily so his head fell free. The movement broke the lingering spell and stirred Jack to action. He arose to his feet with deceptive drowsy ease, as if the look of truth hadn't just passed between them. As she sought to cover herself, he bent and tossed her clothes to her so they landed in her lap. Then, with unhurried motions, he stepped into his trousers and buttoned them with the natural saunter of a man accustomed to dressing himself in front of women.

She, in contrast, donned her dress with an efficacy she hoped would bring the mood back to business. "Very well, tell me," she said, adjusting her bodice over her naked breasts. When he didn't answer, she glanced up to catch him watching her, his hands still at the fastening of his trousers, suspended in midmotion, a fleeting, wistful flicker of remembrance darkening his eyes. He blinked and finished his task.

"What is it you're looking for?" he asked.

"That's none of your concern. All I require from you is your cohort's name. Tell me, and we'll have completed our—transaction."

"What do I get out of this?" he asked, reaching into his jacket pocket and withdrawing a gold case.

She whirled on him, watching as he tapped the cigarette on the cover. "You have the nerve to ask me that?"

"What if I say it's not enough?" he asked, lighting it. "What if I want something more?"

She felt the lazy aftermath of passion seize up and flare into raw rage. "I should have known I couldn't trust you. When did you ever keep your promises?"

He disguised his emotion deftly with a deep puff, waiting until he'd exhaled to answer in a determined tone. "This is getting us nowhere. So let me spell it out so you can understand. I'll help you, but I want something in return."

"What?"

"Half the treasure. We'll find it together and split it—*if* it exists."

She experienced a pang of alarm, but steadied herself. "What do you care? There are plenty of other treasures for you to find."

"Not like this there aren't. This may well be the greatest fortune the world has ever seen—*if* it exists. Enough so that my half will more than buy Birch Haven back."

"You swine!" she cried. "After all that—after what we just— We had an agreement, Jack." She stopped and collected her thoughts, altering her tone. "What am I saying? Trusting you to keep a bargain is like trusting a starving dog with your last meal. But I *do* keep my word. And I'm telling you now, I'm going to find that treasure on my own."

"Call me what you like. It won't change the facts one bit. And the fact is, you won't find that treasure without my help."

This quieted her. Finally, she said, "That treasure's mine. It belongs to me."

"Like hell it does. I have as much right to it as you do. My father died for that treasure as much as yours did. I *paid* for the right to it with two years of my life."

"I won't have it. That treasure is going to show the world my father wasn't the fool they thought him. They laughed in his face for believing something they were too ignorant to even imagine. Well, they'll believe it when they see the new wing in the British Museum named after him and dedicated to his memory. They'll know *they* were the real buffoons. And if they're men enough, maybe they'll even scrape up a morsel of shame for having defamed a man of such faith and courage that he never gave up, even with his last breath. Besides which, that treasure is a symbol of Egypt's heritage. It's going to remain intact, for the world to see."

"What the hell do you care about Egypt's heritage?"

She thought of all Sheila had told her. Diana was

half-Egyptian. But she wasn't ready to think about that now. "That's my business," she said.

"Fair enough. Tell me, then. Once you forced the name from me, how did you intend to get your hands on the clue?"

"I'll offer to buy—"

"Forget it. He won't sell. If you want something from his collection, you'll have to steal it."

"Steal it!"

His mouth crooked in a contemptuous smirk. "Why not? He's stolen practically everything he owns."

"I have no intention of joining you among the ranks of thieves," she snapped. 'I'll borrow them for the time being."

"Them?"

Again, she backtracked, sensing a trap. "Or better yet, I'll copy what I need. There's no reason to steal a thing."

"I know this man," Jack stated, studying the cigarette in his fingers with a thoughtful air. "He won't let you near that collection. To do so would be to admit he has it. He's no fool. The only way you're going to get into his house is to sneak in. And the only way you're going to get there is if I take you myself. So you see, Diana, you have no choice."

She thought quickly. She knew he meant it. He wasn't about to foil his plans by telling her where to find the clues. She'd have to play along for the time being.

"Are we agreed?" he added with a challengingly arched brow.

"As you said, you leave me little choice."

He studied her closely. "Then it's settled. We'll head out late tomorrow night. Meet me at my hotel at—"

"Why don't I just meet you there?" she suggested smoothly. "It will save time and—"

"A valiant try," he grinned. "But I'm no fool, either. Tomorrow. The Savoy. Ten o'clock." Eyeing her gown with a speculative gaze, he added, "And wear something practical. We'll have to climb in." When she said nothing, he insisted, "Will you be there?"

"Oh, I'll be there, Jack, have no fear of that."

She'd be there, all right. She'd let him lead her to the cats, then she'd get rid of him and find the treasure herself.

They came upon the imposing town house just before eleven the next night. The streetlamps sent beacons of light up the dark street. Jack and Diana crouched in the shadow of a group of bushes, peering at the house across the street. It was set back from the road by a long, lushly treed path that was unusual in metropolitan London and spoke of the great wealth of the landholder. As Diana strained her eyes to see clearly, she spotted two guards dressed in long Turkish robes, standing on either side of the front door.

"Ali Pasha!" she gasped.

She didn't need to be told about the owner of the

house. Ali Pasha was the notoriously handsome play-boy son of the Sultan of the Ottoman Empire, who served as Turkish ambassador to the English Court. He was infamous for his expensive tastes in women, horses, and art. But he conducted his business with such public flair and careless abandon that Diana had never suspected him of being the secret buyer of the stolen portion of the collection.

"But the place is surrounded by guards," she whispered. "How can we possibly get by them?"

"I've taken care of that."

"What if he's home?"

"He won't be. I happen to know he's at the French ambassador's ball. It shouldn't break up until well after midnight."

"But how are we going to get in?"

"The same way our fathers got into the tomb of Philip of Macedon." He patted his coat, and there was a dull metallic sound.

"The tomb of Philip of Macedon wasn't sur-rounded by armed guards."

"I told you, I've taken care of that."

"And just how have you done that?"

"Here she comes now."

"*She?*"

Diana heard a swish behind her and in the same instant was accosted by the onslaught of cheap per-fume. Turning, she saw the figure of a plump but attractive woman creep behind the bushes where they lay in wait, squatting low behind the hedge.

"Am I lyte, luv?" she cooed in a thick Cockney accent.

"You're right on time. Diana, meet Flossie."

Flossie extended her hand and grabbed Diana's, shaking it with gusto. "Pleased to meecha, mum. Foine noite fer a romp, eh, wot?"

"She's the distraction," Jack said. Then, ignoring Diana's outraged look, he turned back to Flossie. "You know what to do?" he asked.

Flossie waved a dismissive hand in the air. "Piece o' cyke, ducks. Ain't no more'n a noite's work fer the likes o' me. Don'tchu worry yerself none. Flossie'll keep 'em occupied, she will."

"Good girl." Jack reached into his pocket and took out a wad of bills. "Here's your fee, Flossie girl. And a fiver extra for luck." He tucked the money into the neckline of her low-cut dress, which was drawn tightly across her ample bosom.

"G'won with ye. Ye won't need luck with Flossie around."

She stood and Jack gave her rump a pat before she straightened her clothes and set out across the street with the hip-swaying gait of a tart on the prowl.

Gritting her teeth, Diana forced herself to wait until the woman was safely out of hearing distance, then swung on Jack with glaring eyes. "You hired a whore?"

Jack shrugged. "It was either that or have *you* distract the guards." She could hear the hint of laughter in his voice.

"You fool. You're sending a woman to those men?

Do you know the reputation they have? How do you know they won't eat her alive?"

"That's *why* I'm sending Flossie. I happen to know those guards are regular customers. And they've been known to send for her on the occasions when Ali Pasha's away from home. Which he is tonight."

"But—"

"If you're worried about Flossie, don't be. She likes them. As many, it seems, as she can—"

"I don't need the details!" she snapped. "It just doesn't seem right."

Jack let out a pent-up breath. "Let's get something straight. Flossie loves what she does. She's been extravagantly paid to do something she'd happily do for nothing. Think of it this way. You're keeping the wolf from Flossie's door and she's keeping those guards out of our hair." When Diana opened her mouth to protest, he cut her off. "Better yet, think of it like this. Without her, you don't get inside. So *without* her, you can kiss that treasure good-bye."

"And just how is it you're so intimately acquainted with Flossie's—amorous predilections?"

"Shame on you, Diana," he chastised in a mock tone. "You should know a gentleman never tells."

"As if *you* were a gentleman."

She was almost enjoying the comfort of this banter. It kept her from imagining Jack's wrath when he realized she'd tricked him into finding the clues, then left him to his own devices. But he destroyed that by saying in a silky tone, "Careful, Diana. I might just jump to the conclusion that you're jealous."

"Jealous!" she cried. When he clamped his hand over her mouth, she wrenched free and in a controlled tone hissed, "The *only* thing I could ever be jealous of is the viper who crawled into your bed and bit you while you slept."

"And what would it be like, I wonder, to be bitten by you?"

She clamped her teeth together and refused to speak. He was too quick, and she had more important things to tend to. A swell of laughter drew her gaze across the street, where she could see Flossie leading the two guards toward the right side of the house.

The minute they disappeared, Jack's hand gripped her elbow. "Let's go. But careful now, in case Flossie missed any guards."

As they ran across the silent street, Diana felt one pant leg beginning to come loose. She wore some men's clothes she'd bought earlier that day, but the trousers were too long, so she'd had to roll them up to fit. She paused hastily to tuck them up, then resumed her tread and followed Jack to the left side of the house.

As he reached into the bag he'd brought, withdrawing a rope, Diana went over in her mind once again the steps she planned to take. It was vital that she keep Jack from determining what she'd come to see. Therefore, she must find a way to copy the hieroglyphs while keeping him occupied. She'd have to make drawings of several pieces in the collection. Then, even if he read her notes, he'd have no idea what she was after. A man of instinct and action, he'd never been proficient at reading hieroglyphics, having no patience for the long hours of study required. She'd tried often in the past to encourage him, but now she was gratified that he'd paid her no heed. "What do I need that for, as long as I've got you?" he used to tease. Now it might just work to her advantage.

She'd have to guard her notes carefully, though, until she could get safely away from him. Jack would have no compunction about stealing them from her. But she felt confident that she could throw him off the trail.

Jack had a rope with a distended hook in his hand, which he swung and hurled up to land with a soft thud on the roof. As it slid toward the edge, the hook caught and anchored the rope, dangling it before them.

"I'll go first," he whispered, slipping the bag over his arm. "Once I'm in, wrap the rope around your waist and I'll pull you up."

She nodded and watched as he took the rope in his hands and swiftly scaled the outside wall to the third story window. She held her breath as he took out a thin sheet of tin about the size of a small envelope. This he wedged between the window jambs. The distant sound of a woman's giggle came from the other side of the house, stilling his motions. But he resumed again as the sound drifted off into the night.

Finally, they heard the click of the lock. He opened the window and draped his leg over the sill, slipping inside. In another moment, he was leaning out, motioning to her.

She wrapped the rope about her waist and tied it securely before yanking it to let him know she was ready. He hauled her up a bit at a time, and she used her feet against the side of the building as leverage, climbing the wall as she'd seen him do. She was so focused on her mission, and on keeping her real goal from Jack, that she hardly noticed the height.

Once she was inside, Jack held a finger to his lips and eased the window back in place. It was dark inside. Diana followed him through the maze of oversized furniture and elaborate palms. He stopped before a large bookshelf filled with leather volumes. "He keeps the collection hidden behind here," he told her quietly. When he pressed the bookcase it opened, swinging to reveal a passageway beyond.

"How do you know this?" she whispered.

"I've been here before."

"Of course. I don't suppose he felt he had much to fear from his partner in crime."

He whirled on her, clamping his hand over her mouth and thrusting her back against the bookcase. Her breath caught in her throat at the sudden savagery of the attack.

"Damn it, do you want my help or not?"

Her eyes shot daggers into his, but she schooled herself to nod calmly against his hand.

"Then shut up and do as I tell you. We're just getting started here."

When he took his hand slowly from her mouth, she took a moment to lick her dry lips. But as he continued to glare warningly at her, she couldn't resist the urge to whisper triumphantly, "That was for Flossie. Now we're even."

"Even?" The word sounded foreign on his tongue. "There's no such thing as even between us, sweetheart. There never will be."

He turned and, lighting a candle, pressed his way through the narrow passage, leaving her to follow on her own. On the other side, she saw a door. Jack paused before it, opened his bag, and drew out a sloppy handful of raw meat.

"What's that for?" she asked.

"For this."

He opened the door. On the other side was a long hallway guarded by some sort of animal at the other end. It was a panther. A huge black panther. It was chained, but it blocked their passage. It instantly sprang to its feet and began to growl. Diana froze in fright, pressing herself back against the wall. The panther's eyes gleamed like emeralds as it snarled in warning.

"Why didn't you tell me about this?" she gasped through the lump in her throat.

"Don't worry. It's just hungry. Not backing out, are you?"

He didn't wait for her to answer, but instead tossed forth the meat. The cat lunged onto the mass, snapping and snarling as it gulped it down. Jack motioned Diana to follow. As they approached, the panther looked up, abandoning the remaining food, and sprang toward them in a single mighty bound. If not for the heavy chain, which yanked it back, the cat would have pounced on them and killed them. Jack jumped back, instinctively holding up an arm to protect Diana.

"Maybe it's hungrier than I thought," he remarked.

But Diana barely heard him. She was thinking of his taunt moments before as she stared beyond him at the sleek black animal. Its sinewy power, its savage beauty, the menacing gleam of its immense green eyes, was utterly mesmerizing. An image flitted through her mind, a recollection that ancient Egyptians had once worshiped cats. She stepped to the side and as she did, the feline followed her with its eyes.

She bent and tossed a piece of raw meat and watched in awe as the panther gulped it down. She motioned Jack to sneak past and continued to feed the animal as Jack used his handy sheet of tin to open the door. Then she rose cautiously and, tossing out another piece of meat, slipped around the panther as she backed into the room behind.

Diana turned to find a vast room teeming with antiquities. Glass and wood cases lined the walls, rising to the ceiling, completely filled with jewelry, pottery, busts, funerary objects, weapons, jeweled masks, all manner of ancient and rare collectibles. The body of the room was likewise portioned off with dual-sided cases in a series of rows, each with a narrow aisle to accommodate a person who cared to appreciate the contents. There was a huge limestone sarcophagus with its heavy top angled at its side. Larger statues and obelisks were displayed on pedestals, heading each of the aisles, mounted on walls— on every surface that would quarter them. Gilded caskets leaned against corners and mummies were shamelessly displayed in glass cases. The impression given was that of an excess of wealth, yet it seemed as well organized as any museum. With one cursory glance, Diana's trained eye surveyed the scope of the astonishing display.

She stood staring for a moment, silently absorbing the splendor. Then reality crashed in on her and she turned a biting gaze on Jack. "And you helped him steal all this, I suppose."

He scanned the room. "Only some of it. Look, we'd better be quick about this."

She took a candle from her pocket and lit it to make a hasty circuit of the treasures. As she did, she began to feel overwhelmed. The preponderance of relics, Egyptian, Greek, Etruscan and Roman, was staggering. Ali Pasha, she imagined, must have the largest private collection in the world.

As she scanned the acquisitions and recognized pieces from the ill-fated Alexandria Collection, she marveled at their beauty and delicacy, wondering if any of them really had belonged to Cleopatra. She wished she could spend weeks in here, studying, cataloguing, sketching. But Jack was right to warn her to haste. If they were discovered, there was no telling what might come of it. Ali Pasha couldn't afford to call the police. A man who kept a panther as a sentry would no doubt find some more imaginative way to silence them.

She searched diligently, but she'd already felt Jack begin to stir restlessly when she spotted an alabaster cat about six inches tall resting on a marble pedestal in a far corner of the room. She swallowed nervously and walked toward it. This, she knew, was part of what she'd been looking for. This was one of the sculptures containing clues to the hiding place of the treasure Cleopatra and Mark Antony had hidden. As she approached the object, she could see the exquisite workmanship, the almost translucent shimmer of the alabaster, the finest the world had to offer. As an ancient memento, it was worth a fortune. But as the only discovered vestige of the illustrious queen, it was beyond price.

Quickly, now that she knew what the icons looked like, she scanned the room. There were no other cats. "But there were supposed to be three."

"Three?" Only when she heard Jack's voice behind her did she realize she'd spoken aloud.

She turned away, attempting to distract him as she searched in vain. They had to be here. She couldn't have come this far only to—

"I remember every piece of this collection," Jack was saying thoughtfully. "There was one of every-thing. Except for . . . cats. There *were* three cats. Three perfectly matched alabaster cats."

She spun around, staring at him in horror. Then, trying to alter her look to one of surprise, she said, "I don't know anything about cats."

"The hell you don't. Do you think I'm so stupid that—" He stopped abruptly, as if losing track of the thought. "Three cats. Each with a different clue. That's it, isn't it?" He went to the sculpture and picked it up, turning it over. He stopped, staring at the underside. "I was right. Hieroglyphs. So this is one clue. Where are the others?" Before she could answer, he, too, was searching the room. "They're not here."

"They have to be here," she snapped.

Just then, the panther outside began to growl and fling itself at the door. Diana froze, her alarmed gaze flying to Jack's. "What are we going to do?"

"We have to be quick. Get a rubbing of the inscription. We have to get out of here before your friend here rouses the guards from their fun."

She reached into her shirt and brought out the tools, too panicked now to care that Jack had deduced what she was looking for. As swiftly as she could, she made a rubbing of the message on a piece of blank parchment, pausing only briefly to marvel that Cleopatra herself had no doubt held the same cat in her hand centuries before.

Finishing up, she replaced the statue and stuffed her instruments back into her shirt. Jack was waiting by the door. He opened it and threw a handful of meat just beyond the panther's reach. As it wrenched its chain, attempting to pounce on the morsel, they quickly rushed past. Jack paused and grabbed the meat, tossing it into the cat's mouth, silencing it momentarily and destroying any evidence of their visit in the process.

Then they ran with all speed for the bookcase, squeezing through and setting it to rights. As they did, the trapped beast roared. The sound of it reverberated through the household, turning Diana's blood to ice. Jack darted across the room and was hoisting up the window even as they heard men's voices, followed by the sound of booted feet running up the stairs. He shoved her out the window and she slid down the rope, burning her hands. But the savage roars kept ringing in her ears, prompting her to ignore the pain. Jack was all but on top of her, sliding down behind. When they reached the ground, he yanked upwards on the rope, but the hook wouldn't come loose. Electric lights went on all over the house. Diana saw the room they'd just left flood with light at the same instant that Jack pulled the hook free. He caught it and they began to run, trailing the rope behind. Jack grabbed Diana and, holding her hand in a firm grip, ran with all speed down the street and away from the commotion they'd left behind.

6

A block up the street, Flossie was waiting for them. She thrust out the wad of bills Jack had given her. "Sorry, ducks, I can't in all good fythe accept this. The blokes were called away afore I could give 'em a tumble."

Jack cast a look back over his shoulder. "Keep it, Flossie. You earned it. But we'd all better get out of here fast."

Even as he spoke, he was already beginning to run.

Diana saw her chance and pulled back. "Jack, you make sure Flossie gets home safely. I'll meet you at—"

"Oh, no, you don't. Flossie can take care of herself."

Diana felt the grip of Jack's hand like a shackle. Somehow or other, she had to escape with her prize. She had no intention of sharing it with Jack. If she could get away, she could hide in her hotel for the night and translate the clue. Jack had no idea where she was living. No doubt he'd go to Prudence's house to find her. And Prudence, at first sight of him, would loose the dogs on him.

They left the quiet of Berkeley Square and reached Piccadilly, where the metropolitan bustle of traffic was as tumultuous as any noontime rush. With over six million inhabitants in greater London alone, the city was becoming a capital that seemed never to sleep. Electric lights cast their harsh glare and glitter into the streets, where frolicking crowds poured out of theaters, pubs, inns, and some of the enormous, newly built hotels. The atmosphere was one of carnival-like gaiety and raucous discord. Peddlers sold snacks along the boulevard, and pedestrians paused to sample freshly roasted peanuts or chestnuts. Laughter drifted through the night air to mingle with the smell of horses and industry, then to be drowned out by the screech of trolleys and the disagreeable blare of horns coming from the carriages of rowdies out for a night of sport.

Jack paused, glancing right and left at the nonstop flow of traffic. Across the street, a hack waited for a fare, the driver nodding off beneath the angled rim of his hat while his horse munched away at a bag of oats attached to its head. Jack nodded in their direction then, not bothering to walk the long block to the policeman directing traffic, pulled her through the rush of conveyances and across the street. It took several minutes, dodging carriages and wagons along the way, being forced to stop and wait as a long stretch of unbroken traffic passed before them, or to move back as boisterous young swells swerved toward them, horns trumpeting, in pretense of running them down. All the while, Diana was looking around her, hunting for an opening, awaiting her opportunity.

She found it at last when Jack was negotiating with the hack driver, whom he'd had to shake from slumber. When the driver insisted on being paid in advance at that time of night, Jack dropped Diana's hand to retrieve the money. In the same instant, she heard the clang of a horse-drawn trolley behind her. Glancing over her shoulder, she saw it drawing near on the other side of the street, filled with passengers.

She saw something else: a tube station, one of the stops along the underground rail system. She had to think fast. If she were to bound onto the trolley, Jack could follow her and catch up in no time. But if she could successfully descend into the underground, and make it onto a railway car, she could whisk across town like a bullet, safely beneath the traffic that would hamper her escape. There would be no way Jack could overtake her.

But there was no telling when the next train was due. If she raced down into the station, only to be forced into a long wait, Jack could pounce on her and drag her back to the Savoy.

She decided on a diversionary tactic. As Jack was arguing with the driver, she turned and darted back across the street. By the time Jack had noticed her absence, she'd leapt onto the trolley and was heralding him with a jaunty wave. His money forgotten, Jack sprang after her. But his progress was impeded by the traffic, and by the time he'd crossed to the other side of Piccadilly and was running after the trolley, Diana was several streets ahead.

She felt a temporary relief, but knew it would be short-lived. Jack had always been a swift and agile sprinter, able to cover great distances before growing short of breath. Within two or three stops, he'd have run the trolley down. She looked up ahead, searching for the next tube station. Once she spotted it, she waited for her conveyance to decrease its speed, then jumped from the side and headed for the stairs. She descended a few steps, then paused just long enough to peer over the top and see Jack barreling past.

Laughing triumphantly to herself, she bought her ticket, took more stairs to the lower platform, and came out just as the train was pulling in. As the doors swung open, she dashed in and took a seat, feeling a burst of exhilaration as they closed again and the train swished away from the station.

She was safe. As the train shot through the dark tunnel, Diana crossed her arms over her chest, relishing the feel of the parchment rubbing she'd tucked into her shirt. The urge to pull it out and read the hieroglyphic impression was nearly irresistible. To finally read the words as Cleopatra had written them two thousand years ago! But she didn't dare. She'd save it for the moment when, locked away in her hotel room, she would be assured that no one would be looking over her shoulder.

The thrill of the anticipation reminded her of the reason she'd learned to read hieroglyphs in the first place. Her father had given her two early books, the first ever published about the wonders of ancient Egypt, written by French explorers of a hundred years before. She'd taught herself French just so she could read them. She'd reread them a dozen times each, then spent hours upon hours staring at the indecipherable pictures drawn on the walls of the temples and tombs. The more she looked at them, the more she wondered what the strange writing said. What sort of mysteries and wisdom had the ancients carved into their edifices to pass down to posterity? She knew instinctively that to be able to read the words would create a link of communication with an incomprehensible past. And when at last she'd stood in the British Museum and read her first passage from some time-ravaged fragment of stone, she'd felt tears of awe well in her eyes. It was as if she could hear the voice of someone dead for four millennia speaking to her over the drifting sands of time. It was magical. And now, thanks to all her years of study and discipline, she would read the very words Cleopatra had set down for her eyes.

She was seized by impatience. She heard the turn

of the wheels and in her head, she urged them to go faster. Each stop was agony as she waited for the doors to close so she could be on her way once again. Closer and closer to the moment when a portion of this glorious mystery would finally be revealed.

She all but ran up the street and through the lobby of her hotel. She took the stairs two at a time. She fumbled with her key, her hand shaking as if afflicted. But finally she threw open the door and closed it safely behind. Moving swiftly through the dark room, she switched on the lights.

"What took you so long?" a masculine voice drawled.

She spun about to find Jack Rutherford slumped back in a chair, waiting for her.

"How did you—"

"It's my job to find things," he interrupted curtly. "And to be quick about it."

"Too quick," she grumbled. Then, suddenly aware of the dangerous crackle of his presence in the small room, she decided to change tactics. She smiled at him, all the while fully conscious of the parchment in her shirt. "At least you can't blame me for trying."

Jack stood abruptly and crossed the room in two strides. Grabbing her shirt, he rent it so hard the buttons popped off and the precious drawing fell to the floor. She bent to retrieve it, but he yanked her away with one hand and took hold of the parchment with the other. Then, still holding her arm fast despite her efforts to snatch it loose, he raised the paper and looked at it for the first time.

Diana was seething. "You vile thief," she spat out at him. "You've stolen everything else. How dare you rob me of *this* moment."

If he was listening, he gave no indication. He peered at the paper, then thrust it at her. "What does it say?" he demanded.

She snatched it back from him, saying, "As if I'd tell you."

The ensuing silence was heavy in the room. She could almost hear the echo of her words ringing off the ceiling. She felt his fingers on her arm loosen by slow degrees, until at last he dropped his hand and turned away.

He took some moments to pace the tiny floor, four steps up and four steps back. Then he stopped with his back to her. After a long pause, he turned with a look of calculated curiosity.

"Has it occurred to you that to be of use, this clue must be added to the other two?"

She said nothing, holding the rubbing protectively against her chest, wondering what he was up to.

"I can get those other two cats for you. Or at least find out where they are."

"How?" she challenged.

He gave an expansive shrug, as if to say it was none of her affair. "I have ways. I found *you*, didn't I?"

"I don't need your help. I can find out on my own."

"Not as easily as I can. Unless you'd thought to

use your charms on Ali Pasha. Women, I'm told, are his only real weakness. The women who grace his bed, that is."

Her eyes flashed and he shrugged again, this time with a crooked smile. "Let's bargain, shall we? You read that inscription. If it tells you what you need to know, if you can figure out the location of the treasure with just that one clue, then keep it to yourself and go after it. I'll track you down sooner or later anyway. But if, as I suspect, the other two cats prove vital, you'll tell me what this one says and I'll find out where the other two can be found."

"And if I lie to you?" she dared.

"You won't."

"How do you know?"

He looked at her for a moment, then slowly closed the distance between them. Taking her chin in his hand, he said in an intimate tone, "Because you're a bad liar, Diana. You remember the time in Ireland when you fell from one of the pillars of those Druid ruins? What were you . . . thirteen? You tried to tell me you hadn't hurt yourself. But I could see it in your eyes. I could read your desire to be brave for my sake. But I could also hear your unspoken plea. The wounded girl who wanted to be coddled and cared for. Who wanted the burden of bravery taken from her for just a brief time. So I swept you into my arms and carried you into the forest, where I laid you down in the sweet grasses by a brook and bathed your leg and stroked your forehead and kissed away your pain."

As he spoke, his hand drifted, as if of its own volition, up to her forehead, where he was stroking back the dark hair with a gentle touch. Diana remembered the occurrence well. She'd been in such pain that she'd wanted to cry, but had been afraid he'd make sport of her for not being able to keep up, as he'd done when they were younger. So she'd cloaked her vulnerability in noble falsehood, gritting her teeth and courageously jutting out her chin. But he'd looked into her eyes and swept her up into his arms like some medieval knight saving a damsel in distress. He'd been so romantic, so gentle, so disarming, that she'd abandoned her false pride and accepted the care he offered with a loving, grateful heart.

It seemed an eternity ago. Where was that tender youth who'd kissed and courted her among the mystical ruins of enchanted lands? Had he ever existed? Or had she dreamed him? Had she seen in him only what she'd wanted to see?

He was staring into her eyes at a long-ago memory, still holding her chin in his hand. She could have sworn she saw the same melancholy reflected in his face that she felt in her soul.

She put her hand to his face, feeling the rough stubble of his jaw beneath her thumb. "Where did that boy go, Jack? When did he disappear?"

She saw a flash of pain in the depths of his eyes. "Or did he ever exist?"

She watched as the sadness was replaced once again by the slamming of a bitter gate before the vulnerable grief in his eyes. "If he did," he told her dully, "you killed him."

She was stunned by the hatred in his reply. If he'd hit her, he couldn't have more effectively punished her for reaching out to him.

"*I* killed him!" she exclaimed, stepping back and dropping her hand. "It was suicide, as I recall."

"Believe what you want. I don't give a damn. Do we have a pact, or don't we?"

She was so discouraged by the confrontation that she didn't care. He'd follow her to the ends of the earth, but only to steal the treasure out from under her. What difference did it make? This should have been one of the most exciting moments of her life, but he'd ruined it. The way he'd ruined her wedding day. The way he'd ruined her life. She sighed and said, "Very well."

There was always another day.

But when she glanced at the rubbing she'd made, all other thought disappeared. Here was a message that had waited thousands of years to be deciphered. That had set out from Alexandria for Rome, only to be buried for centuries at the bottom of the sea. Because she, Diana, of all the archaeologists on earth, had been destined to find and interpret it.

She stared at it in silence, feeling the wonder of it seep into her and send chills up her spine.

"What does it say?"

She heard Jack's voice behind her, but he sounded far away.

"It means nothing to me."

"Read it!"

He sounded insistent, as if he thought she'd break her word and keep it to herself. But she knew the words would mean as little to him as they did to her, as beautiful as they were. So she turned to him and read aloud: " 'Who, on the sweetest of days . . .' "

"Who on the sweetest of days what?"

"That's all it says."

"*Who* on the sweetest of days?"

"I have no idea. It would seem to be part of . . . perhaps a riddle."

He let the silence stretch between them as she continued to gaze lovingly at the symbols.

"Then we need the other two lines."

That roused her. "How will you find out where the other cats are?"

"I told you, I have my ways. Just be sure and be here when I return."

The next day, Jack approached the guards at Ali Pasha's door. He was allowed entry, only to be stopped by the East Indian attendant in the grand entry hall. "His Eminence is dining, and will be seeing no one. Return, please, at another time."

"He'll see me. Tell him Jack Rutherford is here."

"Sir, I cannot—"

"Straight away," Jack insisted.

The servant drew himself up in injured dignity and, pressing his palms together before his chest, gave a short bow. "I shall pass along the message, sir, but I must warn you. His Eminence grants audience to no one when he is dining in private."

"Fine. Tell him I'll come back in a few weeks."

The servant left and Jack passed the time by pacing the hall. He had no doubt what the answer would be. Before long, he heard the slap of the steward's slippers as he came back down the stairs. With another bow and an impassive face, the man said, "His Eminence is doing Mr. Rutherford the great and distinguished honor of granting him an audience."

"I'm suitably honored," Jack said with a droll curl of his lips. "Where is he?"

"If you will follow me, sir, I shall show you the way."

Jack curbed his impatience as he proceeded up the steps in the wake of the servant's unhurried stride. They paused before a door at the end of the hall, where an armed guard stood attendance. Jack reached for the elaborate brass doorknob, but the guard snapped to attention and the servant cried in alarm, "I shall announce you, sir."

Opening the door, he stepped inside and gave a low bow, saying, "Mr. Jack Rutherford, Your Eminence." Then, turning back to Jack, he gestured with his hand and said, "His Royal Highness, Ali Pasha the Resplendent, Shadow of God on Earth."

Jack stepped past him irritably. He turned to find himself in an immense room furnished in the Turkish mode. Massive jewel-toned cushions were strewn artfully about the silk rug that seemed to change colors as one moved about the room. Richly tinted, nearly

transparent hangings fluttered daintily. A preponderance of palms and large brass artifacts gave the room
a crowded, opulent feel.

Across the chamber, a man reclined on his side on
a collection of plush pillows, one leg stretched out,
the other knee bent beneath the silver and gold caf-
tan he wore belted with a black sash at the waist.
Well into his forties, he was a handsome man. His
black hair was thick and short, curling about his
head. His skin was the color of café au lait, his brown
eyes large and exotic. He sported a short, cropped
mustache above lips that hinted at cruelty when he
smiled. A prominent nose and a dimpled chin gave
his face character, which he'd learned to use to his
advantage. Even the prim and proper English
maidens of society were known to swoon before his
masculine beauty.

Before him rested a gargantuan brass platter piled
high with rice, whole chickens, and various Turkish
delicacies. He reached forth with a bit of flat bread in
his long-fingered hand, scooped up a mouthful of
rice, and popped it into his mouth, chewing thoughtfully as he gestured to the platter in invitation.

"Come, Rutherford, share my feast. It is my pleasure that you dine with me." He had a deep, resonant
voice, richly accented, with the clipped articulation
and sporadically incorrect syntax of one to whom English is a second language.

"Haven't you *honored* me enough?" Jack asked
with barely concealed sarcasm. "Next time tell your

man to dispense with the formalities. I don't need to be reminded of who I'm dealing with."

Ali shrugged. "It amuses me, the trappings of my station. What for to be a prince, if one cannot indulge oneself with the amenities afforded by one's birth?"

"I can't say I blame you your amusement. Your titles are comical, considering the state of your empire. There are those who would swear the Ottomans are on their last legs. Even your once vast fortunes are trickling through the fingers of your wastrel father in Istanbul. By the time you come into your patrimony, you're likely to find nary a farthing left in the till."

Prince Ali took a small handleless cup of wine, resting it lightly between his fingertips, and sipped. "You tread heavily on my hospitality, Rutherford. But I will indulge you, since I desire it. For what do you think I covet the Cleopatra treasure, my friend? Truly, with such riches, I can restore my beloved country to its former glory. Once, we Turks were feared as none other on earth. When we rode through the desert, men cowered before us and offered their riches in supplication for their lives. I shall reclaim that power and subjugate those enemies who seek our destruction. My name will be whispered with the same awe and fear of my illustrious forefathers. The world will once again lay its tribute at our feet. That is why it is imperative that you succeed. That is why I will tolerate nothing less than complete victory."

"And what if I can only get you half the treasure?"

In a silky tone, Ali said, "That shan't do, my friend. I need it all to achieve my aims."

Jack glanced about the sumptuous room, diverting his eyes from Ali's keen gaze. "Just how did you find out about this treasure?"

"I was watching Sanbourne for many years. The world laughed at him, but I thought he might just come through. And I was correct. Word reached me that he'd made an amazing discovery in Southern Egypt—a pathway to the fabled treasure. I had my people go to him and say, 'This is wonderful. We shall be partners. I shall pay top price. After all, what has England done for you except revile you?' Strange, is it not, Rutherford? I very rarely misjudge people. *Rarely*. But I did misjudge this man. Obviously there was some other motivation, some other factor driving him. When I heard he was ill, I knew he would find a way to send word to his daughter, passing on the legacy he'd given his life to. And that she would have no choice but to go to you for help."

"So you believed in the treasure all along. You even grabbed Birch Haven when you could, all those years ago, because you wagered that a treasure hunter might be of value to you."

"And now you are, my friend."

Jack rubbed his jaw thoughtfully. "I had it all arranged. Five years ago, the loan that would save Birch Haven was nearly in my hands. But at the last minute, it inexplicably fell through. So I had no choice but to sell you the thing you wanted. Was that all part of your master plan?"

"Modestly, I must confess, it is so."

"Brilliant. In one move, you got the best part of the Alexandria Collection, you got Birch Haven, and you got me disgraced and with no alternative but to work for you to get Birch Haven back. Truly a work of genius."

"You flatter me, Rutherford."

Ali took up a cigarette box and handed it forth. Jack took one and lit it. It was Turkish. The harsh smoke burned his throat. "What about Diana? If you think I'll allow you to harm her—"

"I have no interest in harming the woman. After all, she is of value to me as well. Was she not once your other half? Is she not as skilled as anyone in England in the art of reading hieroglyphs? Is she not her father's daughter, who would know his habits and be the only one likely to retrace his steps should that become necessary?"

"And when we're of no more use to you?"

"Come, Rutherford, I'm not a vindictive man. I'm highly misunderstood. I have a great appreciation for the arts, and for people such as you who so selflessly bring them to patrons such as I. On the contrary. My gratitude will be most forthcoming. You bring me the treasure, and I shall sign over the deed to Birch Haven. I ask you, what could be more fair?"

Jack didn't believe him for a moment. Once the treasure was found, the prince would have no recourse but to dispose of the ones who could tell the world where it had gone.

"A funny thing, Rutherford. I believe we had a

break-in last night. So I was correct, was I not? The woman did obtain a clue from her father?"

"The clues are on the alabaster cats."

"So you *were* my visitor last night."

"I should warn you. Even if you had all three cats, you still might have nothing. The clues seem to form some sort of riddle."

"So I shall need Miss Sanbourne to decipher and puzzle out that riddle. And you to find me the treasure once she does."

"Easier said than done. Two of the cats seem to be missing."

Ali scanned the room thoughtfully. "Ah, yes. I lost them three years ago in a poker game. Had I known they contained the clues, I would have been more prudent in my wagering. But as it was, what for did I need three of the same?"

"Then go get them."

"That I cannot do, my friend. They are not in England."

"Then send for them. Without those cats, this farce comes to an end."

"Farce?" With a sudden spring, Ali shot to his feet. He grabbed a long bamboo cane and with a quick decisive motion, smashed it against the platter, sending it crashing to the floor, the food spilling onto the costly rug. In the aftermath, he stood, back straight, broad shoulders squared with the majestic grace of one born to rule. "Have you no fear, my friend?"

"Stop calling me your friend," Jack growled,

unimpressed by the theatrics. "If it weren't for your ruddy blackmail I wouldn't have anything to do with this nefarious scheme. You can make me do your bidding, but you can't make me like or respect you. I'll leave the kowtowing to your servants, *Shadow of God on Earth*."

"You dare to mock me?" Ali cried.

"I don't give a damn about you. I agreed to find the treasure for you, that's all. So get me those cats, or the transaction is null and void."

"You get them. That's what I hired you for. Besides, better for the girl to think you found the clues on your own. I will tell you the name of the man who has them in his possession. But be warned. However tempting the prospect, if you get any independent ideas, you will both be dead before you may act upon them. My spies are everywhere. I will be watching your every move. And if you cross me, Rutherford, I shall take pleasure in forcing you to watch as the girl dies a ghastly death."

Jack raised his gaze to stare levelly into Ali's eyes. "The girl means nothing to me."

"Does she not? I wonder. In any case, bring me that treasure, and you will have nothing to fear. Oppose me, and you shall watch the buzzards pick out the eyes of the woman you once loved."

Jack returned slowly to Diana's hotel, all his recent suspicions confirmed. He'd known Ali Pasha was determined, but he hadn't realized until this day what a diabolically clever villain he really was. To have plotted this all those years. To have had the foresight to snatch Birch Haven merely to hold it over Jack's head. Knowing he could manipulate Jack into helping Diana find the treasure. Knowing he'd need the two of them to find it. Jack knew now that he was dealing with no ordinary man.

And after they found the treasure for him . . . Jack had no illusions what would happen then. He had to keep Diana safe. He'd done everything possible to keep her out of it. But it hadn't worked. Now she was indispensable. If he could find it without her, he'd do so, but she was making that impossible. She wanted the treasure for her own reasons, and wouldn't be bullied into handing it over. He couldn't allow her to search for it alone. With Ali Pasha watching her every move, that could prove deadly.

He had no choice. He'd decide what to do about Ali Pasha when the time came. But first he had to find that treasure.

Diana started as Jack flung the door of her room open without warning.

"Get packed," he said without preamble.

"Where are we going?"

"To get those damned cats."

"You found out where they are?"

"I did."

"But how——?" The grim flash of warning in his eyes killed the words on her lips. "Where are they?" she asked instead.

"Egypt."

It took a moment for the word to crystallize in her mind. When it did, she felt a jolt of fear at the suddenness of it. Just like that? After waiting a lifetime? After all the dreams, all the frustrated desires? It couldn't be true.

Sheila too was in Egypt. Diana had avoided confronting her feelings about her real mother. Now she would have to face them. She'd have to see her again, to sort it all out and come to terms with the truth of her own birth. Nervousness coiled inside her.

But as the realization of what he'd said hit her, she was overcome by an excitement so intense it was like being snatched in the clutches of a cyclone and hurled high into the air. Egypt. She tested the taste of the word on her tongue. A word that symbolized all the majesty, mystery, and exotic adventure of the ancient world. A word that for years had meant glamour and enchantment, the ultimate escape from the harsh realities of her life. A place where she would come face-to-face with all that she was and all she was meant to be.

Her destiny . . .

Cairo
November 1899

The open post chaise barreled down the unpaved, tree-shaded Avenue of the Pyramids at a terrifying pace. It had been a nerve-racking ride from the train station in Cairo, the driver whipping the horse on as if at a racetrack. Hardly the idyllic introduction Diana had envisioned. But then she saw it—the first faint outline of the Great Pyramid looming on the late afternoon horizon. The sight of it stirred in her such a deep awe and excitement that her whole body tingled. Beside her, Jack noted her reaction and said, "You'll never forget your first sight of it. No one ever does."

His words called to mind the initial disappointment of her arrival in Egypt. She'd had only moments, as the steamer approached the dock in Alexandria, to stand alone on deck and marvel at her first glimpse of the place she'd most longed to see. But there'd been precious little opportunity to feel the spirit of the ancient land. The modern buildings of the Mediterranean port had waylaid Diana's desire to delve into the past.

There had been times on the train to Cairo that day when she'd gazed out at the sweeping desert and thought, "This is what I've waited for all my life." But once they'd reached their destination, she'd lost even that. She suspected with a sinking heart that she'd built up such lofty expectations of Egypt that no reality could possibly satisfy them. She'd come in search of the glorious, lost past. Instead she'd found a huge, sprawling city, overwhelming in its blistering heat and teeming masses of people. Ablaze with the dress and tongues of a dozen nations, Cairo was shockingly crowded, dusty, noisy, and alarming in its contrasts—the disturbing poverty of the Arab population and the ostentatious display of wealth brought in by the British colonial administrators. She'd come seeking the land of pharaohs, gods, and legends. But those days were gone. The minarets of Muslim mosques had replaced the obelisks of ancient temples, the calls to prayer singing out hauntingly upon the city five times every day.

She'd discovered instead a metropolis built up with English monuments, English roads sporting carriages full of English tourists vying with carts, donkeys, and endless streams of pedestrians in the congested streets. Arab men wore long caftans with scarves wrapped as turbans about their heads and cigarettes dangling from their lips. The women were dressed in black, heads covered, faces veiled, expertly balancing large baskets on their heads as they wove their way through the throngs. Barefoot children followed the coach, calling out entreaties for chocolate or cigarettes. Hawkers were in evidence everywhere, offering cheap imitations of antiquities—statues, cats, small obelisks, papyrus paintings, bits of jewelry—swearing they'd been unearthed in ancient tombs. The smells of spiced dishes wafted through the still, hot air from stands along the road and up the narrow alleyways. And everywhere, in the station, in the lavatories, on the streets, natives had their hands out demanding *baksheesh*: picking up their luggage, calling a carriage, handing her a towel, offering water and local delicacies, and expecting a pathetic stipend in return. With salaries so meager, the entire system of Egyptian life depended on *baksheesh*, from the humblest street cleaner, to the highest government official. It was considered an insult to refuse.

By the time they'd left Cairo and crossed the Nile into Giza, Diana felt depleted, both physically and mentally, her hopes dashed to bits.

But Jack loved it all. He seemed to thrive in the heat. He handed out coins left and right with a relish. As the carriage raced through the traffic—six lanes of conveyances crushed into two lanes of highway, cutting mercilessly in front of one another in a jumbled system—locals spotted them as tourists and called out with hearty waves, "Welcome to Egypt." Jack took it all in as if he'd come home after years away, grinning roguishly and returning the friendly greetings.

He'd looked at her then, noticing her stunned silence as she'd stared out at the scene, and added more compassionately, "Your Egypt is here, too, Diana. You'll see in time."

Now she glimpsed the first hint of her Egypt looming tantalizingly before her.

The image mesmerized her all the way to the Mena House, a former palace that was now the grand hotel of the pyramids. Built in 1860—at the end of the avenue so that Empress Eugenie, on her visit from France, could comfortably view the pyramids— it stood in isolated splendor. The only hotel nearby, with its views of the last of the ancient wonders of the world, it continued to draw a host of the aristocracy of Europe and notables from around the globe. As the carriage rolled into the forecourt and the sumptuous Moorish facade came into view, Diana was gripped by the impulse to get to her room, splash some cold water on her face, and rush out to explore the exquisite monoliths.

But as she stepped out, she heard a commotion and saw a solid wall of men rushing toward them. They were dressed in European silk suits with fezzes atop their heads—the conical cap with a single tassel that westernized Egyptian men wore. In one hand they held notebooks and in the other, pencils were eagerly poised. As Jack stepped down, the men jostled her roughly aside in their fervor to crowd round him.

"Mr. Rutherford," cried one in heavily accented English. "Mr. Rutherford, is it?"

The others took up the call, each vying to be heard above the din.

"Would you have a word, sir, with the *Egyptian Daily Mail?*"

"Mr. Rutherford, I'm with the *Middle Eastern Times.*"

They called out the names of their papers, the *Cairo Express,* the *Nile Daily,* the *Delta Dispatch . . .*

As she was shoved aside, Diana thought wearily, "Not more of this!"

It had been the same since leaving England. Their thirteen-day journey had taken them through Gibraltar, cruising the North African coast. They'd agreed it would be best to travel independently, disguising their identities and pretending to meet on board. As it turned out, their precautions had proved unnecessary. Shortly out of Portsmouth, Jack had been recognized by a fellow traveler, and had been continually lionized by passengers and crew alike. He'd been wined and dined like royalty, monopolized at all hours, so Diana had scarcely been able to exchange a word with him. She'd known he was notorious in London circles, but she'd had no idea of the extent of his fame among the readers of the penny press. To someone with her scientific inclinations, Jack's pandering to this bothersome fawning seemed the crassest of exhibitionism, the ultimate symbol of how deeply he'd sold out the principles of his youth. Worst of all, he actually seemed to be enjoying the attention, patiently fielding the questions about his celebrated adventures.

It had all but spoiled her trip. As soon as they'd docked in Alexandria, Jack had been accosted by reporters, alerted by wire from the ship, demanding to know what he was doing in Egypt. Everywhere they went, he was followed, hounded for information as to his intentions.

Now the mob of reporters formed a blockade to the entrance of the hotel. One man raised his voice above the rest and called, "Mr. Rutherford, sir, everyone wants to know what brings England's most eminent treasure hunter to our humble land."

Jack, as usual, was handling it in stride. Dressed in a coolly fashionable white suit with a wide hat rakishly tilted on his head, he smiled with an easy, evasive shrug. "What else, my friend? Like all the world, I have a yen to see the pyramids. I've come as a tourist, gentlemen, nothing more."

"We haven't forgotten how successful your last expedition was in Alexandria," someone reminded him as they hushed to hear Jack's words.

"But as you can see, I have no expedition this time. I'm here to view the sights, mingle with the colonial society, and perhaps show my friend here, Miss Allenby, whom I met on the steamer, the wonders of the Egypt I know and love."

One fellow, an Englishman with a pencil-thin

mustache, peered suspiciously through his monocle. "Surely, sir, you don't expect us to believe you have no treasure hunting aspirations? Is it possible you've been hired by the Berlin expedition currently in the Valley of the Kings? We hear they have high hopes of discovering some yet untouched tombs."

"I can assure you, my good sir, that I am not. Whatever they might or mightn't discover will be without my help."

Diana had had enough. These pesky wordsmiths were spoiling the magic of their arrival. Impatient to be off, she pushed her way through the throng, mounted the steps leading to an open terrace where guests were taking their afternoon tea, and entered the cool, dim lobby, leaving Jack to his fate. As she gave her name at the desk, a steward in smart uniform presented her with a red Nile rose and a glass of Egyptian wine. She drank it politely, although it tasted bitter, more like sour grape juice than wine. Having given forth the required *baksheesh,* she was shown to her room.

Once the door was closed behind her, Diana saw, to her disappointment, that her room was at the back of the hotel, and had no view of the pyramids. It seemed yet another in a series of small annoyances. Tossing aside her traveling hat, she shed her clothes and, clad only in a light petticoat, went to the basin and bathed her fevered skin. The cool water felt sensual as it dribbled down her arms, wetting the cotton sheath and bringing sweet relief to her gritty face. A ceiling fan whirred softly overhead, sending down a gentle breeze. She turned quickly, eager to change clothes and be on her way, when she was seized by a wave of dizziness, perhaps brought on by having gulped the wine in her haste to be off.

She decided to lie down for a few moments and collect herself. As she did, she thought of Jack, who was still, no doubt, entertaining the Egyptian press. How on earth were she and Jack to work in secrecy when every step he took was followed with such rabid attention? She thought longingly of all she'd hoped to discover here, the personal as well as the practical. Such high hopes, yet every step she took seemed to be blunted by discouragement and disappointment. In that moment, dizzy and emotionally drained, she felt her dreams to be impossibly out of reach.

She hadn't intended to doze off. One moment she was being lulled by the whirring of the fan. The next thing she knew, she was dreaming of Jack. The way he'd been before. So young, so handsome, so full of optimism and fun. She felt again like the girl she'd been, so happy, so in love—

A knock on the door startled her awake. Her eyes shot open and she bolted up in bed, feeling drained and disoriented, not certain where she was. Without awaiting permission, Jack opened the door and stepped into the room, holding a stack of mail in his hand. Then she remembered.

He glanced at her, then stilled as his eyes slowly traveled over her, resting on the swell of her breasts. She looked down to see that the petticoat was still damp, molded to her like a transparent skin, her dark aureoles clearly visible, her nipples erect. A curious coil of arousal fluttered through her. The dreams were with her still. She saw him once again as the man she'd loved so desperately in the past.

Annoyed and embarrassed, she shifted her position and retorted, more tartly than she'd intended, "Bloody Barnum and Bailey out there. With you acting as ringleader."

He cast a sardonic gleam in the direction of her breasts, then dropped his gaze to the envelopes, as he thumbed through the stack. "You may be well versed in certain talents of your own, but you're an amateur when it comes to this. Watch and learn from a master. Sometimes the best place to hide is in plain sight. Besides which, it afforded me the best room in the house. You should see my view. This, on the other hand, looks like the maid's broom closet."

"Well, Jack, I'm delighted to hear that your notoriety has earned you the sultan's view. But I, for one, am weary of your theatrics. Now, if you'll excuse me, I'm going to get out of this *broom closet* and take in the sights."

"In case you haven't noticed, it's dark outside."

She glanced at the window to see it was, indeed, dark beyond. How had so much time passed?

"Besides which," he continued, "we have serious business here."

She hadn't forgotten their business. She'd only wanted to walk outside first, to make her pilgrimage to the Great Pyramid where she'd been born. But now, on the heels of her dreams, she wasn't certain she was ready. She felt too emotionally flayed to face new truths. Perhaps it was better that she wait, after all. She rubbed her throbbing head and said, "We'll discuss it later."

Jack was watching her keenly. "I went to great pains to come up with this plan. Don't you even want to hear it?"

She wished he'd leave. His eyes on her made her too aware of her every movement. And because she felt like a hot wire on display, she was growing increasingly aggravated by his presumption at barging into her room. "Haven't you been lauded enough for one day?" she asked sharply.

With a wry smile that seemed to take in the reason for her discomfort, he went back to thumbing through the envelopes. "I thought it might come in handy to wrangle an invitation to the Viceroy's mansion. And cross our fingers that he still has those cats."

This caught her attention. She looked up and retorted, "*You're* going to get invited to the Viceroy's? That should be a pretty trick. From what my father told me, these colonials can be more snooty than a Mayfair matron. Reporters are one thing. They'll chase anything they think will sell papers. But the Viceroy's not likely to seek out the company of one with your—notoriety. Unless, of course, he gets wind of your *impressive view.* Surely then he might think you worthy of his company." She didn't bother to hide her sarcasm.

"Well, we *are* in a mood, aren't we?" he asked with an arched brow. "On second thought, this can wait until you're more amenable."

The trouble was she felt *too* amenable. Too vulnerable to his presence. To disguise this fact, she said sarcastically, "You will be sure to alert me the moment the Viceroy sends for you."

"Oh, I will. Have no fear of that."

She wasn't looking at him. She felt him pause, as if studying her, but she refused to meet his gaze. In another moment she heard the door open and close quietly behind him.

Diana couldn't sleep. She'd had a simple dinner in her room, but still she was restless. The pyramids, so close, seemed to call to her. She did her best to ignore the impulse, but the thought of remaining in her room was too confining. To stay inside seemed somehow profane. So at last, after a great deal of deliberation, she dressed and went outside.

When she arrived at the courtyard of the hotel, all was quiet. The front terrace was empty and the carriages had been parked along the far side of the square. Beyond, the nearly imperceptible shadow of the Great Pyramid stood sentinel. The night was warm, a comforting sort of warmth that seemed to embrace her in its caress. An enchanted night that beckoned to her, as if calling her to linger, to remain one with the splendor of her surroundings.

Out here, in the sultry shimmer of the night, she began to tingle with a new and refreshing sense of vibrancy. She passed by the arabesque building and leisurely strolled about the lush green lawns. She glanced up at the sky through the canopy of lavish palms and caught the glimmer of the stars, large and brilliant, twinkling with a radiance that seemed as old as time itself. The Egyptians believed that a person's fate was written in the stars. What, she wondered, gazing forlornly up at them, was written for her?

She'd never known such nights in England. Even in her travels with her father, she'd never experienced this mystical sense of belonging, as if she'd trodden these steps before. The palms, the stars, the distant sounds of someone watering the lawn, all seemed oddly familiar, as if they were part and parcel of a single song that strummed to the beat of her heart. She felt it deep within, a profound rhythm that directed her slow steps. The hush of the night lulled her so her heels on the path rang out like the tinkling of bells.

It was a sensual night that caused her to feel at once a part of all that was, yet singularly aware of her own individual self. With a whisper, her skirts caressed her legs and thighs as she walked, the slither of silk making her body feel strangely alive. She felt the night touch her like a lover's hands, felt the whiff of the warm breeze on her neck like the brush of a courtier's lips. She recalled her dream afresh. Even as her body ached with loss, she felt the stirring of forgotten romantic longings. The need to share the beauty of this night.

And then she knew, with a woman's instinct, that she was being watched. Her body, attuned to every movement, felt the eyes of someone on it, possessing her with his gaze. The hair on the back of her neck prickled. She knew who it was. In that moment, she felt that she'd become the focus of the stars and the palms and the embracing breeze, the very center of the vast and endless night.

She stopped. She could feel the eyes boring into her. Feel the longing, palpable now, seize her in its grip. Feel the hunger of her loins, her empty arms, her discontented lips. The impotence of a woman unloved, with no one to love in return. No one to ease the desire that the Egyptian night had ignited in her blood.

Then she heard the footsteps crunching on the path, coming up behind her with a slow, deliberate gait. She remained where she was, not realizing that she held her breath, only feeling the whole of the universe pause and wait.

The footsteps ceased. She could feel him behind her, feel the heat of his body blast her like a desert gale.

"It came," he said. His voice sounded oddly hushed as if he, too, felt the magic of the night.

She turned and saw him standing before her. In the brilliant moonlight, Jack looked dashingly handsome, so like the man who'd carried her to the rowboat at Birch Haven and spoken of his love. Her heart turned over. She couldn't seem to concentrate. What had he said? She couldn't fathom his meaning.

"What came?" she asked in a voice that sounded parched.

"The invitation." When she stared at him, he added, "From the Viceroy. Dinner tomorrow night."

"Oh, that. Congratulations. Your instincts, as always, are infallible."

He hadn't expected the compliment. He looked at her for a moment before averting his gaze. "A splendid night," he commented.

"Yes. Splendid."

"It reminds me of other nights, summer nights when we sneaked away from our fathers and—"

He stopped short. His eyes caught hers and held as he remembered past delights. Epic nights in mythic lands when they'd gleefully met and stolen moments of such passion that it had seemed all the world had been fashioned just for them. He recalled the moonlight kisses and all the plans they'd made. In the hushed stillness of this night, it seemed that they were innocent again, and hopelessly in love.

"I remember a particular night," he said, his eyes on hers, "when we stole up to the Acropolis."

"We'd been forbidden to go in the dark," she recalled. "Too dangerous, our fathers said."

"But we wanted to see the Parthenon by starlight. We climbed the hill, giddy with rebellion, feeling we'd put one over on them."

"And stared out at the lights of Athens from the Parthenon steps. I remember we swore that there had never been a night such as that one."

They'd done more than gaze out over the remnants of the ancient city. They'd fallen into each other's arms on the floor of the grand temple, and had drowned in passionate kisses and sweetly uttered words. Until the sun had cast a delicate glow in the east, and they'd marveled at how much time had passed without their knowing it.

"Those were happy days," she said wistfully.

"I wish . . ."

"What?" she breathed.

"Sometimes I wish I could find that innocence again. The boy who saw the world as being full of hope and promise. To step back in time, just for one night, and feel as I felt then."

She turned her back, aching inside. "I wish that, too."

Her heart was pounding a rhythm in her head. It seemed that she stood there forever, feeling his electric presence at her back. Then she heard the step that brought him close, and her breath caught in her throat.

When he touched her, she felt her flesh quicken, her blood flaming through her veins like quicksilver, searing her skin. She felt his hands come round her, strong, confident hands that slid up her rib cage to cup her breasts, as if he could feel their need to be pressed in the stronghold of his palms. She felt him pull her back into his arms, his body rock-hard and tempered against her back.

A curl of hunger racked through her, causing her to shiver in his arms. A longing so intense that she felt herself melting into him, desperately wanting the surge of life and fulfillment his hands infused. She felt his breath touch her neck like a promise of bliss. She wanted him so badly that the emotion choked her, threatening hot tears.

Had anything felt so right as having him claim her here, in the Egyptian night, beneath the shadow of the pyramids and the palms and the dazzling stars? She felt with a shudder as she had that long-ago night in the museum, that this was where she belonged. That all the hours of her life had led to this one moment.

Then she heard her name on his tongue. One word that sounded like a sigh erupting from his soul. A word that carried in it the same longing, the same loneliness, the same desperate need she felt inside. "Diana," he breathed, pulling her closer so his arms convulsed around her like a cage of warm, possessive flesh. As if he was claiming ownership of the softness of her body against his toughened frame.

She felt herself belong to him in the hushed stillness of the night. She felt the urge, the powerful, consuming, unshakable need, to turn in his arms and offer her mouth in surrender to his. To give herself to him, opening like a willing bloom, here beneath the palms and the stars. Unmindful of pride or place. Forgetting all she knew as truth, and everything she held dear. A need that blazed through her, erupting like an explosion, blasting from her mind all conscious thought of caution or self-preservation.

She did turn. As if hauled about by some invisible chain, she spun in his arms and lifted parted lips.

Lips that were so empty, so hungry for the remembered feel of his domination. Lips that were all but sobbing for his kiss. She felt, in some suspended state, the lowering of his head. The suspense seemed unbearable, the seconds endless as she waited . . . waited . . .

Then she felt his mouth crush her own, warm and commanding. So good, so sweet. She was fourteen again, a girl in the first throes of love, stealing a moment of impassioned bliss. She moaned into his mouth, felt blinded by the force of his kiss, as images of other nights flashed through her mind. But then she saw him again standing at the altar in chains with the knowledge of his perfidy hot in his eyes.

You betrayed me.

Her senses reeled and panic arrested her. Too late she felt the seizing up of her mistrust. Her betrayal at his hands. Her knowledge that he would hurt her in the end.

"Jack, no," she cried, averting her head so his lips grazed her cheek and settled in the hollow of her throat. She felt her pulse against them, wild and shattered like a snared animal who'd realized the trap only after being caught.

She pushed against his chest, wrenching her neck free, feeling the devastation of loss and loneliness anew, cursing him and her and all the fates for rendering this gift impossible to accept. But fear had claimed her. Fear of herself. Fear of his power to weaken her, to make her believe for one splendid moment that this was meant to be. Fear of what would become of her if she gave in to this awful, aching longing to have him for her own.

He was staring at her, as shaken as she. But like a man who couldn't believe his own words he said, "I want you. It's insanity, I know. Maybe it's the night. I hate myself for it. I hate you for making me say it. But there it is. I want you."

She felt it, too. In England, she could fight him off. But Egypt, with its mysterious sorcery, was thrusting them together with an inevitability that would have seemed impossible anywhere else. She didn't know what it was about this land that should affect her so. She only knew she had to deny it before it consumed her completely.

"But I don't want *you*," she told him in a trembling voice.

"Don't lie to me, Diana," he said roughly.

"And why not, Jack? You lie to me with every breath you take."

Her barb hit its mark. He dropped his hands from her and stared into her eyes with a look of such startled pain that she ached with regret inside. But she couldn't stay. If she did . . .

She turned and ran, leaving him standing alone beneath the stars and the palms and the inky blackness of the night.

8

It was hours before Diana was able to fall asleep. She churned with restless energy, feeling trapped and confined in her room. Her body ached for Jack. The impulse to go to him, to cast aside her qualms, was so overwhelming that she had to forcibly fight the urge. What difference did it make? She asked herself a hundred times. This would be no different from what she'd given him at Birch Haven. But she knew it wasn't true. This *was* different.

When she did finally doze off, she ended up sleeping into the early afternoon. She awoke feeling worn and frazzled. She avoided Jack, taking her meals in her room, locking the door against another unwarranted intrusion. But it proved unnecessary. She heard nothing from him until a cryptic note arrived telling her to be ready for the Viceroy's dinner at six that evening.

She did what she could to disguise the wear and tear of the previous night. She chose an evening gown of silvery lace that hugged her curves suggestively, with an elbow-length, embroidered cape of the same color to wear over it. Even as she tried to deny it, she knew she wanted to take his breath away when he saw her once again. She realized she'd succeeded when she saw the look on Jack's face as she joined him in the lobby. He greeted her with a resentful glare, the knowledge of her rejection still raw in his eyes. But when he caught sight of her, a light of grudging appreciation flared in his glance.

She wondered if he'd broach the subject of the night before. Her awareness of it pulsed between them like a third presence. But he was silent and preoccupied during most of the buggy ride into Cairo.

Finally, she broke the awkward silence by asking, "Just what do you intend on doing tonight?"

He hesitated briefly before answering in a gruff tone. "I intend to get those cats."

His eyes flicked to her, then away, as if he felt as stilted as she.

She tried again. "What do you know of this Viceroy, this Hollowell Blythe?"

"Bachelor. Bit of a ladies' man. Legendary gambler, hence his winning the cats in the first place. But he's no fool. He's heard of me, that's clear, and he'll try to discern why I'm here. We shall have to play our cards close to the vest, to use his parlance."

"How do you know all this?"

"His younger brother was up at Cambridge with me. Told me some lively tales."

She heard the bitterness in his tone and said nothing for the rest of the trip.

The Egyptian driver had taken them the eleven kilometers from the Mena House, swinging north when they hit the Nile and following the river. The fabled waterway was wide here, a murky brown, yet sparkling in the fierce African sun, banked by fertile greenery. It was trafficked by small rowboats and *feluccas*, graceful vessels that had transported Egyptians up and down the river since the dawn of time. The spectacle of the pointed white sails tinged pink by the setting sun, drifting along the water lent the atmosphere an enchanting tranquillity. Diana felt a thrill as she gazed down upon the scene, thinking how this eternal river had sustained life for five thousand years. Considered by her people to be the true mother of Egypt, the Nile was revered for the miracle it had worked in this land, affording food and sustenance in a region where the majority of the arid ground was uninhabitable.

"Gezira Island," said the driver, gesturing before them.

Like Paris, Cairo was built around two islands in the river. The northernmost of them, Gezira, was the bastion of British colonial Egypt. They entered this exclusive world by crossing a stately bridge. Ahead, they spotted the British army headquarters, a collection of administrative buildings shaded by trees, a polo field beyond, and at the southern tip, the neo-classical residence of the Viceroy, Hollowell Blythe.

Outside the wrought-iron gates, several reporters had gathered, evidently having learned of Jack's invitation. It was unusual for newsmen to be so persistent, but they smelled a story and thought it expedient to pursue it. They stepped forth as the buggy slowed, calling out their questions. But this time Jack was in no mood to placate them. He ignored their calls as a guard opened the gates and passed them through.

In the courtyard, an Egyptian footman handed them down with the now accustomed greeting, "Welcome to Egypt," and gestured toward the front doorway. They were ushered inside, where the pastel walls created an impression of cool serenity. Beyond the front hall, Diana could see a large parlor, furnished in formal English fashion, at the end of which was a wall of glass offering a magnificent view of the sail-strewn Nile beyond.

A contingent of guests chatted in the parlor, glitteringly attired, if in the styles of the previous year. As they stepped across the threshold, Diana hanging back behind Jack, an attractive man in his forties with a wealth of blond curls came forth to meet them.

"You must be Rutherford. Hollowell Blythe. So good of you to come."

WRITTEN IN THE STARS 141

"I wouldn't miss it," Jack assured him, shaking the proffered hand. He'd shed his gloom at the threshold, assuming his role of contained yet affable charm. No one would guess the current of tension that had sizzled between Jack and Diana on the ride over.

"If I'm not mistaken," said Sir Hollowell with a keen look, "you were up at Cambridge with my brother Pinky. Don't believe you finished, did you? Pity, that."

Jack met the expected challenge with a cocky grin. "Actually, they ran out of things to teach me at Cambridge. I find instinct to be more profitable than the dronings of decrepit scholars."

"Good show, old chap," cried the delighted host. "Don't much care for the dronings of anybody, myself. Pinky's in Singapore at present. Having a splendid time, by all accounts."

"Allow me to present my companion, Miss Allenby."

Feeling the eyes of their host upon her, Diana unbuttoned her cape and let it fall from her shoulders, displaying the provocatively plunging lace underneath. As she did, the gentleman's eyes all but bulged. He stepped forth with the peculiar energy of a man who has found something much to his liking.

"My dear Miss Allenby, this *is* a pleasure, indeed. Allow me to extend a most hearty welcome to Cairo."

Diana took his hand with a fetching smile, noting that the good man lingered over her palm longer than was politely necessary. She felt Jack's sardonic gaze, but ignored him as she expressed her delight at being included in the evening's festivities. If Jack could so easily step into character, she vowed, so could she.

They were introduced to the other guests. The names flitted through Diana's mind. The gathering was as she'd expected from her father's descriptions, those British citizens who were singularly colonial in their mien. Businessmen, administrators, those highly placed in the military, and a smattering of diplomats, they'd served the British Empire over the years in such exotic locales as India, Aden, and Hong Kong. All seemed to know each other well and to enjoy each other's company, as if they recognized that they were a breed apart. After spending their careers in sun-drenched climes, they would retire to cold, damp England and spend the rest of their lives attending reunions and fondly recalling the good old days. There was an air of community about them that was noticeably lacking in their native land, as if they felt that they were all in the same boat, and must support one another accordingly.

But tonight they were atwitter at having the notorious Jack Rutherford in their midst. Over cocktails, they did their best to entice him to reveal his reasons for coming to the nation that had proved the best treasure hoard in all the world. "We know your claims, my dear fellow, but surely you'll share the *real* reason for your visit with *us*?"

Jack diverted them with insouciant charm.

When they went in to dinner, Sir Hollowell seated Diana in the place of honor at his right hand, while Jack was shown to the chair at the opposite end. As Jack backed into the spotlight by answering their questions with understated accounts of his adventures, the Viceroy set out to beguile Diana into a more lengthy visit.

"While you're here, Miss Allenby, we must journey to Thebes. The group of us, of course. If it's the real Egypt you're looking for, you'll find it more in Thebes than Cairo. It's not so beastly hot this time of year. We shall picnic at the Karnak Temple—the done thing, you know. Jolly fun, setting up a table laden with goodies in the midst of that stupendous shrine. Have you ever ridden a camel, my dear? Good sport, that. The getting on and off is a bit sticky. Bloody beasts charge up like a shot from their knees, you know. But once they're up, it's not such a task. Saturday we're having a rousing polo match, which you should enjoy immensely. Stunning Arabian horses around here, don't you know."

As dinner dragged on, Diana began to wonder what Jack had in mind. He'd made no move, chatting amiably as if he had, indeed, just come for the company. She began to squirm, impatient for the evening to be over. But how did Jack intend to get those cats?

As the dessert dishes were cleared, Sir Hollowell stood, saying, "We'll take our drinks in the garden, if we might. I've arranged for a bit of entertainment."

The guests trooped out onto the lawn. There they

saw an odd sight. An elderly Indian gentleman bowed to them as they approached. He wore a long white robe and had a matching turban on his head, covering his hair. His chin sported a long, grey-streaked beard. In the middle of the lawn lay a long, narrow pathway of glowing coals.

As the guests settled themselves into the garden chairs provided, the Viceroy explained. "This gentleman is a *fakir* from Calcutta. For your pleasure, he will astound us all by walking barefooted across the hot coals you see before you."

"But surely that's impossible," gasped one woman.

"Not at all, my dear. It's common practice in India. We often had such entertainment during my tenure there."

"I've seen it done," said a gentleman. "Truly astounding to behold."

As tea was served to the ladies and brandy to the gentlemen, the *fakir* made a great show of removing his robe. Underneath, he wore a long white cloth wrapped around his waist and loins. He was little more than skin and bones.

At the appropriate moment, the *fakir* went and stood before the path of coals. Silence descended on the guests. The Indian folded his hands before him and closed his eyes in a meditative stance.

"It requires great concentration," Sir Hollowell said in a tone of pride, obviously pleased with himself for having procured such an extraordinary diversion. "We must all remain silent, lest we distract him."

As the *fakir* stepped onto the coals, several of the women gasped, but hastily hushed themselves. They watched wide-eyed as the man proceeded to walk across the coals, in a state of deep concentration. At the end of the path he stepped off and, offering a toothsome smile, bowed to the crowd, who applauded in appreciation.

"A most amazing display," remarked one guest. "However did you find the chap?"

Before Sir Hollowell could answer, Jack spoke in a lazy tone. "If, as you say, this is the done thing in India, I see nothing overly extraordinary in it. This fellow must walk the same path every day of his life. What is it, fifty feet? Now, if it were a hundred, I'd proclaim your party a smashing success."

As he'd spoken, the Viceroy had turned progressively paler, no doubt feeling the barb beneath Jack's challenge. "I say," he cried suddenly, as if the thought had never occurred to him. "Rutherford's quite right. You there," he called to the *fakir*. "Extend the coals to a hundred feet and give it another go."

"But *sahib,* no one can—"

"Of course not. But surely you can make the attempt for the entertainment of my guests. Anyone care to wager on how far the chap makes it?"

Diana watched, appalled, as the bets were taken among the gentlemen. Sir Hollowell, his gambler's instincts enflamed, was now glowing in anticipation.

"The bets are laid, my good fellow. Now *do* be a good sport."

The *fakir* swallowed bravely and murmured, "If you insist, *sahib*."

"Oh, I insist."

It took some time for more coals to be heated in the large bin brought in for the occasion. The guests passed the time debating how far the man could make it on his second walk while Diana glared at Jack, wondering what he was up to.

Finally, all was ready. The *fakir* seemed nervous as he approached the long path of red-hot coals. But he repeated his preparatory routine and once again stepped on.

He walked more quickly this time. It appeared he might actually accomplish his task. But at the seventy-foot mark, he let out a shriek and leapt off the coals, desperately cooling his burning feet in the grass.

A roar arose from the men. Money changed hands and a carnival atmosphere replaced the previous silence. But as they rose to go inside, Jack spoke again.

"You know, it doesn't really appear that difficult. Just a matter of concentration. If I put my mind to it, I daresay I could do it myself."

A startled hush descended. The Viceroy drew himself up, staring hard at his impertinent guest.

"*You* could do it?" he asked through ground teeth.

"I don't see why not," Jack shrugged. "My powers of concentration are rather keen, actually. Of course, we'll never know."

A wicked gleam lit up Sir Hollowell's gaze. "All

too easy to make such a claim. If you're so certain, Rutherford, what say we put it to the test?"

Jack arched a brow. "Are you challenging me, Holly?"

Suddenly the air was rife with tension as the two men stared at one another.

"Since you've broached the subject," Sir Hollowell said, "I should think it only cricket that you put your money, as they say, where your mouth is. What say you to a small wager?"

The *fakir* rushed forth. "No, *sahib,* I beg you. This feat requires many years of training."

Jack glanced at the path of coals. "For such a feat, I'd require more than a *small* wager."

"Ten thousand pounds," Blythe offered.

"Don't be absurd."

"Twenty, then."

"Make it fifty and it's a bet."

Sir Hollowell blanched. In a soft tone, he admitted, "But my good chap, that's all I own."

Again, Jack shrugged. "Very well. If the stakes are too high for you, it makes no difference to me. I am, after all, on record for having offered."

He turned and began to stride toward the house.

"Wait!"

Jack stopped.

Quickly, Sir Hollowell pondered his options. If he didn't accept, he'd have been made a fool of by a man he'd, by now, come to loathe. But it was preposterous. *No one* could do what Jack was suggesting!

Sir Hollowell glanced at the coals, then at the

fakir who'd been unable to make the walk. Finally, he said, "Let me get this straight. We *are* talking about the full hundred feet?"

In a steady voice, his back still to the crowd, Jack said, "Every inch."

"Very well," the Viceroy said quickly. "It's a wager."

Jack turned then with a grin. Diana raced to him and cried, "Are you mad?"

With the hint of a wink, he said, "Let's see."

As the guests stared in astonishment, Jack sat down and removed his boots and socks. Then he rolled up his pant legs and walked toward the coals. Once there, he paused to withdraw a cigarette from his gold case as he calmly studied the situation. Cigarette in mouth, he eased to his knees, then leaned forward toward the bed of coals. Even before the tip of the cigarette touched the glowing ember, it burst into flame. Jack leisurely exhaled a stream of smoke and rose to his feet.

The guests were riveted. Not a sound could be heard as Jack lifted one foot and stepped upon the fiery carpet. One woman fainted in her chair, but was summarily ignored as Jack began his stroll.

"He'll never make it," Sir Hollowell said with complete confidence. "He's a bloody fool to try."

No one else spoke. Jack walked slowly, deliberately, taking puffs of his cigarette along the way. Diana watched with the others, transfixed, her heart all but stopped in her breast.

Jack continued. The smug, doubtful looks were

replaced with increasing awe as he proceeded. He walked steadily, showing no sign that he even felt the fire beneath his feet. As he continued, one gentleman began to count the paces in a soft, reverential tone.

"*Thirty . . . forty . . .*"

Still Jack walked.

"*Fifty . . . sixty . . .*"

The guests were on their feet.

"Seventy . . . eighty . . . good God, how does he do it?"

How indeed? Diana stared at Jack, thinking he couldn't possibly go on.

Ninety feet. Only ten more paces to the end. By now, Sir Hollowell was perspiring heavily. He'd bet everything he had, never dreaming the infernal fellow would go half so far. His lips moved silently as he began to pray with an addicted gambler's desperation.

"*Ninety-five . . .*"

Just then Jack faltered, jerking his foot as if burned.

"I knew it!" Sir Hollowell exclaimed.

Jack glanced his way. Then, placing his foot back onto the coals, he proceeded.

"*Ninety-six . . . ninety-seven . . . ninety-eight . . . ninety-nine . . .*" By this time, the crowd was chanting together in breathless awe.

One more step.

Jack stopped. He brought the cigarette to his lips and inhaled deeply. Then, waiting until he'd exhaled, he took the final step.

Utter silence. They stared in numb disbelief at what they'd just witnessed. Finally, one man whispered, *"One hundred!"*

Jack stepped off the coals. He stood for a moment in the grass, looking down at his feet. No one moved. No one dared to draw breath.

Slowly, Jack lifted his head. He took a last puff of the cigarette, then tossed the butt to the grass. "Holly, old chap, I do believe you owe me fifty thousand pounds."

Sir Hollowell's subsequent desolation cast a pall over the rest of the evening. Soon enough, the guests began to depart. When Jack and Diana were finally alone with the Viceroy, he looked as if he were on the verge of attending his own funeral.

"I'll take my winnings in cash," Jack said.

Sir Hollowell looked up, alarmed. "But, sir, surely you understand, that will take some time."

"I don't have time. I intend to leave tomorrow morning."

"But I can't possibly—"

"Then I'll tell you what. Your collection of antiquities is well known. Give me my choice of—say, two pieces in your collection, and I'll forgo the fifty thousand."

A flush of hope replaced the funereal grimness of Holly's face. "Two pieces, you say?"

"If, of course, you have two pieces that interest me."

"Oh, I'm sure I have two pieces that you'd find

interesting. My personal collection, as you've said, is renowned."

Eagerly, he led them through several hallways until they came to a library at the back of the house. When he turned up the lights, Diana spotted one of the cats at once. It was in a glass case with several other relics, standing tall, gleaming translucently, so lifelike, its tail seemed to curve about the pedestal on which it sat. The sight was deeply moving. She stared at it, her narrow vision blocking everything else in the room, her hands itching impatiently to run themselves along the cool alabaster and tip it up to read the inscription beneath.

Sir Hollowell took out his keys and opened the case. Jack reached in and took the cat in his fist. "There's only one," he commented, not bothering to hide the fact that he knew exactly what he wanted. "Where's its mate?"

At this, Sir Hollowell was roused from his salesmanlike zeal to flash his guest first a look of astonishment, then a slowly dawning realization that this was what he'd been after all along. "I sold it months ago," he said, hesitant now.

"To whom?" Jack asked brusquely.

Holly shot him a suspicious look. "And why should I give *you* that information?"

Jack handed the cat to Diana without so much as a glance her way. She felt the coolness of the smooth stone soothe her itching palms. It was all she could do not to read the inscription then and there.

"Because if you do," Jack told him simply, "and

you include your silence in the bargain, you'll avoid bankruptcy and humiliation."

The Viceroy glanced at the cat in Diana's hands, wondering why it was so valuable to them. He couldn't for the life of him figure it out. He'd have dearly loved to thwart this impertinent scoundrel's designs. Yet he couldn't. This was, after all, a mercifully easy way out of a truly horrible situation.

Bringing his gaze back to Jack's inscrutable face, he said at once, "Done."

9

On the way back to the hotel in the open buggy, they rode for a time in silence. It wasn't the presence of the driver that kept Diana quiet. Now, in the hushed aftermath, she was inwardly marveling at the evening's extraordinary events.

When Jack began to chuckle, as if enormously pleased with himself, she had to ask, "How did you do that?"

"What?"

She heard from his tone that he was taunting her. "Walk across those coals."

"Oh, that. I've seen it done in India many times."

"So you thought *you* could do it? Just like that?"

He shrugged, but when she glanced at him she

could see in the light of the full moon that he was indulging in a cheeky grin.

"Well, I must say, I'm impressed. I never dreamt—"

Jack's roar of laughter cut her off.

"Why are you laughing?"

He threw back his head and cackled his glee. "If you only knew how amusing it sounds to hear such pretty words from you."

"Amusing!" she cried, straightening in indignation.

"Poor Diana. There was a time, I'll admit, when it would have done my heart good to see such admiration in your eyes. But to accept such praise would be to cheat me of my proper due."

"What *are* you talking about?"

"Silly girl. It was a hoax."

"A hoax! But I saw you—"

"You saw what I wanted everyone to believe. I can see I'll have to enlighten you. I happen to know that *fakir*. I met him in India years ago. I spent the day investigating our friend Holly and discovered his surprise entertainment for the evening. That accomplished, it was a simple matter to look up Rashid and arrange a surprise Holly hadn't anticipated."

"That still doesn't explain—"

"Rashid was kind enough to oblige me by supplying a special resin with which to coat my feet. Oh, his trick is real enough. But I had no intention of braving the deed without some—protection. Clever, don't you agree?"

Diana stared at him in amazement. "You black-leg! You scared me half to death!"

"Did I?" he asked dryly. "Really, Diana, I didn't realize you cared."

"Care about a coldhearted schemer like you? I wish you'd burned your soles off, that's how much I care."

"If it makes you feel any better, I did burn one foot a bit. Damned painful," he added, reaching down to adjust his boot. "So if it's heroics you're after, comfort yourself with the thought that the last steps were taken under great duress."

"It serves you right. I should have known you'd—"

"What do you care? I got the cat, didn't I?"

In her agitation she'd forgotten about the cat.

Jack took a match from his pocket and struck it, holding it close in his cupped palm. "What does it say?"

After a slight pause to shift her thoughts, she raised the statue to the light and read, " 'Rose up among the . . .' "

"The what?"

"That's all it says."

"Does that mean anything to you?"

" 'Rose up among the . . . who, on the . . .' No. More likely: 'Who, on the sweetest of days rose up among the . . .' I don't know. The cadence sounds vaguely familiar, as if I should know it. As if it's a quote of some sort. Some Egyptian fable per-haps. Or myth. I can't place it."

"Then we need to get the third cat." He shook out the match and sat back in the buggy, staring up at the night sky but seeing only his own thoughts. "We'll have to figure out a strategy."

"Can we trust Sir Hollowell's vow of silence?"

He considered for a moment. "Normally, I'd say he was a man of honor. But I showed him up in front of his friends. So I wouldn't put it past him to seek some revenge. Which brings me to the next obstacle."

"What now?"

"The man who has the third cat—"

"Professor Hornsby. I've heard of him."

"Hornsby, yes. He's an old rival of mine. We've crossed swords on more than one occasion, when we were after the same find. I've beaten him to the finish line, in fact, three times before. To say he didn't take kindly to it would be a gross understatement. He hates me even more than *you* do. He'd like nothing better than to trip me up now. If Holly warns him we're coming, you can be sure he'll do his best to make certain I never see that cat."

"What can we do, then?"

"All we *can* do is go to Aswan and survey the situation. But even if Hornsby hasn't been alerted, it will take some cunning to get it out of him."

"You excel at cunning," she muttered, still smarting from his deception. "You must have taken a course when you were up at Cambridge, with Pinky."

He ignored her jibe, taking the cat and dropping

it into his coat pocket. "We'll leave for Aswan in the morning. Until then we can't—"

"I can't leave tomorrow. There's something I have to attend to first."

"What?"

Diana hesitated. "It's personal. You'll have to give me the benefit of the doubt."

"It must be important for you to delay this mission, even for a day."

"It is."

"Why not tell me, then? Maybe I can help."

He actually sounded kind. She was tempted to tell him about Sheila. But she held her tongue. She wasn't yet ready to make her secret known.

"Very well," he shrugged. "Have your little mystery, then."

It wasn't like Jack to give up so easily. But the thought of Sheila distracted her. Now that the task was upon her, she was full of trepidation. There was so much she wanted to ask. About the family she'd never known. About her—mother. Even now, the word sounded strange. As the carriage raced up the deserted Avenue of the Pyramids toward the Mena House, Diana quietly imagined the impending meeting. She knew she must come to terms with the truth. But would she ever be able to feel for a complete stranger the affection a daughter should feel for her mother?

After they arrived at the Mena House and Jack bid her good-night, Diana lingered in the courtyard. Once again, the thought of her stuffy room seemed intolerable. She needed to meld into the night, to feel herself part of some larger whole.

She looked about. Stewards were clearing the courtyard of carriages for the night. One was leading a saddled horse her way, intent on retiring it to the stables. On impulse, she went to him and requested the loan of the steed.

"Now, miss? But your dress—"

"Never mind. I'll bring him to the stables when I've finished."

A hearty dose of *baksheesh* quelled his qualms.

Diana bunched up her gown so her legs were free and mounted the horse. A small shaggy bay from the ground, he took on mythic proportions once she was seated on his back. She hadn't ridden like this in ages, but she sensed a bold confidence in the Arabian's stance. As if he was saying to her, "I'll take care of you. You can trust me."

Leaving the hotel, she turned right and rode up the deserted hill. It was dark outside, but the moon was so full, she could see clearly. Her horse carried her as if by instinct, toward the shadow of the great tomb. As she approached, she began to see the silhouette of the pyramid before her, a mighty symbol bathed in moonlight, shadowed by the still night.

Slowly, Diana approached the base of the immense edifice. To see the top, she had to strain her neck back as far as it would go. She'd heard tales of the pyramids of Giza all her life. She'd seen sketches and photographs in the books earlier explorers had left behind. But nothing, neither pictures nor descriptions, had ever prepared her for this sight. If anything could truly be termed colossal, it was this ancient monument. The stones at its base were higher than her head. They rose with astonishing majesty and geometric perfection. Beyond, stretched out before her, were its two smaller companions, appearing mystically serene in the light. At this hour, she was alone, and the surrounding landscape of desert seemed to belong to her. The scene thrilled her, humbled her, frightened her. What was it she'd read? *Man fears time, but time fears the pyramids.*

But this was more than just a testament to human history. This was where Diana had been born. She was returning to her birthplace, to the ghosts of Sheila and Stafford and all that had happened here.

She stopped several paces back. She couldn't bring herself to move too close. She'd thought she was ready. But the image of her parents together at her birth in this very sand was too new, too raw even now. In order to embrace it, she'd have to face the fact that there was a part of her beloved father she'd never known—that, close as they'd been, he'd chosen not to share. Had she ever really known him? Alone in the eerie landscape, she longed for something familiar to hold on to, something to ease the painful knowledge that her father had never told her the truth himself.

The horse tossed his head. Even at this hour, he surged with energy, eager to be off. Grateful for the opportunity for action, she gave him his head and he carried her away.

He took a long path, leaving the hotel and the pyramids behind. Large rocks were strewn upon the sand in their path, but the horse avoided them with uncanny skill. She began to relax a bit, to enjoy the powerful motion beneath her.

Minutes later, the horse stopped. Diana looked up to see the outline of a protruding figure, half-covered in sand. The back of the Sphinx. Her heart gave an erratic skip and she nudged her mount forward.

When they came upon the feline structure from the back, the horse automatically slowed his gait, as if he'd carried untold persons to this very spot a million times before. They circled around to the front, where the human features of the leonine colossus came into view. That face had gazed out upon the desert for untold centuries, guarding the traditional approach to the Great Pyramid. The sight of it enthralled her as it had enthralled Herodotus, Caesar, and Napoleon. It was at once elegant, regal, and supremely enigmatic. The owner of a deep secret, the legendary riddle of the Sphinx.

She sat gazing upon it for a time. The sight of it was a blessed escape. But eventually, reality began to set in once again. She had to go back. Back to the place she'd avoided. She had to see her father, not as she'd known him, beaten and frail, but as the eager, hopeful youth Sheila had known. The part of him that hadn't belonged to Diana. She had to reconcile the two images and somehow claim the entirety for her own. If she didn't, she knew she'd find no peace.

But as she reined her mount around, she stopped

abruptly. A figure was sitting there astride a horse, watching her quietly from a distance.

Jack.

He'd come up silently, watching her, watching the sloped shoulders that spoke of some mysterious despair. He'd been moved by the image of her astride her horse in the moonlight, so beautiful, yet so heart-breakingly sad. Now she sat looking at him as if he were a ghost that had appeared from the spiritual realm.

"I was worried about you," he told her.

"There's no need."

"You were so strange, coming back. I thought you'd be happy about the cat and eager for the prospect of the challenge ahead. Instead you seemed—"

"What?"

"I don't know. Preoccupied. Sad. There was a haunted look in your eyes. I saw you ride off from my window. I was afraid you'd—"

"Be carried off by bandits? Jack Rutherford to the rescue, playing hero once again?"

Her tart tone wounded him. Damn her for always assuming the worst about him. But then, what did he expect? Softly, he said, "Frankly, I thought you might be in trouble. You looked as if you could use a friend."

He could see by the lowering of her eyes that he'd shamed her. She looked so vulnerable, so tender, as if struggling with feelings too raw to face. He knew that feeling. And he still wanted to help, despite her rebuff.

Diana felt his gaze on her. It made her feel small, uncomfortably exposed. The horse shifted beneath her, tugging at the reins. Suddenly she couldn't stand the awkward silence. She didn't want to think. She wanted nothing more than to ride across the desert like the wind.

"Come," she beckoned. And kicking her mount, she trotted off with Jack riding up along her side. As they left the avenue of the Sphinx behind, heading out across the sands, she felt that her horse had sensed her mood. Giving him his head, she kicked him again and he flew off into a full run. It was like no gallop she'd ever experienced. He pounded across the terrain, soaring over the myriad rocks in his path. His gait was thundering, more powerfully thrilling than anything she'd ever known, the pace of a horse born and bred in the desert, running wild. He beat a frantic rhythm, but she wasn't afraid. She was exhilarated. In action, the horse took on a majesty that was breathtaking to experience. She felt that she was riding the back of Bucephalus, Alexander the Great's fabled mount.

She glanced at Jack, pulsing along at her side, and laughed gleefully into the breeze. The sound of the wind they created wailed like a low hum in her ears. It blew her hair into her face, but she gave her head a wild shake and whipped it back. It was a clean wind, not full of dust as she'd expected, purifying her with its kiss.

They bounded on, past carcasses along the way. She felt that she was a natural extension of her steed, and he of the whole earth. She glanced over her shoulder and gasped at the splendor. Behind them, the three pyramids graced the horizon, bathed in the silvery light of the moon. She could feel their power through her horse. He held his head high, his ears pricked forward, sensitive to everything around him. It almost seemed that he knew how spectacular the setting was, this land he called home, and was proud to share it with her in this way.

The more they rode, the faster her animal plunged ahead, gathering speed as if he, too, felt the exhilaration of the experience. She knew instinctively that this Arabian stallion had heart as she'd never known, that he could run all day in the grueling heat and still take the bit in his teeth and run some more. She, too, could have spent the night in just this way.

But after a time, she heard Jack calling her name. She looked back to find him slowing his mount. She squeezed her reins. Instantly, her horse responded, easing to a trot and turning at the slightest pressure back toward Jack. As she rode up to him, she was laughing with delight.

"That's more like it," he said.

He'd stopped on a mound overlooking the panorama of the pyramids. From here, they seemed just steps away from each other. They sat in silence, taking in the scene. Here, on horseback, she felt her spirit rise above its sense of smallness and become one with everything around her. She felt ready to face her fears at last.

"I want to show you something," she said.

Taking off, she galloped back until she'd come to the point of her beginning, the site of the Great Pyramid. She dismounted, and Jack followed in kind, letting the horses wander off a bit as he looked at her with a glint of curiosity.

"There it is again," he said. "That haunted look in your eyes."

She took a breath and told him, "I was born here."

He just looked at her, a small frown puckering his brow.

Slowly, falteringly, she told him the story. About her unexpected visit by Sheila. About her father's past. About her birth on this very spot, where Stafford had held her up to such a night sky as this and called her Diana after the goddess of the moon. She told it all, about the pain of Sheila's betrayal. And how her father had never told her the truth.

When she'd finished, he was quiet for some time, as if absorbing all she'd said. "So that explains it," he said at last.

"Explains what?"

"Ever since we came here, there's been something different about you. Something untouchable. I didn't understand what it was. I felt that it was Egypt. But how could that be? You'd never been to Egypt. But you *are* Egypt in a sense. You look, now, as if you could have risen, fully formed, from the banks of the Nile."

She looked away. "I haven't come to terms with it yet. I longed for Egypt all my life, and all the while without knowing it . . ." She paused and took a shaky breath. "I can almost see my parents here. Happy as they must have been that December night. Yet even so, they seemed fated for tragedy. They loved each other, but it wasn't enough to overcome the circumstances that were conspiring against them. It all seems so futile. I suppose there *is* such a thing as star-crossed lovers, after all."

"We, of all people, should know there is."

"Yes. That's it exactly. You and I are like father and Sheila, in our own way. We had such promise, yet we were doomed. I suppose you never know you're doomed until it hits you. Then it's too late. My father trusted someone he loved and she betrayed him. I made the same mistake. As if we were destined to share the same fate."

The night was so silent, she could hear his breath. Then, very softly, he said, "I still want you."

She turned from him. "Jack, please. You came with an offer of friendship. Would you take advantage of my—"

"Vulnerability?"

She flushed and stepped away. Then she felt his hand on her arm, felt him turn her ever so slowly about.

"No, Diana. But if we were doomed, as no doubt we were, what harm is there in trying to recapture just a bit of it for this one night? Call it comfort. It will never happen again. We both know that. We'll get that last cat—this I vow—and no doubt find the treasure. After that, we'll go our separate ways. So if we want each other, if we take what's offered just this once—without pretense of anything else—honestly, for once . . . where's the harm?"

"Without pretense," she repeated dully.

"We both know what's done is done between us. But God help me, I can't help wanting you. Look at me, Diana. Can you honestly tell me you don't want me every bit as much as I want you?"

"No," she whispered. "I can't tell you that."

Because she did want him. She didn't want to, but there it was. Comfort. Something familiar to ease the hollow ache of her heart.

"You look like a goddess in the moonlight," he said, brushing his knuckles against her face. "Like Isis come to life."

She was scared. She could feel her legs quivering beneath her. She'd run from him the night before, but now she couldn't find the will. So she stood trembling, not looking at him. All too aware of him watching her.

He stepped closer. She could feel the heat of him brush against her, feel her nipples tighten and throb. When she swallowed, it was over a convulsive lump in her throat. But when his hands reached out to grasp either side of her face, when she felt the weight of their powerful grip, her eyes closed and her breath left her with a welcoming sigh.

His hands tightened on her face. It was a gesture of pure possession. Permission granted, he became in that instant a man who knew what he wanted, and was bound to take it for himself.

With his hands cupping her, he lifted her face and dipped his head to hers. At the first touch of his lips, she felt alarmed. Everything in her rushed toward him with such a furious charge that she felt lost and helpless to its demand. When his lips touched hers, a shock jolted them so that they leapt apart. But their lips, so abruptly parted, felt sorely bereft without the pressure of the other's mouth. So they came together with a lunge that nearly knocked them off their feet.

Jack kissed her passionately—possessively, tenderly, lovingly—holding her head, stroking her face, clutching her to him as if he never wanted to let her go. As if he couldn't *bear* to let her go. All rational thought slipped away. As if nothing else mattered but this. Diana felt the sorcery of it. As if she only had to envision what she wanted for him to know and give it to her.

Jack shed his clothes, tossing them aside without so much as taking his eyes from her. He stood before her, bathed by the moon, his hard body chiseled as if by the hands of the gods. Then he reached forth and took her short cape in his hands, giving it a sudden wrench so the button at her throat popped loose as he tugged it free. She felt the slither of the satin against her shoulders before they were bared to his eyes. Without hesitation, with a look of fevered desire, he stripped her of the clinging lace gown that hid the swells and hollows of her body. Then he ran his hands through her dark hair, arranging the glossy tresses about her shoulders, allowing his gaze to wander leisurely down the length of her and back. "You *are* a goddess."

She felt the heat of his gaze drift from her face, across her collarbone, to the prominent thrust of her breasts. Dark blue eyes, as blue as the lapis in Cleopatra's jewels. As he gazed upon her with a gleam of lust, he licked his lips—just once—enough for her to imagine the lap of his tongue against her flesh. She shivered beneath his uncompromising perusal. He didn't hurry. He showed no signs of embarrassment at feasting his eyes upon her as if she were truly a work of art. When he was ready, his gaze lowered, scanning the narrow waist, skimming over the lush swell of her hips, to rest upon the dark curls at the apex of her thighs. She saw him stir at the sight, saw his already impressive erection harden and swell until he took on the look of a statue of breathtaking proportions. She felt the fruit of that look coil within her until she was damp and ready for his impending invasion.

A thrill swept through her, chasing away her sorrow and her fear. Silently, she reached down and ran a finger in her juices, then held one finger out to him, dabbing a drop of her nectar onto his lower lip. His tongue darted out to lick it up. But once having relished it, he was driven mad for another taste. Before her hand had dropped to her side, he'd snatched it up and brought it to his mouth, sucking one finger, then another, then another, like a man dying of thirst.

His hands drifted up her arms to her shoulders, then caressed the curves of her body in a downward course as he lowered himself to his knees before her in the sand. Before she could blink, he'd lunged at her, burying his mouth between her legs. He slapped her thighs open so she stood above him, her legs spread wide, straddling his face as his searing tongue set her to flame.

She stood above him, moaning her delight, feeling like the goddess he'd called her, feeling her power to excite him to such rash, demanding ardor. He moved beneath her, licking her, sucking her, thrusting his tongue inside as far as it would go. But it wasn't enough. He couldn't find the purchase he was after. So he gripped her hands and jerked her back.

Her feet slipped from under her and she fell back onto her outthrust arms. But he followed her, cloaking her body with his, lying heavily upon her until he pushed her backward into the sand. He kissed her madly, stealing her breath as his body crushed hers and his erection branded her thigh. Then he moved, like a man possessed, down her frame, touching, kissing, crushing, sucking, lapping at every inch of her quivering skin. She was delirious by the time his mouth found her again, thrusting her legs open as wide as they'd go, so she felt shamefully, beautifully open before his ravaging demands. The sucking of his mouth mingled like a haunting melody with the whisper of the breeze and her breathless sighs.

Jack thrust her legs up, moving his head for but a fraction of a second as he shoved her knees backwards over her head. He pinned her there, and she helplessly luxuriated in the feel of him claiming her for his own, demanding to taste, to enjoy, to ruthlessly devour every inch of her with his wantonly roving tongue. A tongue that seemed fashioned for a woman's body, a woman's indulgence, a woman's delight. A tongue that knew, as if by instinct, all the secret hollow places that would drive a woman wild.

By the time he lowered her legs, she *was* wild. Because he'd melted her so her only reality was the need to have him come inside. To join with her in a way no other man ever could, or would. She was neither woman nor goddess, but feeling, sensation, a blur of such astonishing pleasure and such wrenching need that she felt if she had to wait a moment more, she'd explode.

He rose on his knees before her, looking more glorious to her than anything she'd expected. No sight had ever moved her the way he did now, gazing upon her with the knowledge of his possession in his eyes. It wasn't that he was just handsome. He seemed to glow with some inner light that wouldn't allow her to look away from his eyes.

She tried. With rebellious fury, she tore her eyes from his, because she knew that if she didn't, she'd lose every ounce of her hard-honed control. But he wouldn't have it. He brought his face close to hers.

He took her head in both hands and held it there, angled toward him. Then he shook her once, and sent her startled gaze flying back to his.

She couldn't find the resolution to resist. Once he'd imprisoned her gaze, he held it with iron determination, the way his fist might grip the reins of a runaway horse. Tight and controlled, pulling her deeper and deeper into the conquering haven of his gaze. And keeping her prisoner of those eyes, he spread her legs without glancing away, his hands knowing exactly where to find her. It was as if he knew that she would not—could not—oppose him in this unspoken command. That she, who'd fought him off the night before, would now, because he ordered it, open her legs for him and whimper in supplication to be taken like a woman knowing nothing but her unquenchable need.

When his hands didn't move, when they held her thighs stretched wide, so she lay spread out before him, but making no move to ease the throbbing that was like a succession of lightning bolts hammering at her loins, she opened her mouth to beg him to cease this agonizing game.

And just as she'd obeyed him moments before, he obliged her with dispatch. With his face close to hers, he took himself in hand and fed his long erection into the moist cavern of her love. Once the head was wedged inside, he gave a single mighty shove that sent him plunging in. He filled her with startling perfection. As if, in that instant, they'd come together to complete the puzzle, to mint a coin that was glorious and whole.

Jack rammed into her with another hard lunge. He paused, then gave another powerful thrust, then paused again, keeping up a steady rhythm. One mighty plunge, then a pause, then another, using his whole body to propel himself into her. She lost track of everything. She felt as if her heart was being hurtled to her throat with his every movement. It was beyond wonderful. It transcended all the milestones of her life. She was transported completely until all sense of self dissolved in the fusion that became *them*.

But while she was writhing helplessly beneath him, he seemed possessed of a strength that was amazing to behold. As if he'd been empowered by the same force that had called her to his side. Keeping her eyes captive with his own, he sent her tumbling to a world she'd never dreamed existed, a world where pleasure and pain and mad, rebellious joy were all mixed up together until one was indistinguishable from the rest. His pleasure was her pleasure. His command was her desire. His breath was the very air she breathed.

Then, in some sudden primal urge, she felt the need for him to take her roughly. And as if he'd read her mind, he tightened his hands on her head and started thrusting with all the raw power at his disposal. As he did, he continued to stare down into her eyes, unflinching as he watched her lose control. She came and came, gasping intoxicated breath, as he watched his effect on her, his power over her. She couldn't look away from his eyes. It was as if he held her captive, and she had no will of her own. Nothing had ever felt so glorious. She felt that she shimmered with the lustrous rays of the moon. He kept plunging into her with rough patience as she came, knowing it would take some time for her to stop. Knowing the magic he was conjuring in her.

And then, when he was well assured of her satisfaction, only then did he relinquish his godlike control. Only then did he allow her to close her eyes as he leaned forth and captured her mouth with his own. As he kissed her blindingly, devotedly, moaning into her mouth, plunging and bucking and driving her back to the brink of madness and beyond. Only then did he allow himself to sate his own lust in the softly yielding burrow between her trembling thighs.

And as he did, as he spilled his seed and they cried out with the explosion of it, they knew the truth that had eluded them in any but this sacred earth. She had only to want and he gave it to her. He had only to command and she yielded all she'd hoarded in the lonely years since they'd been apart. They knew the fallacy of words and promises, of threats and reclamations. None of it was real. None of it mattered. Because they'd been called together by some force that understood their destiny more than they ever had.

Comfort. Something familiar to cling to. Why, then, did it feel like so much more?

10

The light of dawn pierced Diana's eyes. She realized with a start that they'd dozed in each other's embrace. She felt Jack's arm about her, holding her to him like a vise, even in sleep. When she opened her eyes, she saw the glint of his tousled hair, gleaming like a bronze coin in the early sun. His face was serene in sleep, almost boyish, except for the stubble that peppered his jaw like—

She shot up. Memories of the previous night brought a hot flush to her face. She felt her breasts swing free and realized she was as naked as Jack.

What had she done? Was she mad? To have fallen into his arms like a besotted chit because she'd been feeling vulnerable and alone . . .

Her abrupt movement startled Jack awake. He sat up suddenly, looking about for danger. Then his gaze fell on Diana, sitting naked at his side, staring at him with wide, accusing eyes. As his gaze dropped, resting on her creamy breasts, Diana snatched her dress and covered herself.

He yawned and stretched. "It must be true."

"What's that?" she asked, embarrassed.

"That the full moon tampers with men's minds."

"If it tampers with men's minds, it must make women daft."

He arched a brow. "Recriminations so soon? Correct me if I'm wrong, but I wasn't aware of any complaints."

"Last night was a mistake."

"You must be a damned fine actress, then," he commented idly, stretching his arms so his chest expanded to great breadth. "Better than any I've ever known."

She felt a curl of traitorous longing as she caught sight of the hair beneath his leanly muscled arms. Her gaze caressed his scars with fascination. But when she caught his taunting grin, she jerked her head away.

"It won't happen again," she snapped.

"You must have been more deranged by the moon than you've led me to believe. I could swear I made it clear last night that there would be no repeat performance. One last time to—"

"I know what you said," she told him, flushing

anew. *He'd called her a goddess. He'd kissed her like an acolyte worshipping at her shrine.*

"Ah, but then I'd forgotten. You have no faith in my promises, do you? A handy thing, to be so mistrusted. Should the moon cause yet another bout of madness, I could always say, 'What do you expect? I'm a scoundrel at heart.' "

She stared at him, appalled.

"Give way, Diana. We'll blame it on the moon. I'm as eager to be done with this charade as you. The sooner we find that treasure and part ways, the happier I'll be. But you've a mission of your own today."

"Yes," she said, remembering Sheila. "I should be off."

She rose and began to dress in her evening finery. The thought of her mission brought a shiver of agitation. Her hands shook as she attempted to button her gown.

Jack rose and, unashamedly naked, brushed aside her hands and swiftly finished the deed. She felt ridiculous and small, but his help brought a rush of relief.

When he'd finished, he stood looking at her. "Would you like some company?" he asked gently.

She looked up, feeling the look of vulnerability in her eyes, seeing the warm glow of kindness in his. She wanted to deny him, but the thought of facing Sheila alone seemed overwhelming at the moment. She was tired and confused. He seemed so strong, so steady, in the face of her disturbance. So she nodded and said, "If you wouldn't mind."

"Mind? On the contrary. It might be amusing to play the gentleman for a change."

His teasing tone helped to break the tension. "We'll go to the hotel and change. I have her address there."

As he dressed, she turned away and took a cleansing breath. The morning was cool, without a hint of the heat that would steadily creep upon the land. They were in the shadow of the Great Pyramid. She looked up, her gaze scaling its towering height, until she felt dizzy, humbled by the grandeur of the pinnacle. But when she looked out upon the desert, at the smaller pyramids stretching out before her, she felt stirred again by the magic of last night. The ancient tombs stood in isolation amidst a vast expanse of desert extending on one side to the nearby Nile, and on the other to the distant vista of Cairo. In the dawn, the land was tinged carnation pink, gently fused with a delicate tangerine glow. The earth looked soft, the light distinct, as if this cast of brilliant color was unique, belonging to this place and nowhere else.

They walked, leading the horses in silence back to the hotel. Once in her room, Diana stripped off her clothes and bathed with the water in the basin. As she did, images of the night before flashed through her mind. Jack's mouth on her thigh. The smell of his hair. The delicious jolt as he'd plunged inside.

She blushed to think of it. Was that really her, the woman who'd soared with him beneath the glowing moon? Who'd whimpered in need and clung to him as if she never wanted to let him go? What must he think of her? Had she really been such a fool?

She tried to shake off the memory. But as she dressed in a light traveling suit, she could still feel the imprint of his hands on her flesh.

When she arrived outside in the courtyard, the morning was already warm. Jack had arranged for a buggy, but when he saw the address on Sheila's card, his brow puckered in a curious frown.

"She lives in Giza, in the village just across the way. Odd. Didn't you say she was married to a diplomat?"

"Yes. But he died some years ago."

"He must not have left her his property. I'd have thought she'd live in a better part of town. This village is modest by any standard. But it's close. We could walk."

Diana agreed. Tired as she was, she could use the time to collect her thoughts.

They turned left at the Avenue of the Pyramids, then right at a narrow, unpaved street, which took them into a small village. Meager square houses and shops with open doors lined the narrow, winding lanes. Egyptian men sat outside in caftans, smoking from hookahs, pausing to smile and nod as they passed. Women in black robes and veils hurried along with large, flat baskets of freshly baked pita bread atop their heads, avoiding the strangers' glances. Barefoot children paused in their play to call out to them as they passed butcher shops lined with hanging fowl and vegetable vendors arranging their wares. The people paused in their work to watch them pass, but always with a friendly greeting masking their curiosity.

At last they came upon a small two-story white house in a street with many similar structures. Diana stood looking at the door, preparing herself for this fateful meeting. "What should I say?"

"Let her do the talking and follow her lead. I imagine she'll be delighted to see you."

That said, he knocked on the door.

There was no answer.

"It's early," Diana said. "Perhaps she's still asleep."

Jack knocked again, louder this time.

Presently, they saw the parting of the curtain at the front window. A male face peered out. In another moment, they heard a bolt slide and the door was opened a crack. The servant looked out at them, his face alarmed.

"We're here to see Mrs.—" Jack consulted the card. "Mrs. Fayed."

The servant stared at them blankly.

"Do you speak English?" Diana asked. She noted that his eyes were fixed on her strangely. When he didn't reply, she repeated the inquiry in flawless Arabic.

Slowly, the servant opened the door. "You would be Miss Diana, then," he surprised her by saying.

"You know of me?"

"I would know you, miss, from your resemblance to my revered mistress. Please come inside."

Apparently, he was more than a mere servant. He was something of a confidant.

Diana motioned to Jack and they stepped inside. She caught the impression of a small but tastefully furnished sitting room beyond.

When the door was closed, the servant stood wringing his hands. "My mistress has been hoping for your visit. To think you have come at last, when it is too late."

"Too late?"

"My mistress is not here. I was even now on my way to summon the authorities."

"The authorities? But why?"

"My mistress was—taken. Just this morning, I believe. Or perhaps late in the night."

Jack saw the alarm on Diana's face and asked what was going on. Diana quickly explained.

"What do you mean, taken?" she demanded.

"Come," said the servant. "I will show you."

He led the way to a slender staircase and up a flight to a small second floor. From there, he entered a bedroom. It was artistically decorated but the bed was unmade. At the foot of it lay an emerald sheath, which Diana recognized as the dress Sheila had worn for their meeting in England. It had been violently ripped to shreds.

She ran to it and picked it up, feeling chilled. The dress had been severed by a sharp knife, a dire symbol of what could happen to Sheila herself.

"They must have come before dawn. When I brought her chocolate, I found things as you see them. The window was open. They must have climbed in when no one was about. They left only the dress and this."

Numbly, Diana translated to Jack as the servant handed her a piece of paper. On it in English were the words: "When you give me the treasure, I shall give you the woman. Do not think to cross me. Keep the treasure for yourselves, and the woman dies."

Pale and trembling, she handed the note to Jack. When he read it, she saw the start in his eyes. But he masked it quickly and glanced about the room.

"The note was obviously meant for us," she said, watching him with growing suspicion. "It was written in English, which this man wouldn't understand."

"I must summon the authorities," the servant said.

When Diana translated, Jack said, "Tell him he's free to call anyone he wishes. But I doubt it will do any good. They won't find her."

"What does this mean?" Diana asked.

"It means someone is holding your mother for ransom. He wants the treasure in return for her life."

"Who?" she asked.

He glanced at her. He knew who it was. It could be only one man. Ali Pasha had spies everywhere. No doubt they'd witnessed Jack and Diana's rendezvous the night before and misinterpreted the act. They would assume a closeness between Jack and Diana that didn't exist. Obviously, Ali had warned his henchmen to be on the lookout for any sign that Jack might betray him. So they'd snatched Sheila as insurance.

The injustice of it flared anger in his heart. But he couldn't tell Diana. She was headstrong. There was no telling what she'd do. Hadn't she kidnapped him to force his hand? She wouldn't stop until she'd tracked down Ali Pasha and demanded the return of her mother. He couldn't let that happen.

So he met her eyes steadily and said, "Why ask me?"

"I saw your reaction. You know damned well who has her. Why else would the fiend have left an unsigned note? Because he knows you know who he is."

He glanced down at the note in his hand.

Diana rushed at him. "Jack, you have to tell me. We have to find her. She's in danger because of me. That dress is the one she wore to visit me in England. Do you know what that means? That whoever this is, he was spying on us all that time. He knew who Sheila was, and what she wanted. That makes him a formidable foe. I won't pretend I wasn't dreading this meeting. But she's—she's my mother. I want the chance to know her. To know who I am because of her. I can't have her harmed because of me. For God's sake, Jack, tell me who it is!"

He turned from the look of desperation in her eyes. He had to think. Finally he said, "Whoever has her, he's made his stipulation clear. Without the treasure, we have no hope of getting her back."

"We could find her, and take her from him."

"How? Where? No, if I know one thing it's that

he's hidden her well. With the treasure in hand, we have a tool with which to bargain. So the only thing we can do is proceed as planned. Trust me, Diana. We *will* get her back."

"Trust you?" she cried. "When you know who has her and won't tell me? I'd sooner trust the fiend who took her!"

He wheeled on her and grabbed her arms, shaking her roughly as the ransom note fluttered to the floor. "You're not listening. This man has no intention of letting us get anywhere near her. He means what he says. If we don't give him the treasure, he'll kill her. It's as simple as that."

She stared at him in disbelief. "I knew you hated me, but I never dreamt how much. To withhold this information is the vilest thing you've ever done. Have you no feelings at all? Do you care for nothing but yourself? I never even had a chance to be her daughter. I all but rejected her. I couldn't bring myself to give her the love she wanted from me. I told myself it was too new. But the truth is, I felt threatened. She asked so little of me and I turned my back on her. Do you know how that makes me feel? Can't you understand? I *can't* let her die."

"Then we have to get the final clue."

Diana turned away, defeated. "This is my fault. If I'd come at once instead of putting it off, I might have prevented this. But how did they—" Suddenly she stopped. "It was because of last night, wasn't it? They saw us together and assumed we'd want the treasure for ourselves. You said you needed it to get

Birch Haven back. It's the same man, isn't it? The man who holds the deed to Birch Haven has Sheila. Doesn't he?"

Jack refused to answer. He went to the window and looked out. In the distance he could see the top of the Great Pyramid.

After some thought, he asked the servant, who'd been watching the scene warily, "Is there no other staff?"

When Diana angrily translated, the servant said, "I'm my mistress's sole companion."

"I don't understand," Jack ruminated, "why a woman alone would live in such a place. So unprotected."

"To be close to the pyramids," Diana said thoughtfully. She recalled what Sheila had told her. That she'd often walked about the site of the pyramids when her husband was away. That she and Stafford had spent much time there together. The place where her lost daughter had been born. She'd wanted to be close, to relive her memories of happier times. It broke Diana's heart. Because of that lost daughter, Sheila's life was now in danger.

"What if we can't find the treasure?" she whispered.

Jack turned and faced her sternly. "We don't have a choice."

11

Relations were strained as the train took Jack and Diana south to Aswan. Diana spent most of the time staring out the window at the passing desert, brooding about Sheila's fate. Everything in her rebelled against having to rely on Jack when it was so clear he couldn't be trusted. Too, she was angry that his involvement had caused this disastrous turn of events. Had she come so far toward making her father's dream come true, to vindicating his name, only to have the treasure bartered for the life of the woman he'd loved?

But there was work to be done. After passing the city of Asyut, the halfway point in their journey, she turned to Jack and asked, "Why does Hornsby hate you so much?"

He angled her a wry look. "Professional jealousy."

"And what else?"

"I haven't the slightest idea." But there was a twinkle in his eye when he said it.

"I know you, Jack. It had to be something really humiliating to make him hate you this much."

He gave a deprecating shrug. "Well, it might have been the flowers."

"What flowers?"

"The flowers I sent him when he was in that Turkish jail."

"I'll bite," she said, swallowing her impatience. "What was he doing in a Turkish jail?"

"It was a kind of misunderstanding. They thought he was a horse thief."

"And *why* did they think he was a horse thief?"

"Because they found the local magistrate's horse tied to the back of his wagon."

"So he *was* a horse thief."

"Well . . . not exactly."

She gave a sigh.

He shifted in his seat as if better able to gaze down the long road of memory. "Well . . . you remember about two years ago? When every archaeologist in Europe was scurrying around central Turkey trying to find the lost capital of the ancient Hittites?"

"Which you found."

He modestly inclined his head. "Hornsby and I

got the same lead on its location at nearly the same time. I was on my own. He had about twenty cut-throats with him, armed to the teeth, determined to keep me from getting there first."

"You despicable cad! *You* stole the magistrate's horse and tied it to Hornsby's wagon!"

"Let's just say I—came up with a little diversion to help equal the odds. How was I supposed to know he'd end up spending a week in that hellhole of a Turkish jail before they sorted it all out?"

"And you sent him *flowers?*"

He shrugged. "It seemed the gentlemanly thing to do."

"Oh, he must hate you *very* much."

He allowed himself the briefest flash of a grin.

She thought quietly for a moment. "You really *will* do anything to get what you want, won't you?"

When he looked at her, his gaze brought her up short. It was filled with a somber warning.

"Don't be fooled. Hornsby's not a buffoon. He's a scoundrel who's stooped to murder on more than one occasion to further his career. He killed one of my partners in Peru. Long before Turkey. He's the most contemptible man in the profession."

"And he, of all people in the world, has control of the third cat."

"Ironic, isn't it?"

She saw his lip curl in a grimace. He was silent for the rest of the trip.

Five hours later, they arrived in Aswan. It was known far and wide as the most beautiful and conge-

nial of all the cities in Egypt. Though it was four
hundred miles south of Cairo, the region was known
as Upper Egypt, since the Nile ran from its source in
the mountains of Central Africa northward into the
Mediterranean. The climate was more temperate, the
scenery more luxuriant, with assortments of palms
and fragrant, flowering trees. Cataracts, those mammoth boulders that rose in the river like great, softly
shaped monoliths, made it impossible for large
steamers to navigate the narrow channels in this part
of the river. As a consequence, *feluccas* were the pri-
mary mode of transportation. Hundreds of them
could be seen dotting the horizon, their sails gliding
regally in the sun. The banks of the river were lined
with rocky slopes where, thousands of years before,
Ramses II had left his mark, carving his image into a
strut of rock. Aswan had become a favorite resort for
English aristocracy, who wintered here and even re-
tired along the hills overlooking the river, building
English-style homes and planting proper English
gardens.

They arrived after dark, taking up residence at an
outlying hotel inhabited by Egyptians and a few
Nubians. After long, leisurely baths, and under cover
of darkness, they found what Sir Hollowell had told
them was the citadel of the third cat: the retirement
home of Professor Hornsby—a sprawling Victorian
mansion on a rocky outcrop overlooking the Nile.
When he saw the place, Jack let out a low whistle.

"Well, well, well. My old nemesis has certainly
come up in the world. How do you suppose he's

financed such grand digs? He was no great fry when I saw him last. Living in a furnished flat off University Place."

"Obviously, he's come into some property," she said, disinterested.

"I wonder."

"What difference does it make? Let's go get the cat so we can—"

"No," he interrupted. "I want to do some checking first. See what I can come up with that might be of use to us. Go back to the hotel and stay put until I fetch you."

She was hardly eager to obey him like some lackey. But she was exhausted and wouldn't mind a little rest before tackling the next step in their search. So, impatient as she was, she returned to the hotel and tried her best to sleep. But her dreams were fraught with images of the dress Sheila had worn in England, so sadistically ripped to shreds. She awoke feeling vulnerable and exposed, knowing that every move she made was being watched.

She was breakfasting in the dining room on warm pita bread and fresh goat's cheese when Jack joined her, dressed in the same clothes and looking as if he hadn't been to bed. He sat down, tore a piece of bread, and devoured it.

"You're a sight," she told him. "Did you sleep at all?"

"I spent the night making inquiries. Time enough for sleep later. I'll just have some coffee and we'll head out." He signaled the waiter, who brought him a small brass pot of strong Egyptian coffee with a diminutive cup.

"What did you find out?"

He sipped his coffee and sat back in his chair, rubbing his hand wearily across his face. "Interesting news. But I'll have to see what it signifies for us. The first order of business is to find out what Hornsby knows. If he hasn't been warned, I'll play it by ear and see if I can't maneuver him into relinquishing that cat. If he *does* know—"

He left the statement hanging. Gulping the rest of his coffee, he stood and said, "Let's go."

Diana was tense and nervous along the way. Whether Hornsby knew their designs or not, this would prove their biggest challenge yet. She felt that she understood Hornsby's enmity completely. Who knew better than she what it was to be tricked by Jack, and to foster visions of revenge?

She began to plot in her own mind. If Hornsby refused to give Jack the cat, perhaps she could strike her own deal with the man. If he thought she'd use it to foil Jack, maybe he would lend a sympathetic ear. Once she had the final clue, she could lose Jack as she'd always planned and go after the treasure on her own.

But no . . . that wouldn't work. Jack knew who had Sheila and she'd need him in order to instigate the trade. And then she understood why he wouldn't divulge the kidnapper's name. It kept her effectively shackled to his side.

Her hands were trembling in frustration by the time Jack knocked on the door. A servant answered and asked them to step inside. They entered a grand foyer of gleaming marble floors bedecked with fragments of ancient Greek columns. As the servant went to announce their presence, Jack said in an undertone, "Let me do the talking. Remember, he's diabolically clever. Don't give him anything to go on."

She shot him a resentful glance, but remained silent.

Presently, they heard footsteps down the marble staircase. Diana looked up to see a man in his late forties dressed in a crisp white suit with a colorful silk ascot at his throat. His hair was dark, but there were traces of grey about the temples and streaking the close-cropped beard. As he descended, he was looking at Jack with a glimmer of heady triumph in his clear green eyes.

"Welcome to Aswan, Jack. I was expecting you." His gaze flicked to Diana. "This must be the lovely Miss Allenby. Do you prefer Allenby? Or should I just dispense with the farce and call you Diana?"

His tone was cultured and slightly sneering, in the manner of an arrogant professor out to intimidate two upstart students.

"You've done your homework," Jack said dryly.

"Not much happens in Egypt that I don't know about. But come, where are my manners? May I offer you tea? Coffee? Something stronger, perhaps, to take away the sting?"

He was gloating. He had Jack now, after all these years, and he knew it.

"You offered to dispense with the farce," Jack said, "so let's get to it, shall we?"

"Such impatience, Jack. I don't recall this trait in you. You weren't, for instance, in such a hurry when I was a guest in that charming Turkish establishment. You even found the time to send me those beautiful flowers. I've never forgotten that particular kindness, by the by."

"My pleasure, I assure you. But those happy, carefree days are long gone. I think you know why I'm here."

"Ah, yes. The cat I acquired from that idiot Blythe. This is your lucky day, Jack. I'm in a generous mood and shall be more than happy to oblige you."

"What's the catch?"

"The catch is, you'll have to find it."

"Find it?" Jack ground out.

"When I heard you were looking for it, and since it has no huge value to me, I decided to make it the occasion for a test of your *real* abilities. You see, Jack, I've hidden it. If you can find it, you may keep it."

Jack was watching his adversary closely. "As you know, Hornsby—maybe better than anyone—I've always enjoyed a good challenge. But every scavenger hunt starts with a clue."

"Naturally, dear friend. It wouldn't be sporting of me otherwise, now, would it? I shall tell you the cat lies hidden somewhere in the Aswan area."

Jack kept his voice casual. "That's a large territory. There are islands, the city itself, miles of desert, hundreds of archaeological sites . . ."

Hornsby giggled, clearly enjoying himself. "You're right, of course. Actually, I shall give you a rather large clue. The cat lies beneath Aswan's holy of holies. Oh, don't thank me, Jack. It's the least I can do to repay all you've done for me."

As they left, they heard Hornsby's delighted laughter echoing through the hall. "Happy hunting," he called before the door closed behind them.

In the buggy, Diana said, "You're right. He *does* hate you. Even more than I do."

He ignored her. "The holy of holies is what the ancients called the most sacred part of an Egyptian temple. Usually where the altar stood."

"But he said *Aswan's* holy of holies. He must mean Elephantine Island."

It was the area's main archaeological site, just across from the city.

He rubbed his bristled jaw meditatively. "I looked up an old friend last night. A bit of a shady character, but one who usually knows what's going on around here. It seems Hornsby's been involved in some secret operation for the past year. My friend suspects it's an illegal dig. No one knows how he's paying for that big house and those furnishings."

"A sudden reversal of fortune?"

"Exactly. It's obvious he's found a tomb to plunder. But from what my friend has observed, he's going about it rather hurriedly. Instead of taking the booty a bit at a time and selling it off slowly, as would be more prudent. Why the urgency?"

"The dam!" she cried. "They've just begun work on the Aswan dam. And the dam—"

"—will flood the island temple of Philae. When it's completed, the entire island will be underwater for half of each year."

Philae, an island several miles south of Aswan, was the location of the fabled Temple of Isis—the last of the great Egyptian temples to be built by the Ptolemys, and the final holdout for worship of the Egyptian gods. Even five hundred years into the Christian era, people went there to worship Isis, Osiris, Horus, and Hathor, the most beloved of the pantheon.

"Philae," she said, excited now. "Cleopatra herself furnished one of the walls of the main temple. Surely this must be Aswan's holy of holies."

"You're right, of course. So right that it strikes me as being a bit too obvious. He'd be a fool not to think I'd figure this out. Besides which, the temple is crawling with tourists all day long."

Diana had no patience with his warnings. She was certain they'd guessed the whereabouts of the statue and was eager to be off. "That's why we're going at night."

They spent the day gathering the needed supplies. Diana was optimistic, certain they were finally on the road to success. But Jack remained quiet and thoughtful, as if going over in his mind all the ways the crafty and malevolent Hornsby might be leading them into a trap.

Finally, all was ready. Toward dusk, they hired a *felucca* to take them to their destination. The sun rode low in the horizon as they set sail.

This stretch of the Nile was dense with islands and outcroppings of endless shapes and sizes, strewn about the water as if the capricious gods had tossed a handfuls of jewels into the water to fall where they may. None of these islands was inhabited. So when the *felucca* turned into the wind and Diana saw before her the rectangular pylons of a spectacular temple rising from the sea, the suddenness of it took her breath away.

Looking ahead at the serene beauty of the island, she sensed that something monumental was meant to take place here today. That it was no accident that fate had chosen this of all places to hide the final piece of their puzzle.

The temple was exquisite, shimmering in the last rays of the sun. Unlike most of the crumbling temples, this one was largely intact—its isolation offering it a measure of protection. Diana stared at it as they approached, her excitement mounting. She felt the spirit of her father, and wished he could be here to share in this moment.

The last tourist boat of the day had just left. Jack and Diana docked and unloaded the supplies before sending their own vessel on its way. When it was out of sight, they carried their equipment across the island toward the main temple. Diana glanced about. There were no tools, no sign of any excavation.

"Did we guess wrong?" she asked. "What could Hornsby possibly be getting here? And how?"

"Let's have a closer look."

They entered the temple through the Gate of Ptolemy. In the courtyard, likenesses of Isis, Osiris, and Horus greeted them from the walls. Further in, the deities' faces had been chiseled away, desecrated by the fourth century Christians who'd sought to destroy such evidence of pagan worship. The symbol of the Coptic Christians had been carved alongside hieroglyphics in the stone.

They went inside. It was pitch black. Jack lit a lantern, raising it to reveal graceful stone columns with their painted lotus capitals. So lifelike, it was like walking through some Late Kingdom garden along the Nile.

They strolled through the huge corridor in silence, with only the echo of their footsteps breaking the reverential hush. Scanning the walls, they at last came to the one commissioned by Cleopatra. As Jack held the lantern high, Diana gazed at it in awe. A life-size image of the queen was chiseled in the stone in raised relief. She stood in profile, her breasts bared, her diaphanous gown displaying her slimly rounded body underneath. On her shoulders she wore the skin of a leopard to denote her royal status.

It was the most stunning likeness Diana had ever seen. Though carved in hard stone, it was movingly sensual, capturing the allure of the ruler whose quick mind and seductive charm had made her the most famous woman the world had ever known. Diana felt raw emotion choke her. The queen seemed almost to be pointing the way toward her treasure, offering it to them, her chosen beneficiaries.

"The temple's holy of holies would be toward the rear," Jack said. He led the way through a maze of columned halls. At last they found a small, enclosed room at the back. She stopped on the threshold. Inside the rectangular chamber was a tall pink granite pillar, nearly chest high, with a rounded, flat top, rising like a shaft, worn smooth by the rubbing of devoted hands.

Jack had placed the lamp on the stone floor. He stood with both hands resting reflectively on the column.

"The heart of the temple," he said at last. "At one time, a statue of Isis rested on this altar."

"They say the altar is more precious even than the statue. That the altar holds within it all the spiritual energy of those who came to worship for thousands of years."

He ran his hands over the granite. "You can almost feel the presence of Isis here." For an instant, he seemed like the Jack of old, the one inspired to seek out antiquities for the sake of history, and mankind.

She looked about the room to dispel the illusion. "But no indication of what Hornsby's been up to."

Thoughtfully, Jack walked a circle around the altar.

"It's hopeless," she said, the disappointment rushing in on her. "It can't be here."

Jack leaned over and picked something off the floor. A bit of burnt straw. "Someone's been burning a torch here—and recently."

He returned to the altar, rounding it and inspecting it with his hands, as if feeling for something specific. Momentarily, he found what he was looking for—a piece of loose stone. With some difficulty, he wedged it free. He stuck his finger into the hole and the altar suddenly swung to the side with a loud grate. Using his shoulder, Jack pushed it several more inches to the left. The entire altar was mounted on a track, and positioned over a square opening in the floor just large enough for a person to slip through.

"That bastard Hornsby. He's found the tomb of Abhusan."

"Abhu—who? Who are you talking about?"

Distractedly, he said, "An obscure Middle Kingdom pharaoh whose tomb was long thought to be somewhere in this vicinity, but has never been found. Six months ago, a relic bearing his cartouche turned up on the Cairo black market. . . . You stay here—I'm going down."

"Oh, no you don't. If you think I'm letting you out of my sight, so you can tie some magistrate's horse to *my* wagon, think again."

He shot her an irritated glance. "I was only thinking of your safety."

"You were thinking of safely getting the cat and

leaving me behind. You let *me* worry about my own safety."

With an exasperated grunt, he dropped into the opening and she followed close behind. They found themselves in a cramped, narrow tunnel just wide enough for one person to traverse while bending low. They followed it in single file until they came to a larger opening that offered a staggering choice of passageways, a labyrinth of more tunnels shooting out and leading in all directions underneath the island. A maze so vast and intricate that they could easily get lost and never find their way out again.

Jack stood still, thinking. "Obviously, Hornsby has been coming here at night and robbing the tomb. He must have found a map. He's not archaeologist enough to come up with this on his own."

Diana was occupied with other thoughts. "According to Dr. Bouchard's recent studies at the Sorbonne, whenever ancient peoples built a maze, there was invariably some hidden logic to the plan. More often than not, if one bears continually to the right in any labyrinth, one will eventually come to the end without ever getting lost."

"Then we'll go left."

"Left? I just said—"

"I know what you said. But if this *is* early Middle Kingdom Abhusan, who would the tomb's architect most likely be?"

"Imhotep, of course."

"And as everyone knows . . ."

"Imhotep was left-handed."

"So we go left."

They bore left. The darkness was suffocating, the air stale. Only the meager glow of the lantern showed them the way. As they penetrated the maze, Diana began to lose her bearings, feeling lost and entombed. She found it difficult to breathe.

But she went on, looking about to distract herself. In the light she could see paintings on the walls that were so bright and vivid they might have been fashioned only the day before. Warnings to those who might seek to rob the tomb.

Then, all at once, they came out into an area that was wider than the tunnel they'd left behind. Diana stepped ahead, coming abreast of Jack.

"We must be close. Let's hurry."

But he held up a hand. Swinging the lantern, he took a look around. "The earth seems fresher here. Something's wrong."

He took the pack he'd been carrying on his shoulders and tossed it to the ground. Instantly, the earth fell away on two sides, revealing the gaping hole of a trapdoor. With caution, they approached. Below, they saw several angry rows of pointed stakes, some of them stained with what looked like recently dried blood.

Diana shivered at their close call.

"That's the Hornsby touch," Jack said. "He must have lost a man or two here. But he covered it up for us, so we'd have the same surprise."

"You know the most charming people."

Carefully, they inched their way around the

deadly chasm and crept past. Despite her flippancy, Diana followed him now with more care.

"Very common Sixth Dynasty device, by the way," Jack instructed her, now that the danger was past.

"I know. Father encountered something similar at Thebes."

They continued on. In a few minutes more, they came to the entrance of the tomb. It was small, but brilliantly painted with images and hieroglyphs. In contrast, the floor was littered with the debris of hastily smashed crates, cigarette butts, and other telltale remains that gave testament to the looting that had so recently taken place here. A large grey sarcophagus stood empty in the inner chamber, its heavy top cracked, half of it lying broken at its side. And positioned on the other half, as promised, was a luminous alabaster cat.

Diana took a hasty step, but Jack grabbed her arm and yanked her back. Moving stealthily forward, he made an inspection of the grey stone on which the relic sat. "I should have known."

"What is it?"

"Hornsby had no intention of us recovering the cat. He couldn't take the chance of letting us go once we'd found his dirty little secret."

"What are you talking about?"

He glanced at her. She saw a grim look in his eyes. "The cat sits on a spring that's rigged to go off if we lift it. My guess, since we're surrounded by water, is that once the rigging is sprung, the entire tunnel structure will flood and drown us in moments."

"But how could Hornsby possibly build—"

"He didn't. He's attached the cat to Imhotep's last-ditch device to foil grave robbers."

Diana stared at the cat with her heart in her throat. So close, yet it was completely unattainable.

"Can't you place something heavy on it and slide the cat off? That way—"

"Hornsby would have thought of that."

She sank back against the wall, feeling all the energy and anticipation drain out of her. "So the famous treasure hunter comes to a dead end at last. What trick do you have up your sleeve this time?"

He'd been standing completely still, eyes fixed steadily on the cat.

"No trick," he said at last. "We go for broke. You *do* remember how to swim?"

Before she could respond, Jack reached forth and with one bold swipe, snatched the cat from the stone.

For a moment, she couldn't believe what she'd just seen. Then, as if from a great distance, she heard a hissing sound, followed by a succession of thunderous explosions—the dull, heavy crash of huge stone blocks sealing off the passageway by which they'd come. They were trapped. Diana froze in terror.

Without blinking an eye, Jack said, *"Now* you can start worrying about your safety."

All at once, jets of water gushed into the chamber from all sides. The force of it was so great that within a moment, it was lapping about their ankles. Jack scanned the walls all around them and handed Diana the cat. Then, quite suddenly, he stepped to the far corner and dropped to his knees. He felt the surface of the lower wall, even as the water lapped about his shoulders. After another moment, he rose and stood calmly, gauging the rising tide.

"Do something!" she cried.

He gave her a confident wink. "I am."

"What?"

"I'm waiting for the water to rise."

She watched in horrified frustration as Jack stood there, doing absolutely nothing.

The water rose higher . . . higher . . . churning now about her waist.

"Have you gone mad?" she demanded. *"What are you thinking?"*

"Just have a little patience."

"But what are you waiting for?"

He didn't answer. He just stood as he had, watching the water rise. To her chest. Her shoulders. To the base of her chin. In another moment, the water would fill her mouth.

"Now, I'm going to count to three," he said. "Take a deep breath and hold it. You hear me? One . . . two . . . *three*!"

Together, they filled their lungs. Jack dropped the lantern and it fizzled, then died. They were cloaked in darkness, the only sound the roar of the onrushing water. He grabbed her hand and pulled her under. Dragging her behind, feeling about with his other hand, he dove for the corner he'd so carefully ex-

amined. Diana could feel Jack pushing on the lower
wall with his free hand. After some effort, one of the
wall stones swiveled on its axis, opening a narrow
passage.

Using one hand to pull her, the other to feel his
way along the passage wall, Jack begin to swim. Diana felt the abrupt onrush of the Nile's water pressure splitting her ears. Her lungs burned. There was
no clue as to how long the passage might be or where
it led. It was so narrow that as they frantically
plunged ahead, she was constantly banging against
the stone.

They swam and swam, faster, faster, through the
channel. The moments seemed like hours as her
lungs longed to heave for air. She clamped her lips
shut, afraid that she'd impulsively take a gulp of
water. Her legs began to tire from the effort of
propelling her forward. The unreal blackness was op-
pressing. She felt death hovering as it grew more and
more difficult not to breathe. She couldn't hold on.
Her lungs were bursting. Her racing heart was
pounding in her head. It was too much, too long. She
had to take a breath.

She felt them collide into a wall. Then, just as
suddenly, they began to rush upward. They continued to rise, higher and higher, surging up like lava
from the mouth of a volcano. But it was too late. She
felt herself losing consciousness, felt the loosening of
the grip on her lungs.

Then, just as she felt herself slipping to the other
side, they exploded up to the surface. She felt herself

bob above the water. Desperately, she gasped for life. Water shot into her throat and she coughed and choked until at last she could feel the sweet relief of air. Jack's hand let loose as he, too, struggled to breathe. They floated for a time, utterly spent, along the surface of the Nile.

When at last her breath had slowed, Diana felt the weight of the cat in her hand. Buoyed, she looked about and saw Jack in the distant moonlight, swimming for shore. She followed. When she'd dragged herself onto the island, Jack was already lying on the earth, panting heavily.

They lay still for some moments, feeling the good earth beneath them. Finally Diana gasped, "How did you know there'd be a way out?"

"I didn't. I took a lucky guess."

She shot up on her elbows, glaring down at him. "Do you mean to tell me you grabbed that cat on impulse? With no idea of how we were going to get out of there?"

He rolled over, fatigued, onto his back. "What difference does it make now?"

"I think I have a right to know."

He groaned, conveying his unwillingness to make the effort. "All right. If you must know, I put two and two together. Imhotep was a known claustrophobic. I took a bet he'd have the foresight to build an escape hatch in case the pharaoh decided to take him along to the afterlife."

"Fine. But why did you wait for so long before making your move?"

"Don't you know anything? I had to wait until the water pressure inside equaled the water pressure outside, or the stone wouldn't move. God almighty, I'm tired."

Too exhausted to be annoyed by his condescension, she lay her cheek on the cool earth and wearily closed her eyes.

12

*P*resently, she became aware of the cat weighing heavily in her hand. In spite of her terror, she'd gripped it as if her life had depended on it.

She raised herself up and looked at it. It was too dark to read the secret it had to tell. She heard Jack stir and then he said, "Let's go see what it says."

She felt rebellion stir. True, he'd succeeded in retrieving the cat, and had saved her life in the process. For that, she was grateful. But still, feelings of mistrust resurfaced. She didn't want him to know the final clue. Yet what good was the treasure to her now if she couldn't use it to barter for her mother's life?

So she dragged herself to her feet. Her clothes were soaked and heavy. Her legs wobbled as she walked. But the thought that every step brought her that much closer to the attainment of her goal gave her the energy to push on.

They made their way through the darkness of the temple to the altar chamber at the back. There, Jack fished through the supplies and brought forth dry matches, using them to light the spare lamp. The light spilled slowly into the room.

"Take off those wet things," Jack said, "before you catch your death." Already, he was peeling the drenched jacket from his shoulders and unbuttoning his shirt. As Diana struggled with the saturated dress, he tossed his shirt aside and bent to tug off his boots and socks.

When Diana had draped her dress over the altar to dry, she turned and caught Jack gazing at her. She became acutely aware of the petticoat she wore, soaked and clinging to her frame. She didn't have to look to know, from the arrested glitter of his eyes, that he could see every curve, every hollow, every line of her body as if she wore nothing more than a diaphanous veil. And she saw that he was stirred by the sight. Unexpectedly. As if the vision of her body, so tantalizingly bared, had completely caught him off guard.

His words at the Mena House came back to her. *I want you.* Simply stated, without pretense of love or devotion. Lust and nothing more.

She turned her back. She, too, was unsettled by the vibrant charge of sexual tension in the air. What was this? she asked herself. They neither liked each other nor sought to be close. Yet this longing, this damnable desire, was like a persistent hound at their heels. She swallowed hard and balled her fists to fight the curl of hopeless hunger.

She told herself it was the aftermath of their experience. The fight, the battle to live against such crushing odds. The sharing of an accomplishment no one else could comprehend. And the triumph. The heady knowledge that they'd bested a foe bent on their destruction and made a mockery of the conspiring fates. It was only natural that they'd be excited. That their bodies, feeling the renewed surge of life, would leap at the chance to abandon consequences in the face of such a feat. What was danger now that they'd survived?

But still she trembled. Stakes, floods, the risking of life—these dangers paled when compared to the peril she felt as she sensed the heat of Jack's gaze. *I want you. . . .*

She could hear the words echo off the walls as clearly as if he'd spoken them aloud.

She couldn't speak. She knew that one of them must, to break the unbearable tension that turned her shoulders to stone. Yet she dreaded his words. She recalled the look in his eyes as she'd accused him of knowing Sheila's kidnapper. A look of stubborn, immovable will. A look that spoke more eloquently than words ever could of the vindication of her mistrust. He would do what he must, trick anyone he had to, in order to gain his objective. He always had.

Somehow, it was imperative that she remind herself of that now.

His voice was hard and controlled as he asked, "What does it say?"

She had to think for a moment what he meant. She had expected an advance. Had she imagined his look of desire? She turned and looked at him. No. She hadn't imagined it. His voice was sharp, yet his eyes fixed on her with heated craving. Her gaze dropped and she saw the proof of his hunger in the rampant bulge of his soaked pants. She stared at it, her body recalling of its own will the magic of that powerful tool. The unspeakable pleasure he'd bestowed. Then, with an iron will of her own, she remembered the cat. She turned from him and retrieved it.

"One word," she told him. " 'Gods.' And an odd symbol. Something like a misshapen—"

Her gaze flew to his. With a start she remembered. A detail so insignificant that she hadn't thought of it again. Sheila had worn an amulet with that same oddly shaped symbol. Like a misshapen fish.

He was peering at her hard. She dropped her gaze hastily, bent on disguising the knowledge that must surely register in her eyes.

"I don't know what it means," she said softly.

But Sheila would know.

To throw him off the track, she said, "Maybe we should consult with some of the scholars at the Cairo Museum. My father still has a friend or two there, from the old days. If we swore them to secrecy, I'm sure they could be trusted."

Jack was silent for a time. So silent for so long that she felt the urge to squirm. She had to grit her teeth to keep still. She could feel his unflinching gaze on her face. She could only hope she didn't flush and give herself away.

Finally, he spoke. "Let me see it," he commanded.

She passed it forth. His hand brushed hers as he took it, and she felt the spark of raw electric current. Still she avoided his gaze.

He turned the cat over and studied it at great length. Then thoughtfully, he recited, " 'Who, on the sweetest of days, rose up among the gods.' Does that mean anything to you?"

She had to speak naturally, as if the knowledge of her secret wasn't burning in her brain. She couldn't let him know. It was her only armor, her only chance for independence.

"Nothing I haven't thought of before. Part of an Egyptian fable, perhaps. But I know of nothing it would fit."

"And this symbol," he persisted. "It looks like some sort of fish. Is there any myth that speaks of fish?"

"Only one that I know of."

But she said it distractedly. Her mind was busy making plans. If she could somehow find out where Sheila was . . . she could rescue her and find the answer to the riddle in one fell swoop. Without Jack. Then she could find the treasure on her own and claim it in her father's name. Jack and his precious Birch Haven be damned.

"And what's that?" he asked.

Somehow, she must get Jack to tell her the name of Sheila's kidnapper. But how? How to break through his wall of reserve? What could she do that would be persuasive enough to . . .

His grip on her arm startled her back to the present. He was glaring at her fiercely. He towered over her, a black presence seething with manly power, as if he sensed her secret. His fingers gripped her bare arm, hurting her. But a jolt of furious desire shot through him and pierced her like an arrow.

"Tell me," he demanded.

"Tell you what?"

Her voice was breathless.

"The fable. The fish."

"Oh, that."

His eyes were as blue as the most precious lapis. They drew her in so she felt herself drowning in his gaze. She felt again what it was to surge through the water at a terrifying pace. She tore her eyes away and they came to rest on the images carved in the surrounding walls. Lovely images that told a story . . .

And then she knew. She knew the weapon she could use to her advantage.

Slowly, she put her hand on his. A delicate touch, but it seemed to burn him. He jerked his hand away, dropping her arm as if it were a hot brand.

"It's the fable that's told in this very room," she said. She was gaining strength from the knowledge of what she must do. Her voice had taken on a seductive quality, a mysterious tone that spoke of wonders to be told.

"It's the story of Isis and Osiris. See the walls? The images tell the tale. There. Every Egyptian story begins with the words 'It shall be said . . .'" She glanced at him. He was looking at her warily, not sure what to expect.

She went on in the same mesmerizing tone. "Isis was married to the god Osiris. She loved him so dearly that when he was killed, when Set cut up his body into fourteen pieces and threw them in the Nile, Isis spent her life searching for those parts to put him back together again, piece by piece. The pictures illustrate the tale. See? According to the legend, she never found the last piece, which was swallowed by a fish. Even so, they conceived a child, the god Horus, who was also worshiped at this temple. Look at this." She walked to one of the carvings and touched it. "This shows their union. Osiris is making love to her, taking her from behind."

She turned to look at Jack. He'd placed his hands atop the stone altar and was now gripping it, not even noticing that her dress had fallen to the floor as he did. He was gazing at her steadily. But his jaw was set and his face had gone pale beneath the tan.

"She made him whole, and then he took her," he said. His voice sounded choked. His eyes blazed a message that was impossible to mistake.

Diana swallowed hard. The stone room, cold and abandoned, took on a sudden soft, inviting quality.

She felt the heat of raw desire radiate from the walls, surrounding her, enclosing her with its vibrancy, creating an aura of shivering possibility. Succumbing to it, she stepped to the altar and placed her trembling hands on Jack's.

"And what of you, Jack? Would you put *me* back together again?" she asked with a glimmer of unmistakable invitation in her eyes. "Piece by piece?"

He studied her face. Then his gaze shifted to the wall at her back. "What were the fourteen parts Isis put back together?"

She scanned the walls. She could find no reference, but she could feel the charge of Jack's electric presence shoot up her arms. Taking her hands from his, she slowly reached for him.

"The eyes first of all." She took his head in her hands and drew it down. When he closed his eyes, she put her lips to the lids, kissing gently. He looked up and shot her with a hot blue gaze before pulling her close. She closed her eyes and he leaned over her, fluttering his lashes against her lids in tender butterfly kisses that made her sigh with all the force of her feelings.

"Then the ears." She stroked his ears with her knuckles. He shifted and took her earlobe in his mouth, nibbling it delicately as his soft, warm breath penetrated her ear. Her body leapt to life, shuddering in excitement as he wielded his tongue like an instrument, rounding her ear, flitting inside, tugging at her lobe with the courtly coercion of his teeth. She hadn't counted on this. That she'd be so swept away by his touch. But it was too late. She had to go on.

"The lips," she told him, rubbing the tips of her fingers against his bold, sensuous mouth.

"Of course. The lips."

He took her head in his hands and brought his mouth to hers. Her lips parted sweetly, offering unspoken summons for him to steal her breath, to devour her without mercy or restriction. But he didn't. He touched her lightly, running his tongue along the sensitive inner recess of her upper lip. Then he sucked the lower lip into his mouth. She moaned and leaned into him, responding to the gentle pressure, desperately wanting more despite her resolve to take the lead. He took his time. He gave her feathery kisses, drawing slightly back when she pressed for more, teasing her as he explored her mouth with the tip of his tongue.

"And the tongue," she urged, before her own tongue darted into his mouth in supplication, urging him to warm to her bait. He eased back, the tip of his tongue touching hers, circling it, playing with it, luring her toward him, then backing ever so slightly away. His hand reached up, taking her earlobe between his thumb and forefinger, rotating it gently until she thought she'd explode. With a heartfelt moan, she brought her arms about his neck, pulling him closer, until slowly, by infinite, agonizing degrees, he met her lips with his. As she pressed against him, he deepened the kiss. He kissed her for an eternity, savoring her mouth, varying the pressure, nuzzling the plump pads of her lips before delving once again inside. He kissed her with leisurely passion, as though he could spend the night doing nothing more than explore the varied mysteries of her mouth.

She was breathless when at last he grazed her cheek, putting his mouth to her ear, whispering, "What then?"

Her body glowed and shimmered from the internal heat his deliberate mastery had ignited. Her lips felt cold without the fever of his mouth. Her heavy breath filled the room like a seductive hymn.

"The hands." She reached for his, entwining their fingers. He scraped his thumbnail along her sensitive palm, sending chills and hot flashes of desire rushing up her spine. Then he lifted her hands to his mouth and kissed them one by one, as tenderly as the graze of a soft breeze, as lovingly as the most ardent devotee glorifying a shrine. As if nothing on this earth was more precious to him, more treasured, more beautiful, than the two hands he held in his.

As she watched, he took each of her fingers into his mouth, slowly, sumptuously sucking the length of each, keeping his eyes locked with hers. She felt her fingers as she never had before, felt his hot tongue glide along her flesh as he sucked each finger like a delicacy to be relished in the luxury of extended time. Floating, she drew his hands to her and licked each palm, witnessing the flare of lust she elicited. Then, following his lead, she enticed his thumb into her mouth. Slowly, seductively, she sucked it like an erection, hearing his breath deepen in her ears. She wanted more. She was supposed to be the seductress. Yet she craved the taste of every inch of him on her tongue.

"And then?" he asked, his voice sounding husky and highly aroused.

She was having trouble thinking. But her hands moved of their own preference, bringing her palms to his chest. She rubbed the sculpted form of it, the hardened muscles, the scars that spoke of his stubborn rebellion, the thick covering of crisp bronze hair. Then she lowered her mouth and kissed the firm flesh again and again, until her tongue found the nipple and flicked. He drew a jagged breath between clamped teeth, urging her on. She sucked him, licked him, took the raised nub between her teeth and gently nibbled before moving on to the next.

She felt the empowerment of his response. She felt like a woman fully formed, seductive and alluring, ripe in the throes of his desire, spurred on by her hunger to explore all the mysteries of his godlike body, standing before her like a gift meant only for her pleasure. Unbidden, her own story of Isis had taken hold in her imagination. She wanted nothing more than to explore his body with her mouth, her hands, until she could bring him to the brink of shattering fruition and beyond. And in the midst of it, coax from him the truth.

Already his hands were tugging at her clothes. He opened the damp camisole and eased it down, past naked shoulders, letting her female form spill free into his hands. As the garment slithered past her hips, landing in a heap at her feet, he brushed her lavish breasts with the backs of his knuckles, convulsing her in shivers of heart-pounding heat. Then, his hands at her shoulders, he pressed her down, following close behind until the two of them knelt face-to-face before the altar of the goddess of love.

With feathery strokes, he brushed her breasts with his fingers, lightly enough to impel her to move into his hands, to entreat a more demanding touch. He obliged her to some measure, cupping them in his palms, massaging them in circular motions, kneading them with supple appreciation. And when she was more than ready, when she'd adjusted to his tender caress, he took her nipples between the thumb and forefinger of each hand, gently rotating until spasms of lust made her gasp aloud.

As she closed her eyes and threw back her head, his mouth found one breast, anointing it with his tongue as his fingers played with the other nipple in tantalizing, mind-ruffling rhythm. He feasted on her as she sank lower on her knees, awash in dreamy indulgence, feeling like a seductive nymph luring her quarry with a siren's song. She leaned back, her hands on the floor behind her, her arms stretched taut, offering herself more fully.

She felt the power of her womanhood blossom and spill over into a joy and adulation that knew no bounds. Jack moaned deep in his throat, a low, guttural growl, as he savored the benefaction of her woman's bounty.

The story had taken on a life of its own. Without waiting for instruction, he guessed the components she was now too breathless to list. Leaving her momentarily, he cast off his pants, then propelled her up. As she rose, he sat back, his knees raised, his feet flat on the stone flooring, his erection, huge and pulsing, angled against his thigh. He eased her down upon his right knee with her legs sprawling at either side. Then, holding her hands, he rocked her back and forth, her velvety core grinding softly into his kneecap, the hairs on his leg tickling and enticing. She rode him for a time, her hair swishing sensuously along her naked back, her breath sharp and short, coming in little pants as her blood pulsed, simmering . . . frothing . . . bubbling and erupting in a fiery foam.

She knew what she wanted, yet felt herself dangerously close to losing control. With his hands on her hips, he slid her wet sex down his thigh so she landed with a gasp on the rigid spear of his arousal. But just as she was moving against it, silently begging for the invasion she sought, he rolled her so she landed on her back in the heap of discarded clothing. Taking her feet in his hands, he raised one to his mouth, licking the underside until she cried out in licentious urgency. His mouth found her toes, sucking them as shocks of unspeakable hunger blasted through her and settled in the hot, moist cavern between her thighs. She was writhing now, too delirious in her fevered condition to hold still beneath the assault of his tongue. And just when she felt she could take it no longer, just when she felt she'd explode with one more flick of his tongue on her toes, his mouth blazed an unremitting trail along first her ankles, then the curve of her calves, then the delicate underflesh at the backs of her knees. Her legs dropped open, exposing herself to him, wanting him to look, inviting his mouth up her leg until he lay draped before her, delectably nuzzling her inner thigh.

She could no longer distinguish which sensations were pleasure and which were compulsive carnal need. Her head was reeling, her fingers tingling, her loins so sizzling with drenched heat that nothing existed but the gratification of his roaming tongue. His mouth on her thighs made her feel like a raving creature, all animal instincts now, wanting, needing, desperate for release from this dizzying height. Her hips were thrusting madly, crying out in petition for his mouth in the hungry portal between her thighs. The sounds coming from her throat were intonations she'd never known herself capable of, mewling noises that begged as they demanded, that expressed her cravings more succinctly than any words ever could.

Then she felt his mouth at last—at last touch her where she wanted him the most. His tongue moved with unvanquished skill, hurtling her higher and higher until the whole of the universe shattered and exploded, shaking her with unendurable eruptions, one after the other as she came in his mouth, and her body, ravaged by the commotion of her outburst, finally fell limp.

But he didn't cease the voyage of his tongue. He lapped at her unrelentingly until she came again and again, shocking herself, clutching his head, throwing hers back and forth, arching into his mouth with impassioned cries as wave after wave of helpless surrender and intoxicated rapture shook her to her core.

When she finally felt she could take no more, when she had to have him deep inside, he sensed it and rose on his knees before her, looking down. "Now, what," he asked with a knowing twinkle in his eyes, "was the fourteenth piece? The one that made Osiris whole?"

He'd twisted the legend to suit his whim, but she didn't care. She was glowing with pleasure. She felt her hunger stir again as she shakily rose up. "That," she told him, "which would transform him from a god and make him a man."

So saying, she took his vigorous erection between her hands. She caressed it for a time as he hardened further still, marveling at the masculine beauty of his chiseled form. She moved her face closer, catching a whiff of his scent, a heady bouquet of rampant male sex. Then she took him in her mouth until it felt full, thrusting against the boundary of her throat, rounding it with her tongue as she sucked back to the soft and sensitive head. She saw a drop of moisture and lapped it up with her tongue, then took him deeper still, wanting all of him, yet remembering what she wanted from him in return. She varied her strokes, sometimes soft and slow, sometimes charging down on him in her quest to drive him mad. She felt his body clench as she moved, heard his breath pumping like a furnace at full throttle.

His hands convulsed in her hair. She felt his irrefutable control to keep from shooting his load into her mouth. She looked up into his face and caught the glazed look of a man in need of release.

Now was the time.

She rubbed her cheek along the length of him. "I don't know yet how to find the treasure," she said softly, pausing to nuzzle soft kisses along the head. "But I think Sheila can help. If we could find her, Jack . . ." She took him in her mouth again, sucking with heartfelt persuasion. "Tell me who has her, and together we'll . . ." Again she enclosed him with her warm, moist mouth. She felt him tense, and sensed his loss of control. But in the next moment, she felt his hand in her hair. With one savage motion, he yanked back her head so he fell from her mouth, and she was forced to meet the blazing fury of his eyes.

"You scheming witch," he growled in a voice that turned her blood to ice. "So you want to know who has her, do you? So badly you'd sell yourself to me like a filthy limehouse whore."

"How dare you!" she cried. In her wrath, she leapt to her feet.

He followed, grabbing her shoulders, staring at her hard. Even now, he could hardly believe she'd used his desire for her—of all things—against him. He was so angry he felt a mad impulse to throttle something. But just as quickly, the urge passed, to be replaced by cold disdain. Without warning, he let her go, no longer able to bear the touch of her.

She fell back against the stone column and landed in a sitting position, her back against the pillar. She sensed his disgust. The abruptness of it left her too stunned to move.

As she watched warily, Jack bent to scoop his discarded clothes from the floor. When he saw her eyes on him, he stood to full height, looking down on her with a frigid gaze. She couldn't look away from his eyes. He seemed a colossus, standing tall before her, looking down at her unflinchingly, not moving so much as a muscle in his face.

He spoke in a harsh, warning tone. "Don't *ever* attempt to dupe me again," he told her slowly, enunciating every word. "You're out of your league."

With that he turned and stalked out of the room, his clothes clenched in a tight fist.

13

Diana awoke several hours later feeling drained and foolish. For a moment she couldn't think why. Then it all came back to her. Her pathetic attempt to trick Jack. His cold response. And his abrupt departure. She flushed to think of it.

She'd behaved stupidly. Now Jack would never tell her what he knew. She was as dependent on him as she'd ever been.

Her body felt sore from sleeping on the hard floor. Even before lighting the lamp, she could sense that she was alone. Where was Jack? Was he sleeping somewhere?

She decided to seek him out. Perhaps if she apologized, he'd soften and listen to her plea for help. She doubted it. But there must be some way. Even if he didn't relent, they'd be forced to work together to try to decipher the clues. Better to try to ease the tension, for the sake of their mission if nothing else. They couldn't afford to waste time in senseless animosity. Not when Sheila's life was at stake.

Her dress was still damp. It felt tight and clammy when she put it on, but she did her best to ignore her discomfort and, taking the lantern, set out in search of him.

He wasn't in the temple. She went outside and looked around the island. She didn't see him. Then an awful thought struck her. What if he'd left her behind? What if he'd guessed why she needed to know Sheila's whereabouts and had gone off alone to—

Then she saw him. He was standing on a promontory where a column from the Kiosk of Trajan had fallen, a lone figure looking out at the dark Nile. She approached him cautiously, trying to formulate what she'd say. But when he looked back and saw her, he hissed sharply, "Douse the light."

She did so. In the darkness, she saw what he'd been looking at. A light in the distance that didn't belong in this isolated setting so late at night. As she watched it grow larger, she felt a mounting unease. Then, with a jolt of alarm, she realized it was a lantern in the bow of a boat coming their way.

As it drew closer, she could see that it was a large skiff with six men at its oars, rowing steadily toward the island. But who would be making this trip at such an hour?

"Is it Hornsby?" she asked.

Jack was keenly studying the approaching craft. It was close enough now to see that the rowers were Egyptians.

"Could be. He may be coming to make sure he's disposed of us. And to finish the deed if—" He broke off, staring hard. "You stay here. I'll go down and find out."

She watched as he climbed down to a small spit where the boat was docking. Fearlessly, he greeted the leader of the party as the man leaped hurriedly from the skiff. They conversed for several minutes, their voices agitated but not loud enough to hear.

Momentarily, Jack broke away and strode back to Diana. Out of breath, he said, "Hornsby's coming. And he's got a dozen men with him, armed to the teeth. They're only minutes away. Hurry. This boat will take us off the island."

"But where are we going? Who are these—?"

He cut her off, his voice low but intense. "Diana, we have to be very careful here. Say nothing in front of these men. Some of them speak English. This may be our salvation, but it could also be extremely dangerous. Let me handle this, do you hear?"

Taking her arm, Jack led her to the boat where one of the sailors had vacated a seat. As they sat down and the boat pushed off again, Diana could now see the silhouette of a large yacht anchored in a protective cove of a neighboring island. The sailors rowed briskly toward it, the boatswain dowsing the lantern, cloaking them in the dark night. Diana glanced behind and saw the reason for this precaution: a large boat was heading toward the island they'd just escaped.

A thousand questions flooded Diana's mind. Who were these unexpected deliverers? How did they know she and Jack were on the island, much less that Hornsby was planning an ambush? Where were they going? And why was Jack not surprised by their abrupt appearance? She would have demanded an explanation, had she not remembered Jack's caution to say nothing in front of these men.

Moments later, the skiff came alongside the yacht. It was a spectacular ship, all polished wood and gleaming brass surfaces. The plaything of a wealthy man.

A rope ladder was thrown down to the craft. One of the sailors secured it and gestured to the two passengers to climb it. Diana followed Jack, awkward in her long dress, until she reached the rail. As Jack climbed aboard, she glanced on deck and saw a row of sailors watching them in eerie silence, obviously expecting them.

In a daze of shock and suspicion, she looked at Jack and asked in a strangled voice, "You *know* these people?"

"Yes. I know them."

A steward dressed in a fitted white coat was waiting for them. In English he said, "The *Effendi* wishes to speak with you, sir. We have a comfortable cabin waiting for the lady."

Jack turned to Diana. "Go with him," he told her. "I'll come back when I can and tell you everything."

Still numb, Diana let the steward take her to a cabin on the starboard rail. Its luxurious appointments were lost on her. She heard the anchor raise and the engines of the ship roar to life. Detaining the steward, she asked, "Where are we headed?"

"To Nubia, miss. The *Effendi* has a grand palace near Qasr Ibrim. You and Mr. Rutherford will be safe there."

Mr. Rutherford . . . He'd known Jack's name before they'd boarded.

"And who is our host, the *Effendi*?" she questioned, willing her voice to sound casual.

He was quick to cover his blink of surprise. "Why, His Royal Highness, miss, Ali Pasha the Resplendent, Shadow of God on Earth. Who else would offer the young lady such a daring and benevolent rescue?"

Ali Pasha! Her mind reeled back to the evening when she and Jack had broken into his London mansion. The ease with which Jack had obtained the location of the other cats from the notorious Turkish playboy. Had all this been a manipulation? A charade?

Sick at heart, she paced the room for several moments, trying to make some sense of all she'd seen and heard. The evidence against Jack was mounting by the minute. Ali Pasha . . . this sudden rescue that spoke of a vile collusion . . .

She had to know what was going on.

The ship was now under way, steaming due south. Stealthily, she opened the door. To her amazement, there was no one guarding the passageway and she swiftly darted down the corridor. The cabin of Ali Pasha wasn't difficult to find. It overlooked the bridge, with a commanding view of the water, blazing now with lights.

The sailors were all at work at various tasks. It was simple enough to sneak past them to the upper deck, where she spotted an open porthole by the rail. She crept past the cabin door to the side passageway and stood on her toes to look inside.

The cabin was worthy of a sultan, draped in lavish silks. But Diana's gaze was drawn to the two men facing each other in the center of the room. The handsome Turk had just handed Jack a glass of brandy.

She heard Jack's voice. "What are you doing here? This wasn't part of the deal."

"It's a good thing I *was* here," said the prince, raising his glass in emphasis. "I saved your English arse."

"Just what do you intend to do with us?" Jack asked, swirling his brandy, but not drinking.

"Firstly, I shall graciously liberate you from this perilous situation into which you have so clumsily stumbled."

"Then?"

"You have found all the cats?"

Jack hesitated.

"Before you consider lying to me, allow me to issue a warning. My spies have already informed me of the success of your operation."

"Yes, we found the cats. But there's still something missing."

"Missing?" cried Ali harshly. "What is missing? What *could* be missing? You said three cats, three clues. Is that not what you found?"

Jack took a sip of brandy from his snifter. "There's some spark missing. Something to pull all the clues together."

"But what?" Ali demanded.

Jack sighed in exasperation. "I don't know. Diana doesn't know. I think she knows where she can find out. But she's not telling me." He paused, studying the amber liquid in his glass. Then he said, "You took Sheila, didn't you?"

"Who else, my friend?"

"Where is she?"

Ali chuckled. "Safely tucked away in England. Where even *you* shan't ever find her."

"There was no need—"

"Forgive me if I contradict. There was, to my discerning eye, every need in the world. Call it insurance, if you will. Against the likelihood that you and Miss Sanbourne might be tempted to keep the treasure for yourselves."

"You know I can't do that," Jack growled, angry

now. "Because you have *my* treasure. You have Birch Haven."

Diana turned away, leaning her back against the outside wall. *Ali Pasha* held the deed to Birch Haven. And had kidnapped Sheila. And Jack had known it all along. He'd asked her to trust him. And all the while, he'd intended to make his own deal with the Turk.

She had her answers now. But what was she going to do? What *could* she do?

She looked out at the passing Nubian shore, weighing her alternatives. She had to get out of here. If she waited to reach Ali Pasha's palace, there would be no possibility of escape. If she was going, it would have to be now.

Shaking, she grasped the rail, staring out at the dark water churning below. She'd have to take the chance that she could swim to shore undetected. It wouldn't be easy. The river was wide, the banks a great distance. She was dreadfully fatigued by her earlier exertions. Her dress would weigh her down. If she was caught, they'd lock her up and she'd have no further opportunity for escape. But if she made it . . .

Carefully, she balanced herself on the rail, gazing down at the river from what seemed a dizzying height. There was no other way. Taking a quick breath for courage, she dove into the Nile.

An eternity later, Diana dragged her exhausted body onto the rich, dark soil of the riverbank, struggling to pull her drenched clothing behind. She looked back—dripping wet for the second time that evening, her lungs heaving, her overworked limbs burning from effort—to see the lights of the yacht steaming up the Nile. How long would it take for them to miss her? And when they did, how long for them to search the ship? Maybe hours. Maybe just minutes.

She tried to envision the chain of events. Once they were certain she was off the ship, they would turn around and scour the riverbanks, assuming she would make her way back to Aswan and from there back down the Nile to Cairo. But she'd foil them. She'd flee in the opposite direction, into the Nubian desert.

But then what? She'd be hundreds of miles from nowhere, in one of the emptiest stretches of desert in the world. Images of the dead, decaying animals she'd seen from the train to Aswan flashed through her mind, the vultures swarming over them, the jackals lying in wait. Was that her fate? She didn't care. Even that was better than allowing herself to be the prisoner and pawn of these two monstrous villains.

She lay her head in the soft reeds, giving herself up to this new fate. How long would it take her to die out there? Would she lose consciousness before the vultures and jackals noticed her? In the anvil of the relentless sun, she would probably expire long before the next nightfall. Would it be painful to sink into the scorching sand, dying of thirst? Would she feel fang and claw tearing at her flesh? It didn't seem to matter. Nothing mattered. Nothing could be as painful as the agony she'd escaped. The agony of Jack's betrayal.

His words to Ali Pasha came back to torment her. *You have my treasure. You have Birch Haven.* He'd led her to believe he'd help her save Sheila's life. When all he really wanted—*still*—was his precious piece of England.

Out of the hot desert night, a cool breeze suddenly came off the river, touching her cheek like a mother's caress. A sign of hope. A summons to go on. And all at once, Diana lifted her head. Her eyes were brittle now as she stared after the fading lights of the yacht. *"Damn you, Jack Rutherford!"* she cried into the night.

Her situation *wasn't* hopeless. She wouldn't allow it to be. There had to be caravans in the desert, which might offer her assistance. She spoke Arabic in all its dialects. A hundred and twenty-five miles to the east was the Red Sea and the small port of Berenice, founded by Ptolemy II. British ships from India often stopped there on their way to the Suez Canal and back to England.

She would go there. She wouldn't die. She'd get to Berenice if she had to walk the entire way.

She had, after all, a tactical advantage. They didn't know what she'd overheard—that her mother was in England. Jack would assume she would try to get back to enlist the aid of her father's old friends in Cairo. They might spend weeks searching for her there. In the meantime, she would return to England through this back door, and somehow, some way, rescue Sheila and use her help to figure out the riddle of Cleopatra's cats. Then, together, they would end the search for history's greatest treasure and use it to vindicate Stafford Sanbourne—the man they'd both loved.

Most of it, that is. Some small part of the treasure she would reserve for herself. To fund a quest for justice. To right a humiliating wrong. To make Jack Rutherford pay for his epic betrayal.

London
11 December 1899

The night was foggy and cold. Diana huddled in her overcoat behind the bushes across from Ali Pasha's mansion, staking out the situation as she and Jack had done months earlier. But tonight there would be no Flossie and no Jack. Tonight she was on her own.

As she awaited the changing of the guards and her opportunity to strike, she felt a flutter of apprehension. Was it possible that tonight of all nights, after three long weeks of frustration, she would finally come face-to-face with her mother? It seemed a lifetime since that fateful night when she'd overheard the evidence of Jack's betrayal. Even now, she could hardly believe she'd managed the journey. With single-minded determination, she'd made her way across the desert. First on foot, then, when she could trudge on no more, by camel in a Bedouin caravan. They'd taken her to the port of Berenice on the Red Sea, where she'd arrived half-dead and bedraggled to beg the captain of a cargo steamer to take her aboard with the promise that she'd repay him handsomely when they docked in England. Her sorry state—parched, sunburned, her clothes all but ripped from her body—had stirred the good man to pity. He'd supplied her with a private berth and all the food and water she wanted, barely concealing his surprise when, upon arrival in England, she'd returned to the port with three times what her passage would have cost.

So she'd arrived at last in the damp, wintry city that no longer felt like home. After the scorched heat of the desert, it was difficult to adjust to the layers of clothing that barely kept the chill from her bones. But she found a city more alien than the one she'd left behind. In her absence, London had become infested with the fever of the coming new year, when they would usher in the new century. There was a festive, almost manic energy in the air, as if the great city, the center of the British Empire and thus the world, realized the unique position afforded to its privileged generation. Already, parties and balls celebrated the coming epoch. Newspapers speculated endlessly on the fantastic changes the new century would inevitably bring. A massive symposium was being held at the Royal Geographical Society, attempting to predict the state of the mighty British Empire in the year 2000, a hundred years in the future. But the largest gathering was being planned for on New Year's Eve around Parliament, where Big Ben would proudly ring in the new century. Speculation was rampant that the Queen herself would bow to the wishes of the public and attend.

There was a feeling of carnival madness in the air, as if the staid citizens were ready to kick up their heels and celebrate with uncharacteristic abandon. But Diana felt none of their gaiety or exhilaration. The approaching milestone meant nothing to her. All she could think of was finding Sheila before Ali Pasha—and Jack—realized that Diana wasn't in Cairo and pursued her here.

So, moving through the crowds like a stranger, she'd found a small hotel room and, keeping her presence in the city a secret in case Jack made a surprise return, had immediately set out to determine where Ali Pasha could possibly have hidden Sheila. She enlisted the services of a detective, a Mr. Reardon who'd worked closely with the British Museum on various touchy cases involving fraud. He'd quickly discovered that Ali Pasha had three country estates in various parts of England. But after Reardon had staked out those estates and found no activity, Diana was frustrated to find herself back where she'd begun.

She'd first suspected that Sheila was being held here, at Ali Pasha's London mansion. But Mr. Reardon had dismissed it as being too obvious. Having exhausted the other possibilities, however, she was forced to return to her original assessment. The house held the status of an embassy and was therefore legally considered Turkish territory. Police had no authority to enter its grounds. The fiendish prince could keep Sheila a prisoner there for years, and no one could do anything about it. Diana's only hope was to use the element of surprise, to somehow sneak into the dragon's lair and steal her mother before he figured out what was happening.

It was a daunting task, and hardly the kind of thing at which she naturally excelled. But she was able to bolster herself by recalling that moment in the tomb at Philae when Jack had so boldly snatched the cat from its stand, letting loose the floods. She'd faced death then—and again when crossing the scorching desert sands—and had come out the victor. It was proof that she could handle whatever came her way. So, armed with a sense of destiny and a fiery determination for justice, she'd collected the necessary tools and taken a hidden perch to await her opportunity. She knew how to get into the house, and she knew where she could hide once she did. It was simply a matter of snatching the opportunity when it came.

As she waited for the guards to change their posts, she wondered again what she'd find inside. She willed herself not to think of all the rumors she'd heard—and Mr. Reardon's investigation had so chillingly reinforced—about Ali Pasha. How he had served his demented carnal lusts by committing frightful abominations against women—rape, torture, even mutilation. "Things I wouldn't discuss with me own brother," Reardon swore with a look on his face of someone with a secret wild dogs couldn't drag out of him. "I wouldn't want to fall into that bloke's hands," he'd added with a grave shake of his head.

But Sheila had fallen into his hands. Diana shivered. If the danger of the rescue didn't scare her, what she might find when she saw Sheila did.

Just then she heard the coming of the guards who would take the others' places. They came noisily, carrying flasks that they shared with the sentries they replaced. With the master away, his attendants no doubt felt safe in bending the rules. Diana had counted on this, remembering their reactions to Flossie the time before. She tensed, her body poised to spring. Then, when their backs were finally turned in companionable conversation, she sprinted across the road and wove a cautious path to the side of the house.

High above, she spotted the dark outline of the window she and Jack had used to sneak into the house. Reaching into her bag, she pulled out the length of rope with the three-pronged hook she'd had Reardon purchase for her. She swung it high, but her arm wasn't as strong as Jack's and it missed its mark. She swung again, and again it fell short. Gritting her teeth, she took the grappling hook in both hands and flung it up with all her might. This time it clattered against the roof. After a heart-stopping moment when it appeared it would fall free, it bounced a few feet down the slope and held.

With a sigh of relief, Diana tested it before gripping it with firm hands. She placed her feet on the side wall and slowly, pulling the weight of her body up by her arms, began to climb.

But she'd only ascended two small steps when suddenly, out of the still night, she was grabbed from behind.

She gasped aloud, just as a hand clamped down over her mouth, muffling her cry. An arm of iron pinned her back against a sturdy frame. In a flash, her assailant yanked a hood over her head and replaced his palm on her mouth, crushing it with brutal strength.

Diana's terror made her strong. She struggled frantically, kicking and squirming to break his hold. But he pinned her to him, and hauled her up, flailing and gasping stifled screams beneath his hand. She fought him wildly as he stalked away, dragging her with him, her mind frozen on the one thought of escape. But even as she did, some part of her mind, observing as from a disconnected distance, was aware of the pounding of his heart against her back. And she felt, too, with a jolt of horror, the hardening of his erection, as if her struggles and his fight to subdue her were bringing his blood to a boil. She recalled Reardon's warning in that instant. *I wouldn't want to fall into that bloke's hands.*

She increased her struggles to no avail. She felt herself hoisted, then flung against something hard.

Before she could wonder what it was, she felt her abductor beside her, breathing heavily. An abrupt jolt and the crack of a whip told her they were moving forward. She realized they were in a carriage and were moving fast.

She could feel his massive body against her, his arms imprisoning her, pinning her against him so she couldn't move. She ceased her struggles and fought instead to think. What was happening? Was she being taken somewhere to be held until Ali Pasha returned to England? If so, why not take her inside his sanctuary, where she could be held prisoner, safe from any legal retribution? No, this was something more sinister. He was taking her, perhaps, to an obscure place where a body could be dumped. Murder. The word flashed through her mind with ominous velocity. The thought of it panicked her. It was so dark within the hood, so stale and confining, that her mind was playing tricks on her. She had to break free. She jerked against her captor, striking a blow with her elbow into his side. As he flinched, she freed one hand and savagely wrenched off the hood.

She was assailed by a series of passing lights, then plunged once again into darkness. Disoriented, her mind reeled, trying to make sense of her surroundings. As she did, her tormentor set her free, backing into the shadows of the coach. She could hear his breath mixing with her own. She shuddered, wondering who he was. But then a passing light illuminated the face of this brute who'd so cruelly and coldly snatched her.

It was . . .
Jack!

It was such a shock that it took her a moment to absorb it. She'd counted on Jack being in Egypt, turning Cairo upside down looking for her. She was imagining this. Her mind, clutched with terror, had fabricated his face. She waited, breathing erratically, for the next flash of light from the street. When it came, there was no doubt. He sat with his arms crossed, leaning back into the corner of the coach, watching her, awaiting her reaction.

"You contemptible bastard," she said, low in her throat. She was so angry, so outraged, that she couldn't even find the energy to raise her voice.

"Bastard am I? I just saved your sorry life."

It was dark again. He spoke with the sarcastic lilt to his voice that she knew so well. She could almost see the supercilious arch of his brow.

"Saved my life!" she cried, finding the energy now that had failed her. "Have you any idea what you've done?"

"I know exactly what I've done. You were about to make the stupidest mistake of your life. The minute you stepped through the door, you'd have been nabbed by the team of guards he now keeps *inside* the house. Believe me, that's a fate you wouldn't wish even on . . . me."

She lashed out at him, striking his shoulder. "I was so close. Damn you, why can't you leave me alone?"

He grabbed her, jerking her toward him so she landed with a thud on his lap. Pinning her arms again, he circled her with his own and held her hard against him. "I need you, baby, remember? Besides, I'm on your side."

She lurched about, battling his powerful hold. As she did, she once again felt the swelling of his erection against the back of her leg. Furious, she thrust her elbow back, doing her best to deliver a sobering blow. "*My* side? God help your enemies, then."

"After all I've done for you," he chided with something sly and amused in his tone.

"Done for me? Let's just count the things you've done for me, shall we? Why don't we start with the way you conspired with Ali Pasha to have me find the treasure for you, then steal it from me and give it to him. And that's just *lately*."

"No one has to find any treasure for me," he growled, increasing his hold as she struggled madly against him.

"Giving me that sob story about how *someone* bought Birch Haven. You knew all along it was Ali Pasha. If we count up the lies you've told me we'll have a fine tally of *all you've done for me*!"

"You'd better stop now, before you say something you'll regret."

"The only thing I regret is that I ever went to you for help in the first place. *That* was the stupidest mistake I ever made."

The carriage came to an abrupt halt, throwing them both forward. Diana took the opportunity to extricate herself from his hold and slide off his lap to the safety of the other side of the seat. But Jack seemed not to notice. He stepped out and held the door open for her, extending his hand in invitation.

Diana ignored it and stepped down. As Jack closed the door, the driver—a disreputable-looking fellow with a black eye-patch—looked down at Jack and winked. Then he cracked the whip and the carriage sped off.

Diana looked about the dark street. It was full of warehouses. The one they'd stopped in front of was dimly lit behind the shade. Suddenly, she knew where they were. This was their fathers' old warehouse, where they'd jointly stored the antiquities from their various expeditions while cataloging them for display in the museum. She and Jack had spent many fascinated hours here as children, rummaging through the relics, playing games among the piled stores.

"What are you up to?" she asked, her voice seething with suspicion.

"Just come inside."

Her mind worked fast as she glanced back at the dark street. She knew this area well. She could make a break for it and perhaps lose him in the winding alleys.

But just as she was about to whirl and run, he grabbed her arm and pulled her back. "Oh no, you don't," he said, reading her mind. When she tried to pull free, he took hold of her and lifted her, tossing her over his shoulder, gripping powerfully against her exertions to break loose. "Don't you even want to see your surprise?"

"Surprise me by putting a knife in your black heart," she retorted, her voice muffled and breathy against his hold.

He struggled to open the warehouse door. When at last he put her down, she wheeled on him, bent on giving him a piece of her mind, if not the blunt end of her fist. But she stopped when she saw the cheeky grin that displayed his wolfish white teeth. He was looking beyond her. Something in his manner arrested her. Slowly, she turned to see just what his "surprise" might be.

And there, standing meekly in a soft pool of light, was Sheila.

15

The sight was so shockingly welcome that Diana rushed forth with a cry of pleasure and took the woman in her arms.

It was a moment before Sheila responded. Then, tentatively, she brought her arms about Diana's back.

"Thank God you're safe," Diana said.

Sheila said nothing. Presently, Diana became aware of the frailness of the body she held. She disengaged herself and really looked at Sheila for the first time. She was dressed in an English shirtwaist that seemed stiff and foreign on her exotic frame. The beautiful face was drawn and pale, the eyes hollow, haunted. So different from the calm, poised woman who'd told her story on the Wapping docks.

"Are you all right?" Diana asked, taking Sheila's face in her hands. "They didn't hurt you?"

Silently Jack came forth. His grin was gone, replaced by a grim countenance. He took one of Sheila's hands and lifted it for Diana to see. The honey-eyed skin of her wrist just beneath the cuff of her dress was red with welts, the chafed outline of ropes clearly visible.

"Those monsters," Diana swore with fire in her eyes. But then, seeing the suffering in Sheila's eyes, she lifted Sheila's wrist to her lips and gave it a tender kiss. "You mustn't worry," she soothed. "You're safe now. We'll protect you."

Sheila was looking at her thoughtfully, as if surprised by her concern. "You are most kind, child," she said sadly. "But no one can protect me from that man."

Diana took both shaking hands in her own. "Trust me . . . Mother." The word sounded strange but sweet on her lips. "We'll see to it that you come to no harm. This I swear."

With a flicker of something unreadable in her eyes, Sheila looked away.

"You're trembling," Diana said. "Come, sit down. Let us make you comfortable."

She cast a glance about the warehouse. There was a small table where Jack had placed the single lantern, and some old crates filled with straw and draped with heavy quilted blankets that had once cushioned antiquities. Diana went to draw one up to use as a chair, but as she did, Sheila swayed precariously on her feet. In an instant, Jack swept her up into his arms.

"Bring those blankets," he ordered.

Diana shook the dust from one of the blankets and brought it to wrap around Sheila. It was icy cold in the warehouse, and she herself was shivering. Then, working quickly, she scooped out the straw and made a makeshift bed, covering it with another of the blankets. That done, Jack gently laid Sheila down on the soft mass. As Diana fashioned a pillow for Sheila's head, Jack removed a small flask from his back pocket.

"I brought this for her," he explained, handing it forth.

Diana took a moment to give him a reflective look. "That was thoughtful of you," she admitted, staring at him in wonder. She took the flask and held it to Sheila's lips while Jack held her head up so she could drink. When Sheila coughed slightly, Diana took the flask away and eased her down into the bed.

"You need rest," she said, stroking her dark hair from her forehead. "Don't worry. I'm here. I won't leave you."

Sheila opened her eyes and gave Diana a look that was raw with pain.

"I know that what happened to you is my fault," Diana whispered urgently. "But I'm going to make it up to you. We'll find a safe place for you. I'll care for you until you're completely well again."

"You don't understand," Sheila began, but Diana cut her off.

"Do you know what day this is?"

Sheila shook her head weakly.

"Today is the eleventh of December. My birthday. I never knew it was my birthday until you told me. Don't you see what this means?"

Sheila looked at her but said nothing.

"Today, on the day you gave birth to me, we can begin again. We can start to know each other for the first time. On this day, I was given to you all those years ago. Today we've been given back to each other. It's the most precious gift I've ever had."

Tears welled in Sheila's eyes. She looked away so the tears streamed down her cheek into the pillow. Diana leaned over and gently kissed her cheek.

"Don't cry, Mother. This is a happy day."

"If you only knew—" Sheila began in a broken tone. She choked on the words and couldn't continue.

"There's so much I want to know. But we have a lifetime now to learn everything. Hush now. Go to sleep."

Diana lay down beside her, warming Sheila with her arms about her, until at last her breathing slowed and Diana knew she was asleep.

Diana looked up to find Jack perched against the table with the lantern at his back, watching her. His face was in the shadow so she couldn't read his gaze.

She sat up and wrapped her arms about herself, shivering. Without the warmth of Sheila's body, she was beginning to feel the cold in earnest. Jack rose and retrieved the last of the blankets, coming back to hand it to her. She wrapped it around herself gratefully and sat for a moment, looking down at her mother, sleeping peacefully at last.

"It breaks my heart to see her like this," she said softly. "And to know it's because of me."

"She was tied to a chair when I found her," Jack said. "God only knows how long she'd been that way. I got the impression they weren't feeding her much. She's very thin and weak."

"Thank God you found her. But how——?"

Jack rubbed his forehead in a gesture that indicated his fatigue. In a tired voice he said, "I figured he'd stash her in the most unlikely place imaginable, so I broke into the offices of Lawford and Sons—the firm that handles Ali Pasha's London finances—and had a look at the Turk's records. Lawford was paying bills in his name for the most expensive suite at Claridge's Hotel. I knew the prince wasn't here, and wouldn't have need of a hotel suite even if he was, so I asked myself who else could be staying there?"

"And she was there?"

"She was. With a contingent of five guards."

"How did you possibly get her out?"

"I set off the fire alarm. In the chaos, I just let myself into the room and *voilà*."

"And how did you find me? I wanted you to think——"

"That you were in Cairo, I know. But it wasn't hard to figure out. I saw your face in the temple when you recognized that symbol—the misshapen fish. You didn't know what it was, but when you tried to get me to tell you who had Sheila, I suspected she had something to do with that clue. So I stalled the Turk by telling him you'd gone to Cairo to consult with scholars, and while he was organizing his forces, I slipped away and came to find you. I had no luck— you hid your tracks well—but I knew you'd go to the mansion eventually. So I decided to watch for you. After I got Sheila tucked away here, I went back and saw you trying to break in."

"I thought I was a step ahead of you, but once again you were two steps ahead of me. I should have known . . ." She drifted off, falling silent.

After a time, he said softly, "Happy birthday."

She looked up at him again with questioning eyes. "You've given me the best birthday present I've ever had. I was all set to lash out at you. I wanted revenge for everything you've done. And then you turn around and do something so . . . Thank you for that."

Jack shrugged his shoulders as if uncomfortable with the gratitude in her tone.

She felt shaken, confused by his actions. "Why, Jack? Why did you defy Ali Pasha and take Sheila?"

He'd resumed his position at the table, resting with one long leg hooked about the edge. The lantern was once again at his back so she couldn't clearly see his face. But she felt a spark as he lifted his head.

"I told you," he answered, sounding uncharacteristically awkward, as if the question had caught him off guard.

"Because you knew I needed her to figure out the clue of the misshapen fish?"

He didn't answer. Instead, he rose from the table and went to retrieve the flask, taking a long sip. When he handed it to her, she impulsively clutched his hand, preventing him from moving away.

"Is that the only reason?"

He looked at her. Up close, she could see the vulnerable flash of pain in his eyes.

"Drink the brandy," he told her gruffly, easing his hand away.

"Why, Jack?" she insisted.

"What difference does it make?" he asked, sounding annoyed. "For now, we have to figure out what to do with her. I took her early this morning. Ali Pasha's men have been scouring London for her. And he'll have figured out you're not in Cairo by now and will be on his way here. It won't be long before he deduces where we are. We may be safe here for a time, but eventually we'll have to move on."

"Where can we go? He has spies everywhere."

"I have an idea. But for now, you get some sleep."

Diana didn't realize she slept. She was conscious of trying, but her mind was too active. She lay in the darkness for what seemed like hours, listening to the steady breathing of Sheila beside her and the more erratic breath of Jack across the room. She wasn't aware that she dozed off, but suddenly she heard a sound and shot up. The door was open. A man was stepping through. Instinctively, Diana inched closer to Sheila, covering her in a protective stance as her heart drummed loudly in her ears.

"It's only me," she heard Jack say as he closed the door.

She relaxed, but her mind was numb. "Where have you been?"

Jack lit the lantern and Diana shielded her eyes against the light. As her gaze adjusted, she saw that Jack was carrying a well-filled bag. He tossed it on the table and said, "I've been down to Wapping. Ali Pasha arrived there this morning on his yacht, the *Hittite Queen,* which is twice as fast as any passenger liner he might have booked. He brought thirty of his men with him."

She was instantly awake. "Then we have to leave town."

"And quickly. It won't be long before he finds out Sheila's gone."

"But how will we get out? Once he knows she's missing he'll organize his forces and turn the city upside down trying to find us."

Jack looked tired. She wondered if he'd even slept. But he gave her a confident smirk. "We're on the river, aren't we? By boat, of course."

He'd planned their escape on his predawn outing. A long sailing skiff was tied on the wharf side of the warehouse. Jack gave the bag he'd brought to Diana, then bent and scooped Sheila into his arms as easily as he might sweep a coat from the floor. "Bring the blankets," he commanded. "We have a long, cold ride."

She carried the blankets and the bundle outside

into the icy, fog-misted morning. It was still dark, with only a few scattered lights illuminating the river. As she followed behind, Jack carefully laid Sheila down in the bow of the boat. She stirred as he was wrapping her in the blankets.

"Are you comfortable?" he asked.

She was pale and seemed weaker than she had the night before. "Do not concern yourself with me," she said before closing her eyes.

As Diana climbed into the boat, Jack busied himself with the ropes. "Where are we going?" Diana asked. "What are you thinking?"

"Just what you said," he told her distractedly as he struggled with the sail. "We're going to get out of town."

"Ali Pasha's no fool. He'll be watching the Thames like a hawk."

"I realize that," he snapped. "Now stop talking and help me get this thing ready."

A strong, cold breeze was blowing. The minute Jack raised the sail, the wind caught it and sent them floating off from the wharf, taking them up the river. It was quiet in the anticipation of dawn, with little river traffic. Occasionally, they'd pass a large barge bringing supplies into the city. Once, they spotted a police boat coming their way. Diana held her breath, feeling like a fugitive, certain the police would stop them and search the boat. But Jack skillfully averted the craft, losing it in the fog.

Once they were under way, Jack told Diana to look in the bag he'd brought. There she found warm bread, fresh from the bakery. She gave a third of it to Jack and ate heartily, realizing that it had been some time since she'd last eaten. The steaming bread warmed her hands, which felt frozen and stiff.

But when she tried to get Sheila to eat, the older woman shook her head and once again closed her eyes. She threw off the blankets so that Diana had to keep readjusting them. Touching her, Diana realized Sheila was hot with fever. As Jack navigated the boat, Diana dipped a corner of her dress into the frigid river and bathed Sheila's brow. But as time progressed, Sheila began to perspire, even as Diana's teeth chattered from the cold.

"Sheila's ill," she told Jack.

He glanced her way. Diana caught his gaze and read in it the same stark fear. Had they come this far only to have Sheila die?

No one spoke after that. Jack steered the sail, occasionally glancing back to see how Diana was faring. Diana avoided his gaze. She was frightened now. Even if they escaped Ali Pasha, could she protect Sheila? In her condition, prolonged exposure to the frosty air could be deadly. Diana tried not to think of all that might go wrong. Instead, she focused on keeping Sheila warm and bathing her fevered brow.

An hour later, they left the city behind them. After a time, Jack veered the boat and set his course straight toward a thick bank of reeds on the opposite side of the river. Diana sat up in the boat and watched, puzzled, wondering what on earth he had in mind. The boat was heading for the bank with great speed. She opened her mouth to question him but before she could get the words out, the boat plunged ahead, crashing through the reeds. The tall grasses and pussy willows beat against their faces as they barreled through. Diana crouched low, covering Sheila to shield her from the onslaught of vegetation.

On the other side, the channel was clear. As Diana sat up, she saw an overgrown waterway ahead, banked on either side by an ancient stone embankment, veering off from the river.

"What's this?" she asked.

He was gazing ahead and spoke in a distracted voice. "There's a series of canals that connect London with southern England. They were main thoroughfares in the time of Elizabeth, but aren't used much now."

"How do you know where you're going?"

"When I was a boy my father and I spent a few weeks exploring them."

Once again he fell into silence.

"How long will we be traveling?"

"Most of the day."

Diana watched him scanning the overgrown banks. "Why won't you tell me where we're going?"

He gave her a strange look, but said nothing. He was locked in a world of his own, with his own private thoughts, where she had no place. She felt completely cut off from him, as if an invisible wall separated them. She wondered that it should disturb her so. His sarcasm, his anger, his boastful confidence—all these she could handle. His silence seemed daunting. It made her feel he was a stranger.

Yet, she reminded herself, he'd risked his life to rescue Sheila from Ali Pasha's men. And he'd had the grace not to mention the treasure, or the clue he suspected Sheila could decipher. His attitude toward her mother was one of gentle concern. But there was something closed and mysterious in his actions and his silence. Diana sensed there was a great deal he wasn't telling her, and wondered why.

They spent the day traveling in silence, sipping the brandy in Jack's flask against the chill wind, making their way through an intricate system of waterways. In some places the canals were wide and open, in some they were so narrow, the sides of the boat scraped against the stone embankments on either side. They came upon willow trees so overgrown, their branches spread down into the water, blocking the way. They had to pull themselves through the branches, Diana shielding Sheila's face. When the wind failed, Jack jumped out of the boat and found a long, narrow tree limb that he used to pole them through the weeds.

As the day wore on it mercifully warmed up. The fog dissipated and patches of meager sun broke through the thick covering of winter clouds. Sometimes in the distance they'd see farmers at work in their fields, clearing their furrows of winter debris, or a farmhouse whose chimney smoked with a welcoming fire. But mostly they passed no one as they pushed on along this discarded anachronism that seemed, on reflection, a remarkably efficient way to travel.

Diana did what she could to nurse Sheila most of the day, coaxing her to sip the brandy that she hoped would break her fever. The hours wore long, and she was consumed with worry about her mother's fate. She grew impatient, wanting nothing more than to get Sheila out of the elements, to a warm bed and a fire, where she could perhaps make her some nourishing broth.

Then, late in the afternoon, as the sun was setting once again, Jack stood up in the boat. He put a hand to his forehead to shield his eyes as he peered off into the distance. Diana glanced about and slowly, she began to recognize her surroundings. They'd come out of the canal onto the very river where once—a lifetime ago—Jack had rowed her in the sun and asked her to marry him. Birch Haven. He was taking them to Birch Haven.

But Ali Pasha owned Birch Haven. Surely, this was madness. Surely, he would guess at once where Jack had gone.

She turned on him to voice her concerns, but when she saw him, her words dried in her throat. He was standing like a statue, gazing out upon the approaching land with a look of such love and peace that her heart turned over in her breast. She'd never seen such a serene, contented look on his face before.

It was the look of a man who was going home.

16

Diana sat on the side of the bed, holding Sheila's hand. The older woman, under a pile of blankets, her black hair damp with perspiration, was still in the grip of fever. But Jack had brewed a concoction of herbs he'd gathered and Diana had been feeding it to Sheila in hopes of lowering her raging temperature. Once again she was murmuring in her sleep. She tossed her head from side to side as if agitated. Diana leaned closer, trying to understand. But Sheila spoke in a language she couldn't comprehend. It sounded like Greek, but was a dialect Diana didn't know. Occasionally, Sheila cried out Ali Pasha's name. It chilled Diana to hear the fear in her voice.

She stroked her hot brow. "It's all right, Mother. I'm here."

Under her touch, Sheila sighed and settled into a more peaceful slumber.

They'd been at Birch Haven for a week now. Jack hadn't taken them to the main house as she'd expected, but had guided the boat a mile upriver. There, secluded by a patch of forest, was a small cottage that had been the first home of his ancestors before they'd cleared the land and built the main house. The subsequent generations had used it as a hunting lodge. But it had lain empty for years. Ali Pasha, who hadn't been to Birch Haven since acquiring the deed, would likely not even know of its existence.

Once he'd carried Sheila inside and settled her in one of the small bedrooms, Jack had collected the herbs and made the medicine while Diana had brewed some broth. They'd cleared the place of dust to make it livable, and had found a pantry full of tinned staples. When the cottage was clean and tidy, Diana took up her post by Sheila's side, staying with her night and day, administering the herbs, bathing her hot skin, feeding her broth and brandy. She rarely left her side, even when Jack urged her to sleep. She dozed fitfully in a chair by Sheila's bed, waking at every sound. By now she was exhausted. But she wouldn't leave Sheila for any length of time. She couldn't. Not until Diana knew she was out of danger.

Life had settled into a tranquil routine. Jack disappeared for hours at a time. Diana assumed he was spying on the main house, looking out for Ali Pasha's men. In the evening he came back with fresh meat, which he cooked while Diana fed Sheila broth. Then he coaxed Diana into the small sitting room, where they ate quietly by the fire, talking about Sheila's progress. Jack seemed a different man. He was satisfied to sit quietly over a brandy, looking into the fire and thinking his own thoughts. He never mentioned the treasure or the threat of Ali Pasha, never said anything that would cause Diana concern. He seemed to sense that all her energies were needed to make her mother well. To her surprise, Diana found that she was soothed by the amiable domesticity. Sometimes, late at night, she sat holding Sheila's hand and thought with a sense of wonder, "This is my mother," and a rush of love and contentment would fill her heart.

She wondered more than once if this was what her life would have been like if she and Jack had married all those years ago. The sense of family was a bittersweet balm.

"Di . . . ana . . ."

She was brought back to the present by the sound of Sheila's voice. She looked down and saw that her dark eyes were open and clear. Touching her forehead, she felt that it was cool.

"You're better," she smiled. "Thank God."

Sheila was looking about her, puzzled.

"Don't worry," Diana told her. "You're safe. We've been here for a week. You've been very ill."

Sheila's eyes fixed on Diana's face. She watched her with an odd, confused expression. "You've been with me all this time?"

Diana nodded.

"I felt you here. But you're so tired, child. Why did you waste your time nursing me?"

"It wasn't a waste of my time. After all, you're my mother."

Sheila looked away. "That you should sacrifice yourself so for me . . . you cannot possibly know the guilt I feel."

Diana reached forth and took her hand. "Mother, look at me."

Slowly, Sheila met her gaze. But her eyes were guarded. Diana leaned over her, gazing into her eyes, grasping her hand in both of her own.

"I know I wasn't the daughter you'd hoped to find. I know I disappointed you when I couldn't accept you as my mother right away. But that's over now. When I found that Ali Pasha had taken you, I knew I had to find you. I had to give us the chance to know one another. And when I saw you . . . when I saw how they'd mistreated you . . ."

Sheila flinched. "I cannot speak of that man."

"You don't have to. Not now. What I'm trying to say is that all my life, I wished that I could have a mother who cared about me the way other mothers seemed to care for their daughters. I wanted someone to love me, to take care of me. But when I saw you so ill . . . something changed inside me. I no longer wanted to selfishly take what I had been denied. I wanted nothing more than to nurture you, to give to you, to try and make up for all the years when you suffered without my father and me. And I've found that the emptiness I felt for so many years is gone. It's made me happy to do what I could for you. Can you understand that?"

As she'd spoken, Sheila's eyes had welled with tears. "I do not deserve—"

"Hush. You mustn't say that. The past is gone and forgotten. We have a new chance, a chance that was nearly stolen from us. The present is all that matters now. We can start fresh from this day."

Sheila wiped her eyes and took some breaths to compose herself. "You are not what I expected," she said softly. "You have been so very kind to me. I never thought—" Again she halted, closing teary eyes.

Diana watched her for a few precious moments. Seeing Sheila's improvement, she thought of the question she had to ask. It burned in her suddenly, yet Sheila was still weak. Perhaps it was too soon . . .

As if sensing Diana's hesitation, Sheila opened her eyes and looked at her once again. "I feel there is something you wish to ask me."

"Yes," Diana admitted, "but if you're not up to it—"

"No," Sheila sighed. "Perhaps it is best that we speak now."

Slowly, Diana reached beneath the sheet and withdrew the chain Sheila wore about her neck. She picked up the amulet that lay side by side with the cartouche Sheila had shown her all those months ago. A golden symbol, like a misshapen fish.

"I noticed this at the dock, when you showed me the cartouche with my name. What is it?"

Sheila glanced at it, clearly surprised. "Why, that is the island where I was born."

"Island? I thought you were born in Egypt."

Sheila's lips trembled as a new rush of tears spilled from her eyes. "There is so much to tell. I cannot think now how to begin. I feel so—"

"It's all right," Diana said quickly, realizing this was taxing her mother more than she'd anticipated. "You're tired. We can talk about it another time. Sleep now, so your fever won't come back."

She replaced the amulet and tucked the covers around Sheila, who watched her every move. As she leaned over to kiss her mother's cheek, Sheila moved the blankets aside and took Diana's hand.

"Cyprus," she told her. "I was born on Cyprus."

A bolt of lightning seemed to sear Diana's mind. But just as she was about to repeat the word, she heard Jack's voice behind her.

"Cyprus!"

She turned and saw him standing in the doorway. His eyes met hers and she felt the shock of recognition that she knew mirrored her own.

"Sleep now," she told Sheila. She doused the light. When she turned toward the door, she saw that Jack had gone.

. . .

She found him in the sitting room. He'd taken a book from the shelf, brown with age, and was looking at a page. When he glanced up and saw her, she noted the excitement in his eyes. He handed the book to her and she saw a map of Cyprus—an island that did, indeed, look like a misshapen fish.

"I should have known," he said.

She set the book aside. "No. I should have known. It's Homer."

"Homer?"

She scanned the bookshelf and found some volumes of Homer's poems. Searching the contents, she came at last upon what she was looking for. "The riddle. Here it is. The clues are lines of Homer's *Hymn to Aphrodite*."

She held forth the book and he read aloud: " 'The Cypriot, who, on the sweetest of days, rose up among the gods.' "

"I knew it sounded familiar, but I haven't read Homer since I was quite young, and I couldn't place it. But it makes perfect sense. Cleopatra worshipped Isis. Loosely speaking, Aphrodite is her Greek counterpart. Cleopatra was Greek, so it was the perfect choice."

"I'm afraid you've lost me."

She looked at him, her excitement mounting. "Aphrodite is said to have risen from the sea at Cyprus. In ancient writings, when someone referred to 'the Cypriot,' he wasn't speaking of a citizen of Cyprus. He meant Aphrodite, *the* Cypriot. Cleopatra chose lines written about Aphrodite to show that the treasure was hidden at the birthplace of the Cypriot at Cyprus."

"I remember now. There's a huge rock just outside of Paphos, where legend has it Aphrodite was born. About here." He grabbed the map and showed her the spot on the western end of the island.

Their eyes met. "Then it has to be there. Or somewhere close to that spot. Cleopatra and Mark Antony were fleeing the disastrous battle at Actium with their treasure. It would have been a simple matter to make a detour to Cyprus and hide their cargo before returning to Alexandria." She paused, thinking. "I don't want Sheila to know yet. It could be too dangerous for her."

"Agreed."

The room was silent, throbbing with anticipation.

"Now what, Jack?"

He met her gaze, his eyes glittering like blue diamonds. "Now we go to Cyprus and get that treasure."

"But Sheila—"

"We'll take her with us. When she's well enough to travel, we'll tell her we're taking her back to her birthplace, where she'll be safe. Something."

"And Ali Pasha?"

"Once we have the treasure, we hold all the cards." Suddenly he stopped. "Do you smell smoke?"

She sniffed the air. There was a faint, distant aroma of something burning. She glanced at the fireplace. The fire wasn't lit.

Jack strode to the door and threw it open. "It's outside."

She heard the panic in his voice. By the time Diana made it down the steps of the front porch, he was running frantically in the direction of the main house.

In the distance, she could see the faint outline of smoke above the trees. The night had cleared, and a three-quarter moon filtered the ground with dappled light. Without thinking, Diana ran through the forest in Jack's wake. By the time she reached the meadow she was panting, her throat burning from the cold air. But she could see the fire ahead. It was coming from a structure past the rock gardens. She ran across the field, tripping along the way, until at last she came to the site.

Up close, she could see that it was the gazebo by the river that was on fire. Jack had ripped off his shirt and was desperately beating at the flames, his muscles straining with effort.

Diana ran to the barn. Inside, she found a musty horse blanket. She raced back to the gazebo with it and joined Jack, pounding at the flickering flames until perspiration ran down her face. A gust of breeze carried the flames from one side of the trellis to the other. Jack chased it as Diana pounded away, her arms aching, her lungs filling with smoke so that she coughed as she worked.

At last they succeeded in beating out the fire. Diana stood, breathing great gulps of fresh air, staring at the smoking shell.

The silence in the aftermath was eerie. She could hear Jack's ragged breath. He stood staring at the structure, his shirt dangling limply from his hand.

"It isn't even mine anymore," he said in a choked, defeated voice. "But I couldn't stand to see it destroyed."

Diana saw in the moonlight that there were tears in his eyes. She was so shocked that for a moment all she could do was stare.

"You really do love this place, don't you?" she whispered.

He glanced at her and she saw the despair in his eyes. "My father built this gazebo for my mother, so she could sit in the evenings and look out at the river. When I was young, I'd run out here every afternoon with a book and climb into her lap in her big wicker chair. She used to read to me for hours, rocking gently. I can't think of it without remembering the sound of her voice as the sun went down over the river."

Diana recalled the summer Jack's mother had died. He was ten and she was five. She'd caught him crying in the loft in the barn. He'd grabbed her dress and had shaken her and sworn her to secrecy. After that, he'd mentioned his mother only once. It was as if she'd never existed. But that fall, when he'd returned to school, he'd been called up time and again for fighting with his fellow schoolmates. When she asked him why, he'd said coldly, "They think they're better because they have a mother and I don't."

He'd worn that same look of loss and desolation that he wore now.

She went to him and put a hand on his arm. It was solid, strong, yet it trembled with emotion. "I'm so sorry, Jack."

"For what?" he asked gruffly.

"For not understanding what this place meant to you."

He glared at her, suspicious, waiting for the kick he felt would surely come.

"Finding Sheila has changed me," she told him softly. "I can't explain. But I feel things I never felt before. I know what that gazebo meant to you. For the first time, I can feel your pain. What it means to you to lose your home."

His eyes softened. The look he gave her was one of gratitude and a touching vulnerability.

"And when you risked your life to save Sheila—I know you did it for me. It's something the old Jack would have done. It made me realize that—"

"What?"

She couldn't say the words. Instead, she stepped closer and pulled him to her, holding him in her arms. It was a moment before his arms came about her, but when they did, he held her in a close, convulsive grip. He smelled of smoke. Barechested, he was beginning to shiver in the cold night air. Her heart breaking for him, she stroked his hair and murmured, "Forgive me."

He pulled back slightly and took her face in his hands. He searched her face, his eyes full of wonder, as if gazing upon something he'd searched for and never found.

"If I could only believe that you meant it."

"I mean it, Jack, with all my heart."

In the soft moonlight, he saw the sincerity of her words shining in her eyes. Slowly, he lowered his head, his eyes fixed on her lips. She lifted her face to welcome his kiss. She watched as his lips moved closer . . . closer . . .

But suddenly his gaze flicked from her face to the gazebo at her back. His hands fell from her and he left abruptly. She stood for a moment, feeling cold and abandoned. But when she turned she saw that he was shifting through the debris of the charred gazebo.

"This fire was started deliberately," he told her in a hard tone. He held something in his hand. When she drew closer, she could see a piece of burnt straw.

"But who—"

Suddenly her eyes flew to his.

"Sheila!"

They ran for the cottage. With Jack in the lead, they raced across the field, plunging into the forest, the tangled vegetation brushing their legs as they forged ahead.

As they came to the rise above the clearing, Jack came to an abrupt halt. Below, outside the cottage, they could see a group of men and horses, the men carrying torches and speaking in muffled tones. The cottage door was open, spilling light onto the porch, where a single man stood, giving orders.

"The fire was a diversion," Jack said softly. "Those are Ali Pasha's men. I recognize their leader, Abdul, the one on the porch. There are too many of them. We have to get out of here while we can."

"But Sheila," Diana reminded him.

"We'll have to leave her."

"I can't leave her. I *won't* leave her."

"There's nothing we can do here. We can figure out something once we're safely away—"

She put her hand on his in a pleading gesture. "I can't leave her to those men. Who knows what they'll do to her this time? Jack . . . please."

He turned and looked at her, then heaved a sigh. He glanced back at the clearing, then at her again. A fierce determination hardened the features of his face.

"All right. Wait here. I'll see what I can do."

With a resolute stride, he walked down the rise and into the clearing, straight into the heart of the horses and men. They spotted him at once and a hush descended on the group. As he strode forward, they stared at him as if they couldn't believe what they were seeing—a barechested man, his back and arms scarred by the lash, unarmed and stalking into their midst, showing no indication that he even knew he was in jeopardy.

One man, shaking off his shock, made a move. From the porch, Abdul called, "Take him alive."

Two of the men rushed at Jack. As they grabbed for him, he stepped aside, using his leg to trip each in turn so they went tumbling behind him like a pair of carnival fools.

He had barely even broken his stride. He just kept walking as three others charged at him. Without skipping a beat, Jack leapt into the air, kicked the first of them in the face so he went crashing to the ground. Then, landing on his feet, Jack interlocked his hands, driving one elbow into the gut of the second man attacking from his left, then the other elbow into the stomach of the third attacker on his right.

The horses were agitated by now, circling the clearing and creating mass confusion as they blocked the paths of the other men. Watching, Diana could barely believe what she was seeing. Jack moved as if he wore an invisible shield that would keep him from harm, mowing the men down as if they were nothing more than gnats to be swatted out of his way. She was uncertain whether she should stay where she was or follow him in case he should need some help. She stepped forward, to the edge of the clearing. But Jack called, "Wait there."

Still he walked with a determined clip straight toward the cottage. There, five men had gathered in front of the porch, forming a protective wall before their leader. To Diana's horror, she saw one of them raise a pistol and aim it at Jack. But the leader saw it and barked out, "I said don't kill him." Reaching down, he knocked the man's arm, deflecting his aim, so the shot fired in the air. This sent the horses charging wildly about the clearing, snorting and whinnying shrilly.

Jack didn't stop.

"Get him," the leader called. "Hold him down."

There was a mad scramble as men converged on Jack from all sides, leaping at him so they came together in a pile on top of him. But somehow, in the scuffle, Jack slipped out from under them and left the men struggling with each other, unaware that they'd lost their prey, and Jack, without the slightest hesitation, took the last few steps up to the porch.

Abdul was staring at him as he would a madman, shocked and disoriented by Jack's relentlessness. The sheer confidence of Jack's stride now caught the leader off guard.

Taking advantage of the moment, Jack reached out and grabbed Abdul by the throat and pushed him into the cottage. Once there, he squeezed the man's throat until he turned a beet red, then abruptly released him. Abdul dropped to his knees, choking.

Jack didn't pause. He swooped into the bedroom, scooped Sheila up into his arms, and carried her out again. Jack stalked past the pile of men, who were just beginning to disengage, toward one of the horses. He put Sheila on her feet, bolted onto the horse, and pulled her up behind him. "Hold on to me as tightly as you can," he told her. Sheila was weak and dazed, but she wrapped her arms about Jack's waist and held on. Jack reached over and grabbed the reins of a nearby horse.

As she was watching this, Diana felt a presence behind her. Suddenly, five men had surrounded her. They grabbed hold of her, some crushing her arms, another seizing a handful of her hair. In their zeal to contain her, they were yanking her between them so her arms strained in their sockets. She struggled, tugging back, kicking at them to try to beat them away.

She was terrified. But she glanced up to see Jack veering the horses around. He saw her then and she called to him, "Go! Get away!"

As she did one of the men slapped her soundly in the face.

Jack gave his horse a thunderous kick. The horses tore forward at a full gallop. He charged into them, rearing his horse in the air, using the other to scatter the men. In the confusion Diana was thrown free. Jack landed a blow to one man's face, then bolted forward at a gallop. As he passed her, he reached down, grabbed her arm, and threw her up onto the back of the other horse. Then he tossed her the reins and they rode back through the clearing, Jack scattering the other horses before him. They tore across the field toward the main house with the startled horses loping off in all directions, then galloped off into the night, leaving the confused melee behind.

For what seemed like ages, they rode hard through the dark countryside, Jack leading the way. Exhausted, Diana finally called to him to halt. She was breathing rapidly, her heart still pounding. But she gazed at Jack in the moonlight with shining eyes.

"That was the most extraordinary thing I've ever seen," she gasped. "They couldn't touch you!"

Jack looked back over his shoulder with an irritated air. "I got lucky. Any one of them could have shot me. I just took them by surprise."

"You were wonderful," she told him.

He ignored her praise. Turning in the saddle, he asked Sheila if she was all right. She was still clinging to his waist. "Yes," she told him weakly. "Because of you, I am."

Jack turned to Diana. "Any bright ideas for what our next move should be? I've about run out."

"We go back to London," she said.

"London?"

"We underestimated Ali Pasha. He won't give up. Cyprus is in his part of the world. We were fools to think we could ever get there alive."

He was peering at her keenly. "What are you saying?"

"I'm saying that we should try to make a deal with him."

"What deal?"

"I want to offer Ali Pasha half the treasure in return for safe passage *and* Birch Haven. It's the only thing that makes any sense."

Jack seemed frozen in the saddle as he stared at her.

"It's a fair compromise," she continued. "I've got what I want, my mother. You'll get what you want, Birch Haven. And half the treasure is better than none. Why shouldn't he go for it? It's worth a try."

"You mean to tell me—you're willing to give up half the treasure—for Birch Haven?"

"So you can keep the home you love, yes. I told

you earlier that I understand. What you did just
now—Jack, you deserve to have Birch Haven back."

He sat looking at her for a moment. Then, reining
his horse close, he put his hand to her cheek. He said
nothing, but his touch was so electric, it made her
shiver.

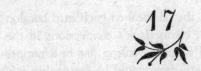

*J*ack and Diana stepped out of the hansom cab in front of the forecourt of the British Museum. Across the classical portico was a huge red-and-white banner:

INTO THE TWENTIETH CENTURY
THE GLORY OF THE BRITISH EMPIRE, 1900

A crowd was streaming into the building, eager to see the special exhibits celebrating the splendor of the past as a way of welcoming the imminent new century. Each of Britain's colonies had sent a display of its ancient native culture: India, Yemen, Australia,

New Zealand, Seychelles, East and South Africa, Hong Kong, and Egypt.

As they moved through the crowd, Diana was relieved to see a contingent of bobbies and some plain-clothes detectives she recognized from her tenure at the museum. They were here to guard the valuable exhibits, but their presence would ensure Jack and Diana's safety in this vital, and very public, meeting with Ali Pasha.

Three days ago, they'd sneaked back into London with Sheila in tow. Using Jack's connections in the underworld, they'd found a rooftop flat in a remote corner of Soho, where they would be reasonably safe and Sheila could recuperate. After settling in, they'd sent a message to Ali Pasha's house, requesting a meeting. This exhibit would provide them with the perfect neutral ground, a public forum where Ali Pasha wouldn't dare try to overpower them.

They made their way to the Egyptian wing, where the lavish trappings of the Fifth Dynasty nobleman, Ti, were the Anglo-Eqyptian contribution to the grand exhibit. Only recently unearthed in a huge *mastaba,* or tomb, in Saqqara, the find had aroused much excitement in scholarly circles earlier that year.

Circumventing the tourists gawking at Ti's sarcophagus, they spotted Ali Pasha at the far end of the room. His henchman, Abdul, stood at his side, glowering angrily as they approached. He fingered his throat, no doubt remembering how Jack had choked him at the cottage just a few nights before, and silently vowing revenge.

But Ali Pasha, standing tall and noble like a desert sheik, stepped forth with a charming smile brightening his handsome face. "Ah, Jack! My dear friend! I was so delighted to receive your gracious invitation."

He extended his hand, but Jack ignored it. With a philosophical shrug, Ali turned to Diana.

"And Miss Sanbourne. Always a pleasure. How fares our mutual friend, the enchanting Sheila?"

Diana bristled under his cheery tone. She thought of how Sheila had been so cruelly mistreated by this animal, of how she had moaned his name in her nightmares, and seemed certain she would invariably fall into his clutches again. *He will not allow me to get away. He will find me and take me back, I am certain of it.*

Now Diana glared at the prince. *"My mother* is recovering slowly, no thanks to you."

Ali threw back his head and laughed heartily, as if she'd just told him the most delightful piece of gossip. "You must convey my salutations to the good woman. I'm told my men thoroughly enjoyed her company. Be sure to tell her she is welcome in my household at any time."

"You cad!" Diana cried. "Abusing innocent women to feed your foul ambitions."

"Innocent?" Ali laughed. "What an amusing creature you are, Miss Sanbourne. It is no wonder our friend Jack fancies you so."

Jack shifted impatiently beside Diana. "Let's skip the small talk and get down to business, shall we?"

"But my friend," cried Ali, "you haven't even glanced at these wonderful new archaeological finds. Surely your heart beats faster at being so close to another looted grave. I should think it would make you proud to know that yet another of the world's treasures resides in this great repository of British cultural arrogance."

"We're here to make a deal," Jack told him curtly.

Ali beamed, spreading his hands wide. "All business, you English. You must learn to enjoy life more. Take time for the small pleasantries, as we Turks do."

"Do you want to hear it or not?"

"Most certainly. I am—as you English say—all ears."

Jack moved closer and lowered his voice. "We're both in a no-win situation here. A stalemate, if you will. The only thing that makes sense at this point is to make a compromise."

"A compromise," said Ali, glancing at his henchman. "What an intriguing idea. And just how would we go about arranging this—compromise?"

"We'll split the treasure. You get half, Diana gets half as her father's discovery, and I get Birch Haven. Something for everyone."

"I can see how, indeed, such an arrangement would make you happy. I suppose you'd allow me to send some of my own men along to ensure your—good will in this matter?"

"If we get certain guarantees of safety in return."

Ali stroked his jaw with his long-fingered hand.

"An interesting proposal. And I must say, a typically British one—reasonable, logical, civilized. But there's just one problem with it."

"What's that?"

Maintaining his easy, conversational tone, Ali said, "Half the treasure won't do. I want *all* of it."

The firmness with which Ali said the word "all" left no doubt of his resolve in the matter. Jack looked at Diana, then back at their opponent. "I'd say you're in no position to be so greedy at this point. Don't forget that Diana and I know where the treasure is. You don't. Isn't half the treasure better than none at all?"

"Unfortunately, not much. You see, Jack, to be perfectly frank, I am in a bit of a devilish situation. As you know, the four-hundred-year-old empire of the Ottoman Turks has been crumbling for the past hundred years. Everywhere. Armenia, Syria, Palestine, Greece, Mesopotamia, Arabia. Unless something is done, I could be its last ruler."

"Empires rise, and empires fall," Jack said unsympathetically. "That's history."

"And sometimes they rise again. You see, Jack, I have been busily planning a renaissance of my ancestors' great empire. I have spent years making strategic alliances in each of these regions. And I intend to seize the occasion of the new century to finally make my move, and ride its momentum to create a *new* Ottoman Empire."

"And to do that you need lots of money—money you don't presently have."

"Sadly, that is so. I have armies all over my father's empire that expect to be paid *before* they move. So alas, I need all the money I can get my hands on. But I need all the treasure for another reason. You see, Jack, this particular treasure is not just gold. It is, in a way, the sanction of history, the mandate of heaven. Its recovery at the dawn of this new century will be seen by my superstitious people as the greatest of omens. With it in my possession, they will rise up behind me, they will die to the last man at my bidding, they will crush anyone foolish enough to oppose me."

Diana felt her blood turn cold. She'd given no thought to exactly *why* he'd wanted the treasure so desperately. Now she saw him not as a greedy fortune hunter, but as a maniac with an agenda of evil.

"We'll never help you," she cried.

Her voice echoed through the hall, drawing curious stares. Jack raised his hand to caution her. "And once you've reestablished your empire, then what?"

Ali dropped his air of cordiality as if snatching a mask from his face. His charm vanished. In its place, his eyes took on a demented gleam, turning his features cold and cruel. "Then the desert will run red with blood."

"You'll create a tyranny," Diana said.

"Tyranny?" Ali snarled. "Yes, a tyranny. Every minor official, every sultan, every peasant who ever dared to spit in the direction of Istanbul will die a horrible death. The world shall see a holocaust that will put all the other holocausts in history to shame."

"You're out of your mind," Diana gasped.

Ali turned his blazing eyes to her. "Look at you. So sanctimonious. So morally superior. In what way do you differ from me? You British have stolen half the world and looted most of its treasures. Your fathers alone are two of the greatest thieves in all of history. Look around you. This venerable British Museum. What is it but a grand and ostentatious celebration of theft?"

Diana stared at him, horrified. Mad as he sounded, his words struck a chord of truth.

Jack looked at her, then back at Ali. "So it's all or nothing," he said. "Then it'll have to be nothing. Because there's no way in the world we're going to aid your little march to glory."

Ali looked from one to the other of them shrewdly. Then he fixed his gaze on Jack. "You may change your mind when your beloved ancestral estate is about to be turned over to the Hadley Mining Company."

"What!?"

"Oh, didn't I tell you? My mining engineers tell me Birch Haven sits on the richest deposit of coal in middle England. I've been negotiating with the Hadley people for months now, and I've finally decided to close the deal. On New Year's Eve, every structure on Birch Haven is scheduled to be demolished."

Visibly shaken, Jack glanced at Diana. She remembered the tears in his eyes after the destruction of just the gazebo. She knew that this threat had to be killing him. He was so stunned, he couldn't find words to speak.

"Think about it, Jack. Noon on the thirty-first. The dawn of the new century. Give me what I want before then or the grounds you so revere will become an eyesore—one huge, open-pit coal mine."

18

*T*aking numerous diversions to make certain they weren't followed, Diana and Jack returned to their flat in Soho to decide what to do next. But there was no obvious next move. They couldn't very well give in to this madman. So Birch Haven was doomed.

For the next few days, Jack left the flat several times for long periods. Diana guessed he was seeing barristers to ascertain if there was any way to legally break Ali Pasha's hold on Birch Haven. She didn't have to ask how he'd fared in the meetings. From the dejected expression on his face each time he returned, she could see there *was* no way.

Christmas came and went with no one in the

mood to celebrate. Diana tried to lift their spirits with a festive meal, but Jack barely touched it.

As more days passed and the deadline neared, Jack withdrew more and more inside himself, sinking into an absorbed depression that unsettled Diana deeply. Often, late at night, he'd go out for hours at a time, coming back with liquor on his breath. She'd never seen him like this. He rarely slept. In the early morning hours, he could be found slouched back against the wall of the window seat, staring out the bay window at the rooftops of London, trying to think of a way out of his impossible situation.

Diana felt his pain. Her only solace from this turmoil was the time she spent with Sheila. They shared a room, and as Sheila grew stronger, they began to talk—haltingly at first, like strangers trying to become better acquainted. Sheila steered clear of talking about her past, or her family. Diana sensed that it was too tender a subject still. But she spoke a great deal about Egypt and the cultural heritage Diana had inherited. Not about the ancient glory, which Diana already knew, but about the last two thousand years, during which Egypt had been under the control of one foreign power or another.

"These two millennia," she said with quiet passion, "have caused our people to be fatalistic. They will tell you that to be conquered and dominated is our fate. But I tell you, it is less fate than the greed of evil foreigners like Ali Pasha that has humbled and humiliated us for these many centuries. Once Egypt was the wealthiest, the most scientifically advanced, the most resplendent kingdom on earth. Now look at us. We've been stripped bare by vultures. Even our precious antiquities—our sacred heritage—are being systematically looted by all the nations of the world. As long as there are men like Ali Pasha, Egypt will be enslaved."

Sheila wanted to know everything about Diana. Soon, in the hours when Jack was away, Diana found herself telling her mother stories of her childhood: her closeness with her father, their summer trips that were the focus of Diana's school years, her loneliness and longing for a mother she could confide in. She found herself divulging personal feelings that she hadn't thought of in years. And she told Sheila about her past with Jack. As she spoke, she realized with a sense of wonder that the bitterness was gone. That she was beginning to see her past in a completely different context.

Something was changing within her. As Sheila listened, surprisingly perceptive and empathetic to Diana's suffering, Diana found that the pain had vanished. It was as if she were speaking of someone else, someone who, being young and determined, had been blinded to all that was transpiring around her. She found in Sheila an intelligence and simple wisdom that cast her experiences in a different light. She felt that her heart was opening, embracing feelings that she'd long since suppressed and denied. Though Sheila spoke little of herself, Diana was growing to love her. Their long talks gave her a sense of comfort and security she'd never known. These were the sort of conversations she'd so longed to have with Prudence, but was denied. It was as if she was fulfilling her entire frustrated childhood in these weeks.

But Sheila was an amazingly astute woman. When she felt strong enough to join them in the sitting room and saw for herself Jack's disheartened appearance, she was alarmed.

One night, after they'd watched his eyes grow sadder and sadder and his disappearances longer and longer, Sheila turned to Diana.

"Jack is in great turmoil."

"I know."

"He loves you very much."

Diana's startled gaze met Sheila's calm dark eyes. She was surprised that her mother could divine this from her short time with them. But when she'd recovered, she said softly, "I know that, too."

Sheila leaned forward in her chair and took Diana's hand in her own. "Your Jack is dying," she told her. "If he loses that which is so important to him—his home, this Birch Haven—he will not survive it. I promise you. It will be his spiritual death."

These words shook Diana to her core. She felt the hopelessness of their situation churn like a whirlpool inside.

Diana began to watch him more closely. She could see in his bleak eyes that he'd given up. That he knew he had no choice but to let Birch Haven go. She could see, too, that Sheila's words were true. Jack was dying inside. She agonized over it. She told herself all the reasons why Birch Haven must be sacrificed. Ali Pasha was mad. He'd use the treasure to let loose a bloodbath, and it would be on their heads. Then there was her father, who'd suffered and sacrificed for most of his life to find this treasure that only he had the courage to believe in. What of him? It was only reasonable that Birch Haven be sacrificed. Yet when she looked into Jack's dead eyes, it broke her heart.

The night before the deadline, she couldn't sleep. She felt the threat of what was about to happen hang over her like the blade of a guillotine. Finally, after tossing in her bed for hours, she knew what she had to do.

It was six in the morning. Diana stepped out from the bedroom into the sitting room. As usual, Jack was perched at the window seat, staring at nothing. He hadn't shaved for a week. His jaw was bristled, his eyes soulless, as if he no longer cared about anything.

She sat down beside him.

"I want to give in to Ali Pasha," she said. "I want to give him the treasure."

Jack didn't even look at her. He shook his head. "No. We can't."

"We must," she insisted. "We can't let him destroy the thing you love most in this world."

"We can't give in to him," he said in a spent tone. "I may have done some despicable things in my time, but Ali Pasha is operating on a whole different level. He's pure evil. We can't support his quest."

"We'll tell him where the treasure is. You'll get the deed to Birch Haven. Then we'll find some way to stop him."

Jack closed his eyes, shutting her out.

Desperation filled her heart. She knew now she had to try to convince him. "Jack, if you lose Birch Haven it will kill you."

"What if it does?" He sounded as if he no longer cared, as if he'd already given up his will to fight.

She worded her appeal carefully. "That night on Ali Pasha's yacht, when I overheard you talking and found that you'd betrayed me, all I wanted was revenge. At that moment, I would have crowed with joy to see you in this situation. I would have taken what I wanted and said to hell with you and your precious piece of England. But I've changed, Jack. I can't explain it, but knowing Sheila has changed me. I know now why you did all that you did. I understand your desperation. I'd do anything to protect Sheila now—give up anything to have her with me. It would have killed me to lose her, knowing that I'd never have the chance to know my real mother. But I didn't lose her, Jack, because you saved her. You can say what you like. You can tell me it was because of the treasure. But I saw it in your eyes that night. You did it for me. And I realized then that you still loved me."

Nothing but silence followed her words. She sat, waiting. Finally, he heaved a sigh and said wearily, as if it no longer mattered, "I never stopped loving you. Even when I thought I hated you."

"I know. Because I never stopped loving you. I knew that when you risked your life to bring Sheila back to me. Because you knew it would destroy me if something happened to her. Just as I know it will destroy you to lose Birch Haven."

He said nothing. He remained as he was, his head back against the wall, his eyes firmly closed.

Desperately, she seized his hand. As she spoke, she felt tears well in her eyes. "Jack, don't you understand? I don't care about what Ali Pasha might or might not do with the treasure. I don't care about my father's name or a new wing in the British Museum. I care about *you*. It's breaking my heart to see you like this. I know that if you lose Birch Haven you'll cease to exist. I can't stand by and let this happen. I love you too much."

He opened bleary eyes and looked at her.

"I love you, Jack," she repeated quietly.

By now tears were streaming down her cheek. With one hand he touched them, looking at the drops with a sense of wonder. "You really mean that?"

"I've never meant anything more."

The air around them seemed suddenly lighter.

"You love me that much? To give up everything you've worked and fought for?"

"I love you a hundred times more than any treasure. And yes. I'd give up anything—for you."

He pulled her to him and held her close while she cried into his chest.

"We've been so awful to one another," she

sobbed. "We've hurt each other so cruelly. I know now that it was my fault as much as yours. I wanted what I wanted so badly that I couldn't see anything from your point of view. My selfishness blinded me completely."

He lifted her head and wiped the tears from her face. "You *have* changed."

"You remember the story I told you in the temple?" she asked. "Of Isis and Osiris? How she made him whole and brought him back to life? I'm not trying to trick you now. You told me you sometimes wished we could find our lost innocence again. I want that, too, more than anything. I want to go back. Before that night when you came to me at the museum, knowing you'd stolen the collection to save Birch Haven. I want to wipe the slate clean. Begin again, as if none of it had ever happened. I want to do for you what Isis did for Osiris. To make you whole with the one gift I have to give. That which you love better than anything."

Once again, she saw the tears in his eyes. The look he gave her was so tender, so full of hope and love and gratitude, that it made her feel her heart was about to burst.

"Can't we begin again, Jack? Can't we take Birch Haven and begin to build a new life together? As if all these years and all this pain had never happened?"

He drew her close. His arms were strong about her, so that she felt safe and protected. She felt his old vibrancy restore her hope.

"We can," he said as his own tears bathed her cheek.

They stayed, holding each other for some time, feeling a sense of peace. But eventually, Diana became aware of the hour. The decision had been made. The time for action was upon them.

"We have to hurry," she told Jack, glancing at the clock. "There's a train to Bedford at nine o'clock. It's a two-hour trip with all the stops along the way. Once there, we'll have to hire horses and ride out to Birch Haven. With any luck, we'll just make it before noon. You shave while I dress. We'll leave a note for Sheila, telling her where we've gone."

Like a man coming out of a dream, Jack did as she'd commanded. When they were ready, they went out into the early morning, groggy from their lack of sleep, but fueled by a keen sense of urgency. It took some time to make their way to Euston Station. They arrived before nine, but the northbound train was delayed for half an hour. Diana paced nervously, all too aware that thirty minutes could make all the difference.

When they'd finally boarded, the journey seemed excruciatingly slow. They stopped seven times along the way. Each time, Diana glanced at the clock, counting the minutes, willing the passengers to hurry off and the train to be on its way. When at last they reached the town of Bedford, they were left with only a half hour to spare.

They rented horses at the inn, pacing nervously as

the groom methodically saddled them as if he had all the time in the world. When at last the mounts were ready, they raced the five miles to Birch Haven, galloping all the way. The horses were lathered and out of breath by the time they reached the rise that looked down on the estate. They'd made it with but moments to spare.

Below them, the entire estate had been roped off. The county sheriff and a dozen of his men were there to provide security and keep the area clear of curious neighbors. The Hadley Midlands Mining Company was there in force, with excavation equipment and miners ready to move into place. And on the edge of the throng was a contingent of Ali Pasha's men, whom Jack and Diana recognized from their scuffle at the cottage the week before. If they harbored any hopes in the back of their minds that the Turk might be bluffing, this settled the question once and for all.

As he saw them ride up, Ali Pasha strode toward them with a beaming, welcoming smile. "Ah, my friends. So you made it after all."

Jack was staring at the main house. Positioned all over it, and on the grounds before it, were what looked like small, brown boxes. He dismounted and asked curtly, "What exactly is going on here?"

The prince held something in his hand. This he tossed to Jack, who caught it neatly. It was a stick of dynamite.

"Swedish dynamite," Ali said with a grin. "The best in the world. There are five hundred pounds of it spread strategically around the estate, awaiting the single push of my plunger."

Diana dismounted and came up beside Jack. "We've come to agree to your deal," she told him, her loathing of the man choking her voice.

With a brittle, amused smile, Ali looked at Jack and shook his head. "You English. You never fail to amuse me. Your love of gardens and symmetrical estates and your utter contempt for the rest of the world and its people. You really are so trivial when you stop and think of it. But you, Jack . . . perhaps you're more like us Turks than I'd assumed. Women mean little to us, after all. I offered you a choice. The desires of your woman or that little patch of earth you see before you. I should have known when it came down to it that this place would be more important to you than this mere woman."

He was smirking. But Jack had gone pale. He glanced at Diana, and she could see that something had changed in his eyes. He stared at her for a long moment. As he did, it seemed to Diana that he was looking at her for the first time. Then, abruptly, his features hardened and his eyes took on a determined glare.

"No," he said.

"No?" mimicked the prince.

Turning to him, Jack sneered, "You can take your deal and shove it up your foul Turkish arse."

"Jack, no," Diana cried, wheeling on him.

Ali Pasha's eyes flashed anger. "You think I bluff, my friend?"

"I don't give a damn if you're bluffing or not."

Diana grabbed his arm. "Jack, please, don't be a fool."

Jack turned to her. "I can't go through with it, Diana. I don't know what I was thinking."

"Jack, you must. Forget what he said."

"No, he's right. When you offered me this gift, all I could think of was what I wanted. But what of you, Diana? What of all you've worked for?"

"Jack, think," she urged frantically. "You love Birch Haven."

He looked down on the imperiled land, the house and gardens his ancestors had built with their own hands. "Yes," he said wistfully. "I love this place. I've fought with everything I have to keep it. My father died for it. And I'd die, too, to save it." His voice choked with his emotion. He paused, taking a deep breath, fighting, as he'd fought for his home, to compose himself, to overcome the awful pain of his decision. Diana could see his struggle. It took all the courage he could summon to say these words, to face the doom of his dream.

Finally, he turned to her and took both her hands in his. They trembled against her palms. "But I love you more. You were willing to sacrifice everything for me. And I must find the strength to do the same. But I can do it, Diana. I'd give up anything for you. All my hopes and dreams, all I've fought for—" Again his voice choked. But his hands tightened on hers. "You know why, Diana? Because I've found them all in you. You're worth the loss of all this and more."

Tears prickled Diana's eyes. "Jack, you fool," she said, loving him more than she ever had.

Ali Pasha glowered his contempt. "You don't believe me, Jack?" He walked over to the plunger that would set off the dynamite and put his hand on it. "You think I bluff? You think I will be so touched by your foolish sacrifice as to change my mind? I never bluff. You have one more minute, Jack. One more minute to spare your precious home."

Jack looked deeply into Diana's eyes. He saw there all her love and pride overflowing with her tears. She saw his final struggle before his face cleared, his decision made. Dropping her hands, he turned and strode toward the Turk, squaring his shoulders. The two men stood face-to-face taking each other's measure.

"Think what you will be giving up," Ali warned.

"But think, *my friend*, what I'll be gaining."

With those words, Jack raised his foot and slammed it down on the plunger.

An immense explosion shattered everything around them. The impact of it knocked them all to the ground, the sound of it splitting their ears. A mammoth cloud of dust and dirt blotted out the winter sun so it was suddenly as dark as midnight.

As everyone rose slowly to their feet and gazed down at the destruction, an apocalyptic awe settled over them. No one moved through the long minutes during which the dust cleared. And then, gradually, they saw the result of Jack's noble sacrifice. Where Birch Haven had once stood, there was nothing but a huge gaping hole in the earth.

Diana went to Jack and put a trembling hand on his arm, feeling heavy with sadness.

"Now I'm free," Jack said softly, looking down at the devastation that had once been his home. He turned to Ali. "Free," he snarled, "to do what I should have done long ago. Free to kill you."

The sheriff stepped forth hastily, crying, "Now, see here—"

But Ali raised a silencing hand. "Kill me, will you?" he taunted.

"You have no hold on me now," Jack growled.

"No hold?" Ali asked, raising a brow. "Are you sure? What about Sheila?"

"You don't have Sheila. We do."

"Are you quite certain of that? Are you sure we haven't been watching your little hideaway in Soho for the past three days? Waiting for you to leave so we could grab an even better insurance policy? I was hoping you would make it easy on me and accept my offer for your land. But you see, Jack, I'm a man who believes in careful planning. I thought there might be an off chance that you loved this slip of a girl more than I'd realized. So I had my men pay a visit to your little love nest while you were on your way here this morning."

"You lying scoundrel," Diana cried.

Ali shrugged his shoulders. "You don't have to believe me. Go back. See if your Sheila's there."

Jack looked at Diana. The color had completely drained from her face. She was staring at Ali Pasha with horrified yet disbelieving eyes.

Ali laughed. "Now that you've chosen the girl over the estate, Jack, your next decision should be simple. Tell me where the treasure is and you get back the girl's long-lost mother. Tonight, Jack. Don't tell me, and the woman dies."

19

Diana was beside herself on the train back to London. Every stop seemed endless. She couldn't contain her impatience. Yet fear kept her in her seat. The wheels of the train seemed to pound a rhythm in her head, echoing the words in her mind. *What if it's true? What if it's true?*

"It can't be true," she said to Jack. "He's bluffing."

"He doesn't bluff."

"But he could be this once, couldn't he?" she cried.

Jack saw the desperation in her eyes. "Maybe. He could have told us that to keep me from strangling him then and there. That's possible."

But Diana knew he was being merciful. She knew in her heart that he didn't believe it any more than she.

"If it's true," she asked over and over, "what are we going to do?"

There was nothing to do but wait. As soon as the train chugged into Euston Station, Diana jumped off, running through the depot, to leap into a cab. Jack was right behind her. They raced to Soho, and as Jack paid the driver, Diana flew up the flights of stairs to their rooftop flat. The moment she entered the room, the truth slammed her in the face.

The sitting room was a shambles. Chairs and tables had been overturned, spilling the contents to the floor. A spot of red stained the carpet. Diana was bending over it as Jack came in. She looked up at him, trembling. "It's blood."

Jack pulled her up and put his arms around her, holding her close.

"You gave up Birch Haven for me," she said, her voice muffled by his coat. "And it wasn't enough. It's never enough. It was all for nothing. Oh, Jack, how you must hate me."

He pulled back and looked her in the face. "I don't hate you," he told her forcibly. "I don't regret it. To tell you the truth, when I looked down and saw it gone I felt absolved. Maybe . . . maybe it can help make up for what I've done to you."

"I know you're trying to be kind, but—"

"I'm not being kind. Diana, I love you. Those aren't just words. On the yacht in Egypt, when I saw that you were gone, and I realized what you must have heard . . . I knew how hurt you must have been. I knew I had to do something to make it up to you. So I decided to find Sheila for you myself. But it was more than that. With you gone it was like . . . like half of me was missing. I knew then how much I loved you. How much I need you."

"But Birch Haven—"

"Birch Haven was an albatross. It's always stood between us. I saw that when Ali Pasha said I was choosing it over you. I've faced the worst and it's not so bad, so long as I have you. I'd do it again, to see you look at me the way you did—with pride in your eyes. The way you used to look at me. I'd give up anything for that."

He stroked her face tenderly. She could see by the warmth in his eyes that he meant every word he said.

"Jack, what are we going to do?"

"I don't know," he said, his frustration apparent in his tone.

"He'll kill her, won't he?"

Jack hesitated. She could see that he wanted to ease her mind. But her eyes pleaded with him to tell the truth. "Yes," he said finally. "I think he will if we don't give him what he wants."

"But how can we possibly do that? After all we've been through? Knowing what we know? Can we selfishly save one life when so many others will die because of it? And yet—" She choked on the words. "She's my mother. How can I—"

She couldn't finish. But her words hung in the air. *How can I let her die?*

"Now I know how you felt when you knew you had to sacrifice Birch Haven."

"I should have killed him long ago," Jack said.

Diana's heart was breaking. "We can't give in to him. But Jack . . ."

She looked up at him with teary eyes.

"How can I let her go?"

She couldn't bear to see the pain and helplessness in his gaze. Tearing herself away, she ran out of the room, down the flights of stairs, into the cold. She ran until she could run no more, and then she walked. Endlessly, step after step, trying to escape the horror that followed her like a ghost.

Finally, she came upon a park and sat down on a bench, completely disheartened. Homes surrounded the square. Children were playing, laughing. Houses were being decorated, servants running to and fro. The activity was somehow eerie to Diana. It seemed to her that the world should have stopped. Yet there was a bustle and excitement that clashed with the sorrow in her heart. Then she remembered it was New Year's Eve. At midnight, they would ring in the new century. And if they didn't give in to Ali Pasha's blackmail, Sheila would die.

She watched the children with burning eyes. One mother came out to button up her daughter's coat. Diana's heart seemed to catch in her throat. She thought of her midnight talks with Sheila, of how they were slowly becoming close. She thought of the

fulfillment of caring for her, of the pleasant sense of
domesticity she'd found with Jack and Sheila at
Birch Haven. She thought of all the years when she'd
cried herself to sleep, wondering why Prudence
seemed to despise her so. She thought of all the plans
she'd had for the future, making up for the years she
and her real mother had lost.

Tears slipped silently down her cheeks.

Then she felt someone sit down beside her. She
looked up and saw Jack. He was a welcome sight. He
seemed to offer sanctuary from the turmoil of her
thoughts.

He took her hand and sat quietly for a moment,
watching the children play. Finally, he said, "We're
going to give in."

The words were like balm to her wound. But she
said, "No—we can't. It's unthinkable."

"Sheila's a real person. She lives, she breathes.
She's more important than whatever nebulous people
out there Ali may or may not hurt. They're not real
to us. Sheila is. She's placed her trust in us. We're not
going to let her down."

"Can you live with that decision?"

"Can you live with the alternative?"

She dropped her gaze.

"Diana, you said it yourself. You were willing to
sacrifice everything you wanted, everything you'd
spent your life working for, to give me the one thing
I wanted. I want to reciprocate. The treasure is mean-
ingless to us now. Your father's dead. We can't help

him. But Sheila's alive. If we can save her by paying a ransom, that's exactly what we must do."

"And then? When we tell him where the treasure is?"

Jack hesitated. "Let's just get Sheila back first."

Ali Pasha's house had been extravagantly decorated for Christmas. He wasn't a Christian, but he outdid every other mansion in the area with candles and greenery and a life-size manger scene on his front lawn. Just beyond the wise men, the front portico was full of guards. When Jack and Diana approached, the guards stood back in formation, watching them as if they were expected.

Diana churned with nervous excitement. She couldn't wait to see Sheila, to know once again that she was safe. Her mind was filled with all the horrors Ali Pasha might have inflicted on her. She had to clench her teeth to keep her emotions in check.

They were shown inside, to the side parlor. In a moment, Ali Pasha came in, wearing his Turkish robes. He greeted them with his usual beaming smile, every inch the gracious host. "May I assume this time that you have come to deal seriously at last?"

"We've come to negotiate a trade," Jack said curtly. "A map showing where the treasure is in exchange for Sheila."

"Excellent. A fair trade. But how am I to know if the information you give me will be correct?"

"The minute you see the location, you'll know it's true. It will seem obvious to you."

"How intriguing. Do you have the map?"

"Not here," Jack said. "The exchange will have to be made in a public place. Where there can be no chance of a double-cross."

Ali put his hand to his chin in thought. "Then let us meet in the most public place of all. Tonight, at midnight, all of London will be gathered in the streets before Parliament to stand witness as Big Ben rings in the new century. We shall meet there at, say, a quarter hour before midnight. In the meantime I shall ready my yacht for departure. Just in case you have any second thoughts once the exchange is made."

It was almost eleven. Diana waited impatiently in the flat for Jack to return. He'd gone out to spy on the loading of the Turk's yacht to see if he might figure out where Sheila was—and determine if there wasn't some way of stealing her away before the appointed meeting. Diana had been praying for his success. But when he walked in, she could see from his face that he'd failed.

"No luck," he told her. "We'll have to go through with the exchange as planned."

She did her best to swallow her disappointment. "Are we doing the right thing, Jack?"

"We're doing the only thing we can."

"My heart tells me it's the right thing. I can't wait to get Sheila back. But my conscience bothers me, Jack. To give him that treasure, knowing the terrible things he intends to do with it—Can't we give him false information?"

"No. He knows the clues that were written on the cats. Cyprus will seem so logical to him that he'll accept it in a flash. But he's clever enough to see through any trick we might devise."

"And what if we give him the treasure and he doesn't give us Sheila?"

Jack paused for a moment, meeting her eyes with a steady stare. "Then I'll kill him just as fast. And he bloody well knows it."

The scene below Big Ben was like the Queen's Jubilee, Guy Fawkes Day, and the Feast of Fools all rolled into one. The crowds from London's pubs had spilled out and moved here, drinks in hand, sloshing over from the steady movement. The regular Hyde Park contingent had moved here en masse from Speakers' Corner and were engaged in lively debate, some casting forth predictions for the new century, some vociferously shouting them down, arguing the technicality that the century wouldn't turn for another year—1901. But most eyes were beginning to gravitate toward the huge hands of the clock, which indicated that only fifteen minutes were left in the nineteenth century.

The crush of the gathered crowd prevented their coach from reaching its destination. They paid the driver and stepped out into the mob of merrymakers. The carnival atmosphere, the heat and sweat of the sheer mass of humanity, swirled about them like a circus gone mad. Jack shoved and stiff-armed his way through the crowd while Diana struggled to keep close behind. Finally they came to Parliament Street, where they spotted Ali Pasha, standing by his coach with a detachment of bodyguards.

Ali Pasha greeted them with his wide, charming smile. "You're late. I was beginning to fear you'd had a change of heart."

"We're here," Jack called over the noise of the crowd.

"Where's Sheila?" Diana demanded.

The Turk's gaze flicked to the coach. "She's very close. You'll see her in a few minutes' time. I promise you—as Allah is my witness."

"Let's see her now," Jack said, taking a step toward the coach.

But Ali held up a hand and two of his guards stepped forward to block Jack's path. "Tut, tut, Jack. You're not in charge here. You can have the woman when you've given me the treasure."

Jack glanced at Diana, who gave a slight nod. Then, turning to Ali Pasha, he handed forth the map he'd prepared. The prince quickly unfurled the paper and stared at it. He smiled again. "By God, Jack, you're right. It *is* obvious. What fools we are not to have guessed it from the start. Cyprus! Cleopatra was queen of Egypt *and* Cyprus. Aphrodite's rock. Where else?" He threw back his head and laughed. Someone from the crowd, seeing his glee, slapped him jovially on the back. His two henchmen immediately grabbed the man by the arms and hurled him back into the crowd. But the prince scarcely seemed to notice.

Diana seized the opportunity to run to the coach and fling open the door. For a moment she stood, rooted in shock and horror, hardly believing the sight before her.

"It's empty."

Jack whirled on Ali Pasha. "You miserable bastard! Where is she?"

Ali Pasha slowly lifted his gaze toward the illuminated face of Big Ben, three hundred feet above them. Ten feet or so above the clock was a row of open arches. In one of them, they could see several figures moving about. Figures that might have been workmen or someone planting fireworks. But on closer inspection, it was apparent that one of figures was a woman.

"As I promised, there she is," Ali said. "And at exactly midnight, just as the fireworks light the sky, my men are going to fling her to the unsuspecting crowd below. I'm sure you'll agree it will make a most spectacular display. An omen, perhaps, for the fate of the mighty British Empire in the coming century."

"But *why*?!" Diana cried. "You have what you want. Why kill this innocent woman?"

The twinkle in Ali Pasha's eyes turned into a glacial hardness. "Because she betrayed me. And there is no mercy for anyone who betrays me."

Jack took a knife from his coat pocket and made a

lunge. But as Ali's men charged, drawing their own knives, the prince caught Jack's arm. "You know, Jack, if you hurry, you may just make it up there in time to save the woman. But if you take the time to try and end my humble life, there's no chance at all. What's it going to be?"

20

*J*ack took one look at Diana, then, glancing up at the clock, turned and charged into the crowd. Hurling aside everyone in his path, he made for the south entrance of the clock tower with Diana following, trying to stay as close to Jack as possible. She glanced upward. She could no longer see Sheila, but she saw that only five minutes were left until midnight.

As the huge minute hand clicked into place, she heard the crowd roar, *"Five!"*

Ali Pasha had stationed two men at the door. As they saw Jack approach, they drew pistols. His knife still in hand, Jack charged them without the slightest hesitation. As the nearest of them raised his arm to fire, Jack dove for his feet, knocking him to the ground. The gun discharged in the air harmlessly. The crowd, assuming this was the first of the fireworks, let out a cheer. The second man raised his pistol, aiming at Jack on the ground. Jack instantly flipped his knife around so the blade was in hand, then hurled it at the man. It hit him directly in the throat. He dropped to his knees, gurgling blood.

The first man was on his feet, rushing Jack again. As Jack knocked him unconscious with a single blow of his fist, the crowd roared, *"Four!"*

Opening the door, Jack entered the building. As Diana followed, he raced up three levels of stairs. At the top of the third level was a huge spiral staircase that reached up to the clockworks. It was silent in here, eerily so after the noise and confusion of the crowds outside. Diana could hear their breath echoing off the walls.

Pausing a moment to catch his breath, Jack heard the muffled cry of the crowd outside roar, *"Three!"*

With a new burst of energy, he began to run up the spiral staircase, round and round, his footsteps thundering up the metal steps. Diana, panicked by the diminishing time, screamed, "Hurry, Jack, hurry!" even as she barreled up after him.

A hundred feet up, Jack stumbled, hitting his knee sharply on a step and falling back. Diana rushed to help him. As he lay there, breathing hard, the crowd below yelled, *"Two!"*

Without looking at her, Jack surged forward and resumed his frantic climb. In another hundred feet he was within view of the platform area above the clock-works. He could see four men and one woman—Sheila. Two of the men held her arms in position to hurl her to her death. The crowd roared, *"One!"*

Desperately, Jack charged ahead. Taking two and three steps at a time, he bounded up the remaining stairs. The Turks noticed him for the first time. The crowd began to count down the seconds of the final minute of the century.

"Fifty . . . forty-nine . . . forty-eight . . ."

The two who weren't holding Sheila charged him. Jack grabbed the first one with both hands, fell back onto the floor, and with his feet positioned against the man's stomach, rolled back in one motion and sent the man flying into the air and crashing down the stairwell, past Diana, to his death.

"Thirty-nine . . . thirty-eight . . . thirty-seven . . ."

The second man had thrown himself on Jack. They were now rolling on the floor, struggling. Neither had a weapon.

"Thirty-two . . . thirty-one . . . thirty . . ."

One of the men holding Sheila had withdrawn a gun and was trying to aim it at Jack, but couldn't get a clear shot as Jack struggled with the other man on the ground.

"Twenty-eight . . . twenty-seven . . . twenty-six . . ."

Jack finally managed to pin his opponent to the floor. Diana saw the other guard take aim. Thinking fast, she glanced about and noticed a huge pulley suspended from a heavy chain, obviously used to lower workmen into the clockworks below. She reached for it, hoisted it behind her, and swung it at the man.

"Eighteen . . . seventeen . . ."

It hit him in the head, knocking him cold just as his pistol discharged. The deflected bullet hit the man Jack had pinned to the floor. He struggled for a moment, then fell back, dead.

Jack looked up at her in astonishment. "Thanks," he said.

"Twelve . . . eleven . . . ten . . ."

With only seconds to spare, Jack and Diana both rushed toward Sheila and the one remaining guard. But they were too late.

"Three . . . two . . . one . . ."

The sky erupted in fireworks. The roar of the crowd was suddenly deafening, everyone yelling, *"Happy New Year!"*

Calmly, the guard pushed Sheila over the ledge.

Diana's shriek mingled with Sheila's muffled cry. But as Diana looked down in horror, she saw that Sheila had hit the jointed hands of the clock as it touched midnight, her dress catching on the minute hand so that she hung precariously from it. She was bleeding profusely, apparently cut by the hand's sharp point.

From behind, Jack grabbed the guard with a choke-hold to his neck, and squeezed hard. Then he relaxed his hold and the man slipped dead to his feet.

The minute hand—some fourteen feet in length—clicked off the first minute of the new century. As it did, the pressure caused Sheila's dress to tear several inches and made her tenuous hold on life even more precarious. The fireworks continued to explode in the air around them, distracting the crowd from the awful scene above.

As Jack and Diana frantically tried to figure out how to rescue her, the clock clicked off another minute. The dress tore another few inches.

"There must be a rope or something we can use."

"There's no time," Jack told her. "I've got to climb down."

"The pulley!" she cried.

Eyeing it, he said, "Perfect." He grabbed the chain and said, "I'm going to hold on to this end and go down. The chain is attached to another pulley in the ceiling. It'll support me if you can hold on tight to the other end. But you're going to have to lower me down. And when I get her, you'll have to pull us up. Can you do that?"

The clock clicked again and Sheila screamed in terror.

There was no time now for Jack to climb down. "Grab the other end of the chain and hold tight," he ordered. Holding his end, he leapt off the ledge just as the clock clicked again. The final threads gave way and Sheila fell just as Jack snatched her arm.

The impact had pulled the chain through Diana's fingers, threatening to fly out of control. But she managed to grab it and, with the support of the pulley in the ceiling, contain its free fall. Jack and Sheila hung high above the city, depending on her to pull them up. If she lost control of the chain, they could go crashing to the earth below. She prayed that Jack could hold on to his end of the chain and Sheila at the same time.

It took all her effort just to keep the chain anchored in place. She tried to pull back, to raise their combined weight, but she didn't have a fraction of the capacity required. Suddenly, she realized the chain was burning in her hands. How would she ever find the strength to hold it, much less hoist them up? She was consumed with horror. The lives of the only two people she loved in the world were literally in her hands.

Panic paralyzed her. In her mind, she saw her hands give way, saw the chain slip through her numb fingers, saw Jack and Sheila fall to agonizing deaths.

But then she heard Jack's voice calling from below. "You can do it, Diana. You can find the strength."

Find the strength. From where?

Then she thought of Ali Pasha, no doubt laughing as he sailed away to Cyprus. The treasure was one thing. What did that matter now? But if he claimed the lives of these two most beloved people, he'd have won.

Suddenly, the chain was light in her hand. Suddenly, she knew she could do it. Because she had to. Because there was no other way. She gripped the chain tighter and began to pull, throwing the full force of her body into each tug, thrusting backward as she took one step, then another, then another. Her arms were nearly ripped from their sockets. Her body throbbed and shook. But she pulled again with all the power at her disposal.

Finally, she heard Jack climb over the ledge, his voice saying, "I'm afraid she's in a bad way, Diana."

They laid Sheila carefully on the floor. Then Jack ripped the bottom of Sheila's dress. As he did, Diana saw the blood on his hands.

He gently turned her over and Diana saw the long gash in the dress that showed the deep wound in Sheila's side. "She's lost a lot of blood."

They used the strip of cloth he'd torn off as a compress, attempting to seal the wound.

Alarmed by Sheila's ghostly pallor, Diana said, "We have to get her to hospital."

"I'll carry her. You run ahead and see if you can find a cab somewhere."

"Oh, my God," Diana gasped as she glanced at Sheila's side. Already, the compress was soaked with new blood. How much longer could she last? "Hurry, Jack."

"No." It was Sheila's voice, already sounding distant. "Wait."

Diana bent over her. "Mother, we have to get you to a doctor. You're badly hurt."

Weakly, Sheila's hand reached up to touch Diana's cheek. "It is too late."

"No," Diana cried, tears of panic stinging her eyes. "Don't say that. It can't be too late. I won't allow it."

"Diana, listen to me." It was taking every ounce of energy that Sheila possessed to voice the soft words. "I cannot die like this."

"You're not going to die." One of Diana's tears splashed on Sheila's cheek.

"I cannot leave you with this on my conscience."

Her tone frightened Diana. She did, indeed, speak with the conviction of one who knew she had only moments left to live. Diana looked up at Jack and saw the certainty in his eyes.

"I think you'd better listen, Diana."

Her lower lip began to tremble. She took Sheila's hand in hers. "You have to hold on. You can't leave me now, not when I've just found you."

"My poor Diana. You have been so good to me. How can I ever tell you this? You will hate me so."

"I could never hate you," Diana sobbed. "You're my mother."

"No." The simple word seemed to hang in the still air.

"Please don't try to talk now," Diana pleaded.

"Diana, my child . . . you must listen. I have not much . . . time. I have come to love you as any mother might. How could I not? But I do not . . ." She took a painful breath that seemed to hiss through her lungs. "I do not deserve your grief."

Diana sat perfectly still, her eyes riveted on Sheila's face.

"I am not . . . your mother."

"Of course you are."

"The story I told you was true. But it did not

happen to me. Your mother—the real Sheila—was with your father when he died. She was sent by Ali Pasha."

Diana sat back on her heels. She was numb. She could see this woman—this impostor—lying so pale and suffering before her. She could hear her whispered words. But she couldn't seem to feel her own body. She felt frozen in a nightmare from which she could never escape.

"In the story I told you, the diplomat . . . your mother was married to . . . was Ali Pasha."

"No!" Diana cried.

"It was he who forced her to give you up, and threatened to take your life if she would not. But he wanted the treasure. When Stafford was ill in Egypt, he sent Sheila—your real mother—to nurse him. When Stafford died, Ali Pasha tortured the clues out of her and, when she had confessed . . ."

"What?" Diana whispered.

"He killed her."

There was a long silence. Diana couldn't bring herself to move.

"Then who are you?" Jack demanded.

"I was a servant and confidant of Sheila's. After giving up her child, she would have nothing to do with him. Because I resembled her, and because he needed an outlet for his anger, the master—used me as his whore. But that does not matter now. The only thing that matters is that your mother loved you dearly. She thought of you every day of her life. She constantly told me so."

Diana was weeping now, her heart breaking.

"And this masquerade?" Jack growled.

Sheila spoke haltingly, fighting for breath. "The master made me do it. He threatened to kill me if I did not. He placed one of his men to keep watch over me—the servant you no doubt saw at my home in Giza. He even kept me tied and starved after the . . . fraudulent abduction in case you succeeded in . . . rescuing me. If you did, I was to return to him. But I could not. He was so cruel. Having tasted of your kindness, a kindness I had never known except from my mistress Sheila, I could not bring myself to return to that . . . beast. So I betrayed him and . . . stayed with you. That is why he has done this to me. He is a monster. Evil as you cannot even imagine. He must be . . . stopped."

"A fine time to tell us," Jack growled. "You could have told us long ago and spared us all this. We would never have had to tell him where the treasure is."

"That is a regret I will have to take to my grave. I just could not bear to see this poor child lose her mother once she thought she'd found her. And . . . I never dreamed that I would love her so. I never had a child. I never had a moment of happiness. I selfishly wanted that . . . joy. I dare not ask you to forgive me."

No one spoke for a time as Diana looked at the dying woman. Finally, she said, "Forgive you for giving me a mother's love? For letting me know, even for a short time, what that was? You've honored me."

After a slight pause, she asked, "What's your real name?"

"Daria. Please, my child . . . take the necklace I wear. The Cyprus amulet is mine . . . but the cartouche with your name . . . your mother wore it always, hiding it from her husband. She would want you to have it." Weakly, she touched the gold. "They say . . . if a person wears a piece of jewelry long enough . . . that something of that person's soul remains."

Diana gently took the necklace and placed it around her own neck. Then she lifted the woman's hand and kissed it tenderly. "Thank you, Daria," she said. "Is there anything I can do for you?"

Daria gripped her hand. "The light is fading, Diana. There is nothing you can do for me. But if I were your mother . . . I would tell you this: Never forget . . . the responsibility you owe . . . to the half of you that is Egyptian. Honor your mother . . . by honoring your . . . heritage."

With that she died.

Diana continued to hold her hand. Jack let her sit in peace, saying nothing.

Eventually, her tears stopped and a heavy recrimination took its place. "She's right. Honor that heritage. What have I done? I've put it in the hands of a madman."

Jack's eyes hardened on her face. "Well, baby, maybe we can take it back."

21

"*I*'m going to leave you now," Jack said. "Will you be all right?"

"You're going after him?"

"Yes."

"But what can you possibly do?"

"Obviously, I can't chase them down the Thames. They're on the fastest ship afloat. But . . . if I were to get across southeast England, I might be able to cut them off as they come out of the Thames estuary. Perhaps at Southend-on-Sea."

"But it's the middle of the night. How would you possibly—"

"There's a two A.M. express out of Victoria Station." He spoke distractedly, as if thinking aloud. "It only stops twice before arriving at Southend-on-Sea."

She could see his mind calculating the distance to the coast, the speed of the *Hittite Queen,* all the variables that went into the equation.

"It's a long shot, but with luck, I may just be able to pull it off."

But what if he *did* succeed in catching up with them? What then? He would be one man against fifty. It seemed hopeless in any case.

Diana looked down on Daria's pale and lifeless face. She thought of the woman's murderer speeding so happily toward Cyprus. The urge to be part of *anything* that might have a chance of stopping him was overwhelming. "I'm going with you. There's nothing I can do for Daria now."

"I think you'd better stay behind this time. What I'm thinking is extremely dangerous."

"I don't care—I'm going. Don't even think of trying to stop me. He killed my mother. And Daria, who was the closest thing to a mother I've ever known. I have to help in any way I can."

He took her face in his hands and studied her determined gaze. Then he kissed her and said, "All right, let's go."

They finally found an available cab, but in the push of the crowds it took them nearly an hour to arrive at Victoria Station, with only fifteen minutes to spare. They quickly boarded the Southend express. The nearly empty train departed right on time. As it began to gather steam, a drunken reveler ran up beside them, beating on the window. "Happy New Century," he cried.

"Let's hope so," Jack muttered.

As the train chugged through the dark night, Jack was silent, planning in his mind. Diana, too, was quiet, giving him room to breathe. She knew he needed time to formulate some plan of action for when they arrived at the coastal town of Southend-on-Sea. In her own mind, the situation seemed impossible. Jack wasn't even armed.

But the questions that sprang to mind were stilled by a more powerful consciousness—the realization that no matter how hopeless their mission seemed, something had, indeed, changed inside her. She found that she had unconditional faith in Jack. That whatever the outcome, whether they succeeded or not, Jack would do his utmost—his absolute best. For them.

At Grays, the first stop along the way, Jack left the train and returned only moments before the porter closed the door.

"I cabled ahead to Southend," he told Diana. "There's an outfitter there—a Mr. Bartley—who supplied the ships for my father's expedition to the Frisian Islands, just across the channel. I've asked him for the fastest sloop he can find."

"And after we get the ship, what?"

"Then we pray for a strong wind."

They arrived at Southend-on-Sea just as the pale pink glow of the new dawn broke the horizon. The sloop was waiting for them at the dock. As Jack had requested, a rifle had been placed inside. While making the final arrangements with Bartley, Jack glanced up and saw that his calculations had been correct and luck had been with them: the *Hittite Queen* appeared several miles to the southwest, where England's great river met the open sea.

"If that's your quarry," Bartley commented, "I'd say Poseidon smiled on you. The winds are to the southeast. You should be able to cut them off handily."

They stepped into the narrow sloop. Jack cast off the lines and raised the sail. As it caught the friendly southeasterly wind, Diana shivered in the blast of the cold breeze. Seeing this, Jack put one arm around her to warm her as he controlled the rudder with the other.

They sped effortlessly through the water, setting a diagonal course that would cut off the *Hittite Queen* before it could enter the Straits of Dover.

The ship grew larger and larger in their sights. As it did, some of the crew began to spot them. At first they stared at the tiny craft in puzzlement. But as Jack maneuvered the fleet ship closer still, some recognized him and sounded the alarm. Men poured onto the deck, shading their eyes with their hands as they looked out at the apparition in the ever-brightening sea.

By the time Ali Pasha had come on deck, resplendent in flowing robes that buffeted in the breeze, Jack had brought the sloop within shouting range of the larger ship. As the Turk spotted him, he broke into a disbelieving grin.

"You English!" he cried, his voice shaking with laughter. "You really do astonish me. You just won't give up, will you? But tell me. Were you able to save the damsel in distress? Miss Sanbourne's—*mother?*" Again he cackled in glee, the sound of his laughter carrying with the breeze.

Diana flinched, but Jack ignored the jibe.

"You know, Jack," Ali Pasha called, "this is by far the most insane stunt you've ever pulled. All I have to do is give the word and you'll go down in a hail of bullets. I do believe the strain of my outsmarting you has relieved you of your senses."

Leisurely, Jack picked up the rifle. The men on deck instantly took cover. Only Ali Pasha stood firm.

"Fools!" he cried. "He's one man against fifty!"

The men rose tentatively. As they did, Jack took aim at a water casket attached at midships near the mainsail. He fired. The wood splintered and the liquid began to pour out, spilling over several bales of supplies that were secured to the deck below.

This amused the prince even more. "You really *are* crazy, aren't you? Do you think we might die of thirst before reaching the French coast?"

"Are you sure it's water?" Jack called, lowering the rifle.

Suddenly a voice yelled, *"Effendi,* it smells like kerosene!"

The smile vanished from Ali Pasha's lips.

Jack reached into his pocket and took out the

stick of dynamite that Ali Pasha had so arrogantly tossed to him at Birch Haven. "Remember this?" he called, flipping it in his hand. "Swedish dynamite. The best in the world. Isn't that what you told me?"

Numbly, Ali Pasha turned and stared at the bales on deck that were now drenched with kerosene. The arrogant sneer he'd worn was slowly transformed into a look of dawning horror.

"Knowing your fondness for the stuff," Jack called, "I thought I'd leave you a batch as a little surprise *bon voyage* present. You made a big mistake when you told me you were busily preparing your ship to sail. In the rush of activity I had no trouble passing myself off as a longshoreman. Your men didn't even give me a glance as I carried that box of dynamite on board. You surprise me, Ali, old pal. You're not usually so careless."

As Jack spoke, Ali glanced about the deck at the seeping kerosene, his concern rising. But suddenly, his face brightened. "And how do you intend to light it, my friend? Strike a match and toss it over?"

"Watch and see."

In one lightning motion, Jack raised the rifle. As Ali hit the deck, Jack took aim and fired. The bullet expertly glanced off the metal band at the kerosene-drenched base of the mainsail. The spark it made instantly ignited the fluid.

Rising to his feet, Ali Pasha screamed in a panicked voice, "Throw yourselves on it. Extinguish it! Now!"

As the men frantically and hopelessly tried to

stamp out the flames, Ali turned and stared at his adversaries. As her eyes met his in recognition of what was about to happen, Diana whispered, "This is for my mother."

The ship exploded. The sound of it split the dawn. The blast hurled Jack and Diana high into the air. They hit the water hard some twenty feet away. As they did, their sloop cracked in two like a matchstick. The pieces sank like rocks, leaving Jack and Diana abandoned to the frigid grip of the North Atlantic waters. The ocean erupted and they rode the crest of a mighty tidal wave, rising and falling with the churning tide, being sucked under and having to fight with life and limb for the surface. When the wave passed them, they looked back to see that the *Hittite Queen* had simply disappeared. An instant later, they were showered with its splintered wood and shreds of canvas.

In the aftermath, Diana began to feel the cold. Jack found a large piece of floating wood and helped her to grab it, using it as a makeshift life preserver. But as she took hold of it, she realized she had no feeling in her arms and legs. With the excitement over, her adrenaline had ceased to flow. The cold water was draining the life out of them. They couldn't hope to last more than a few minutes.

Numbly, she reached over and clutched Jack's icy hand with her own. Already, his skin was beginning to turn blue.

"I'm sorry, Diana," he gasped. "I misjudged the impact of the explosion."

"It doesn't matter," she told him, her breath feeling like frost in her throat. "We stopped him. We have that satisfaction, at least."

Jack glanced back, toward the distant shore, hoping to see some sign of rescue. There was nothing but the empty sea. "We'll have to swim for shore."

"I can't move my arms."

"You can—you will. The movement will warm you. Come, Diana. Swim."

She tried. She swam, holding onto the flotsam, but her clothes were heavy, weighing her down. Her limbs refused to respond. She looked ahead. It was miles to shore.

"I can't," she gasped.

"You have to. Hold on to me."

He held her with one arm and swam with the other. But it wasn't long before he, too, faltered. His breath was coming hard in frozen wisps.

Diana felt her senses slipping. She pulled back and collapsed on the float, gasping for air. "We're going to die, Jack."

"We're not going to die. Don't say it. Don't think it. Baby, try to hang on."

She looked at him, and saw that he hadn't yet given up the struggle for life. Ali Pasha was right. He never gave up. But he would have to give up on this. "It isn't so bad," she said when she saw the fear in his eyes. "I can accept it."

He, too, was numb with cold, so numb he felt he couldn't force his limbs to obey his will. But with superhuman effort, he lunged toward her and snatched her in his arm, shaking her.

"We're not going to die," he growled.

"It's all right, Jack. To die with you is a privilege."

"You're not going to die," he screamed, shaking her again. "Do you hear me, Diana? Don't do this to me. Don't let me think that I brought you to your death. You have to fight. You have to live for me. I love you, Diana. I *need* you. Goddammit, swim!"

"I can't."

"Swim!"

But Diana just looked at him with peaceful, resigned eyes. "I feel complete, Jack. I finally have you. Nothing else matters. Kiss me, Jack. Just one last kiss. That's all I ask."

It took every ounce of effort to wrap her arms about his neck. His lips were like ice. But he kissed her deeply, passionately, like a man urging her to live with the gift of his breath. It was the last thing she knew as she felt her body slip lower into the briny depths.

EPILOGUE

"So this is what heaven is like," Diana sighed.

She felt the water enclose her, warm, luxurious, as clear as crystal. So unlike the frigid, inhospitable depths of the North Atlantic where, just a month before, she'd almost met her death. She swam with long, leisurely strokes through the blue Mediterranean that gently caressed the western shore of the enchanted island of Cyprus. The warmth embraced her, nourished her. She turned onto her back, floating, her arms extended, her face kissed by the sun, and sighed with pleasure.

It seemed a miracle that they were here at all. In those last desperate moments, she'd given up any hope of rescue. But the outfitter Bartley had seen the explosion after all. After she'd lost consciousness in the frozen waters, Jack holding her close, trying desperately to warm her, for God only knew how long, Bartley's rescue ship had finally appeared—to wrap them in blankets and hurry them to shore for long, hot baths to prevent the ravages of frostbite.

Once they'd sufficiently recovered, they'd given Daria a small memorial service, then sent her body back to Egypt to be buried in a Muslim cemetery. With Ali Pasha gone and all physical threat with him, they'd taken the opportunity to heal, to regroup, to reaffirm their love for each other. But they were both archaeologists by instinct and breeding. The secret of the Cleopatra treasure burned within them, and they knew they couldn't deny it for long.

Now she and Jack were swimming in the shallows around a huge rock just off a sandy stretch of beach, a rock that rose from the sea like a miniature Gibraltar. Off to the side, further out to sea, were other, smaller, rocks. But this mammoth boulder, Aphrodite's rock, dominated the setting.

Jack, with a small raft in tow, had been unsuccessfully searching the contours of the rock, seeking the opening his instincts told him had to be here somewhere, most likely just below the waterline. Diana dove under the water like a playful porpoise, cutting him off from his work, breaking the surface in a swirling effervescence of foam. Happily, she wrapped her arms about his neck and kissed him, throwing him off balance so they tumbled together into the sea.

"Can you feel the magic of this place?" she asked, her lips to his.

"I feel the presence of a treasure," he reminded her with mock severity. "And I feel frustrated that I can't get to it."

She dropped her head back and looked up into the deep blue sky. Her gaze roamed the adjacent green hillside dotted with the ruins of the temple of the goddess of love.

"There's more than treasure here. Can't you feel it?"

He'd been all business, but now he grinned as he saw the sparkle in her eyes. "Feel what?"

"The sensuality in the air. It's all around us. Like magic."

"It is special," he conceded.

"Is it any wonder the earliest Greeks set their most precious myth right here, on this very spot? Aphrodite rising from the foam, in all her glory. Do you realize, Jack, that since the dawn of history, lovers have come on pilgrimages to worship at this shrine? To anoint themselves in these waters, to make passionate love in the warm sand. I feel the spirits of them all, all the lovers who've come here down through the centuries, as if all the love they'd shared had been absorbed by the rocks and the sand and the sea. Left here for us."

"Something else was left here for us. By two other lovers."

"Lovers who sacrificed all they had, even their own lives, for each other. Because they knew that nothing else matters in the end."

With an arched brow, he teased, "Nothing? So you don't want to find the treasure."

"I found my treasure in you."

The teasing tone was replaced by a look of tender devotion. He bent his head, catching her lips with his, kissing her lightly at first, then deeper, harder, until his arms at her back crushed her to him, lifting her out of the water as his mouth sweetly tasted hers. Somehow, she found herself lifted in his arms, one arm about her shoulders, the other cradling the backs of her knees. He held her as if she weighed no more than the white cotton petticoat she wore. Her head was spinning pleasantly, his mouth igniting her senses as the sun warmed her body.

"Your kisses make me drunk," she sighed against his lips.

He lifted his head and looked down at her. The petticoat was soaked, clinging to her like a second skin, outlining the firm round breasts with their dark nipples below her mother's necklace, and the gentle curve of her hips. She felt the jolt of his hot gaze, as if Zeus himself had flung a bolt of lightning from the heavens, striking her heart.

"The hell with the treasure," he growled.

He ripped the cloth from one breast and devoured it in his greedy mouth. As he did, his hands moved like a sorcerer's, stripping her of her sheath so it floated off in the water. They clung to each other, passionate now, feeling the spirits of all the lovers who'd come before them permeate their souls. Diana was awash in a sea of love, surrounded by bliss, bubbling over with sweet, sensual sensation. Jack's arms were rough and strong, his mouth possessive.

"You're the real goddess of love," he whispered as he carried her up out of the sea and laid her on the welcoming hot sands. Sands where Cleopatra and Mark Antony had no doubt loved, knowing their time together was near its end. Sands that had hosted hot embraces and sibilant sighs as Aphrodite herself, no doubt, smiled approvingly down on them. When Jack entered her with a powerful thrust, Diana felt that they represented, in that instant, all who had passed before them. That she embodied all the women who looked at their men with love and trust burning in their eyes, and that Jack embodied all the men who'd shielded, protected, found bliss at their lovers' altars. A goddess and a god.

Diana lay in Jack's arms, feeling whole, complete, at one with all eternity. He, too, seemed deeply satisfied, content to lie back lazily in the sand.

"It's so beautiful here," Diana said. "I wish we could stay here forever."

"Why can't we?"

She leaned up on one elbow, looking down at him. "Do you mean it?"

"Why not? Birch Haven's gone. We need a new home. We can build a villa up on the hillside. With a view of this spot."

"Oh, Jack, I'd love that. You see? This spot *is* magic. It's given you a wonderful inspiration."

"You're my inspiration." He took a strand of her dark hair in his fist and drew her down to kiss her. But suddenly, his lips lost their force. His head drew back and his face took on a look of wonder.

"Diana! I think I know where it is!"

"But . . . how?"

"I have that feeling of . . . certainty that I get sometimes. I don't know how I know, but I know."

"Where?"

"Wait here."

He stood up quickly and ran, naked, diving into the water. Swimming several strokes toward the rock, he suddenly dove under the water. Several minutes elapsed. Diana stood, staring at the calm, empty sea. More minutes elapsed. Longer than any man could possibly hold his breath. Panic struck her. But as she started to rush toward the surf, Jack's head suddenly bobbed out of the water.

"I found it," he called. "There's a passage down here that I'd overlooked. It comes up about ten feet into the rock. There's air there, Diana. A cave!"

Working swiftly, he pulled his watertight bag of supplies off the raft. "The opening is just below me here. It's about three feet wide, and seems secure. Wait a few minutes, then follow me."

With that, he dove under the water again.

Diana stood trembling on the beach. Could this possibly be it at last? After all the years of searching, all the lives lost? Was there really a treasure here? Or was it all a folly? She thought of all her father's hopes and dreams and whispered a little prayer.

Taking a tremulous breath, she followed in Jack's wake, diving under the water. She opened her eyes, felt the slight sting of the salt, but saw the passage in the clear sea. The opening was about seven feet below the surface. The passageway was as dark as a moonless night. She felt a moment of anxiety at swimming through, but remembered Jack's words. Feeling her way along the rocky walls, she swam through the tunnel, holding her breath.

On its other side, she emerged out of the water and into stale air. And the sight of Jack's strangely impassive face as he held a torch he'd just lit.

"Is it here?" she asked.

Jack looked at her, then extended the torch away from his body, illuminating part of what she could now see was a vast cave, flashing with glimmers of multicolored lights, glinting with sparkles as bright as stars on a cloudless summer night.

Jack took a step forward and his torch illuminated more of the cave. Every corner was piled high with gold, silver, boxes of precious jewels . . . emeralds, rubies . . . the wealth of Egypt's glorious past.

He took two more steps, to the center of the cave. Still holding the torch out, he circled around, surveying the full extent of this impossible treasure trove. The immensity of it had struck him dumb. There were no words to describe its splendor, its sheer magnificence.

Diana rose from the water and stepped over to

join him. She couldn't speak. Somehow, the silence seemed sacred, as if the two of them were standing in the sanctuary of a church. They both felt the presence of the two lovers who'd left this legacy here, wanting to protect it, hoping to use it for a higher purpose than lust for possession.

Taking another torch from Jack's bag, Diana lit it and began to make a closer inspection. She marveled at these objects that put her face-to-face with history, as if these two millennia hadn't passed. Cleopatra's scepter . . . the pear-shaped crown of Upper and Lower Egypt . . . and the personal—a comb, a perfume flask, a knife and fork, a drinking cup, all in the finest gold . . . and finally a scroll, positioned on a small serving table as if waiting for them.

She secured the torch in a crack in the wall, then picked up the scroll. With held breath, she unfurled the ancient papyrus. It was written in Greek, in an artistic hand. Cleopatra's hand.

Jack came up beside her. "What does it say?" His voice was soft, reverential.

" 'Beware those who would use this treasure for their own ends and rob from Mother Egypt what the gods intended to be hers.' "

Later, after they'd emerged from the hollow of the great rock, they stood amidst the piled-high stones and broken columns of the ruins of the temple of Aphrodite. The charm of Cyprus surrounded them on all sides, with verdant hills and sandy beaches, strewn throughout with the ruins of Greek temples and Roman amphitheaters. The small white houses of the citizens shimmered in the golden light of the sun. A lovely jewel set to perfection in the glittering blue sea.

From high on this hill they held a panoramic view of the coastline where Aphrodite's rock rose proudly from the sea, so stealthily hiding its precious secret. They had barely spoken since reading Cleopatra's admonition.

"It seems I've spent most of my life looking for this treasure. And now that we've found it, it strikes me what a responsibility it is."

"Almost a burden," he agreed. "But how can we possibly fulfill that responsibility? When Egypt continues to pass from one foreign power to another? Ripe for the plunder of men like Ali Pasha . . ."

"And people like us."

"Us?"

"Ali Pasha said we English are the greatest thieves history has ever known. In a way, he's right. Your father, mine, all of us—our motives may have been pure, we may have wanted to preserve history and share it with the world. But the effect is the same."

"What are you trying to say, Diana?"

She turned to him. "Jack, that treasure belongs to Egypt. Not us, not the British Museum. It's as if Cleopatra herself had handed us a sacred trust."

"You want to leave it hidden!?"

"Egypt isn't ready for it yet."

She watched him, dreading his reaction. It was a

great deal to ask, after all they'd been through, after all they'd sacrificed. Daria . . . Birch Haven . . They'd come at last to the end of a long journey. But the world wouldn't know.

All at once, Jack's face broke into a devilish grin. "I love this," he said.

"Would you mind so much?" she asked, startled.

"I wouldn't mind at all. What a grand trick to play on the world. Keep it hidden. But what about you? What about your father's memory? His reputation?"

She hesitated, weighing her words carefully. "I have to believe that if my father had read those words, he'd have come to the same decision. Someday when Egypt is a great nation again, when a rightful ruler comes forward, someone who will protect this heritage from colonialists and greedy pashas and religious fanatics . . . then we—or our descendants—will hand it over. To stay where it belongs."

"Our descendants," he said warmly, pulling her into his arms. "I like that idea."

She smiled. Finally, they were completely in accord. "Maybe we can build that villa we were talking about right here, where we can look down the hill and watch over our charge. And maybe together we can work to help each country keep her own treasures. Help to pass laws and—"

"And raise those descendants."

"You're not taking me seriously," she scolded.

His grin vanished and his face grew thoughtful and intense. "You're wrong. You've made me realize that what my father told me is true. That what we do is more important than the work of kings. That we've been given a sacred trust. I understand that now—I *feel* it—because of you. So we'll guard Cleopatra's treasure and keep it safe, as she would have wanted. Until Egypt is ready."

Diana felt her love for him spill over. "Welcome back," she whispered. "The real Jack. The Jack I've always loved."

He took her face in both hands and looked into her eyes. "Will you marry me, Diana? Will you help me remember always who I am? Who I've become because of you?"

All she could say was, "Yes," before his lips drowned her in their own sea of love.

Ever what my order told me is true. Then what we do is done against all the world's kings. That we were once given a sister, that I understand that he—I ... his presence ... of you, so we'll seize whatever treasure and keep it safe, as she would have wanted ...
Your crypt is ready.

Dark figures rose before a still creek. Welcome rest, she whispered. The soil ... pale. The jaws bit at one loved.

"I will not give up hope, hands shot nailed into her eyes. "I will not marry me. I come ... with ... my murderer there, who I am, who I've fought forever or live."

All other could suppress ... he saw before the line she would ... it to ... I turn to see of love.

About the Author

Katherine O'Neal is the daughter of a U.S. Air Force pilot and a fiercely British artist who met in India in the fifties. The family traveled extensively and lived for many years in Asia. Katherine is married to William Arnold, a noted film critic and author of the bestselling books *Shadowland* and *China Gate*—a man she feels makes her heroes pale in comparison. They make their home in Seattle, but continue the tradition of travel whenever possible. Their daughter Janie spent a year in France as an exchange student.

Katherine loves to hear from readers.
Please write her at:

P.O. Box 2452
Seattle, WA 98111-2452
and enclose a self-addressed stamped envelope for a response and news of forthcoming books.

Bestselling Historical Women's Fiction

⚡AMANDA QUICK⚡

____28354-5 SEDUCTION ...$6.50/$8.99 Canada

____28932-2 SCANDAL ....$6.50/$8.99

____28594-7 SURRENDER ....$6.50/$8.99

____29325-7 RENDEZVOUS ....$6.50/$8.99

____29315-X RECKLESS ....$6.50/$8.99

____29316-8 RAVISHED ....$6.50/$8.99

____29317-6 DANGEROUS ....$6.50/$8.99

____56506-0 DECEPTION ....$6.50/$8.99

____56153-7 DESIRE ....$6.50/$8.99

____56940-6 MISTRESS ....$6.50/$8.99

____57159-1 MYSTIQUE ....$6.50/$8.99

____57190-7 MISCHIEF ....$6.50/$8.99

____57407-8 AFFAIR ....$6.99/$8.99

⚡IRIS JOHANSEN⚡

____29871-2 LAST BRIDGE HOME ...$5.50/$7.50

____29604-3 THE GOLDEN
             BARBARIAN ....$6.99/$8.99

____29244-7 REAP THE WIND .....$5.99/$7.50

____29032-0 STORM WINDS ....$6.99/$8.99

- -

Ask for these books at your local bookstore or use this page to order.

Please send me the books I have checked above. I am enclosing $____ (add $2.50 to cover postage and handling). Send check or money order, no cash or C.O.D.'s, please.

Name _____

Address _____

City/State/Zip _____

Send order to: Bantam Books, Dept. FN 16, 2451 S. Wolf Rd., Des Plaines, IL 60018
Allow four to six weeks for delivery.

Prices and availability subject to change without notice.   FN 16 9/98

Bestselling Historical Women's Fiction

❧ IRIS JOHANSEN ❧

____28855-5 THE WIND DANCER . . .$5.99/$6.99

____29968-9 THE TIGER PRINCE . . .$6.99/$8.99

____29944-1 THE MAGNIFICENT

ROGUE . . . .$6.99/$8.99

____29945-X BELOVED SCOUNDREL .$6.99/$8.99

____29946-8 MIDNIGHT WARRIOR . .$6.99/$8.99

____29947-6 DARK RIDER . . . .$6.99/$8.99

____56990-2 LION'S BRIDE . . . .$6.99/$8.99

____56991-0 THE UGLY DUCKLING. . .$6.99/$8.99

____57181-8 LONG AFTER MIDNIGHT.$6.99/$8.99

____57998-3 AND THEN YOU DIE.... $6.99/$8.99

❧ TERESA MEDEIROS ❧

____29407-5 HEATHER AND VELVET .$5.99/$7.50

____29409-1 ONCE AN ANGEL . . . . . .$5.99/$7.99

____29408-3 A WHISPER OF ROSES .$5.99/$7.99

____56332-7 THIEF OF HEARTS . . . . .$5.50/$6.99

____56333-5 FAIREST OF THEM ALL .$5.99/$7.50

____56334-3 BREATH OF MAGIC . . . .$5.99/$7.99

____57623-2 SHADOWS AND LACE . . .$5.99/$7.99

____57500-7 TOUCH OF ENCHANTMENT. .$5.99/$7.99

____57501-5 NOBODY'S DARLING . . .$5.99/$7.99

Ask for these books at your local bookstore or use this page to order.

Please send me the books I have checked above. I am enclosing $____ (add $2.50 to cover postage and handling). Send check or money order, no cash or C.O.D.'s, please.

Name _____

Address _____

City/State/Zip _____

Send order to: Bantam Books, Dept. FN 16, 2451 S. Wolf Rd., Des Plaines, IL 60018
Allow four to six weeks for delivery.
Prices and availability subject to change without notice.   FN 16 9/98

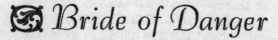